Feet of Clay

A Twisted Truth Novel

Jack Watts

5 MOON PRESS

Published by Five Moon Press, Atlanta, Georgia.
Sales, Marketing, and Distribution services provided by Fitting Words LLC,
105 Hazel Path, Hendersonville, Tennessee.

ISBN: 978-1-942557-73-9
Cover Art: Dwayne Bassett
Internal Design: Colin Hawk

Printed in The United States of America

Unless we can look the darkest, blackest fact full in the face
without damaging God's character, we do not yet know Him.

—Oswald Chambers, July 29, My Utmost for His Highest

There are three things a man should do with his life:
Plant a tree,
Have a child, and
Write a book.
He should plant a tree to feed those who will come after him when he is gone.
He should have a child so that his name will endure.
And he should write a book so that the purpose for his life will be known forever.

—Old Hebrew saying—

Jesus . . . said, "You know that the rulers of the Gentiles lord it over them, and their great men exercise authority over them. It is not this way among you, but whoever wishes to become great among you shall be your servant, and whoever wishes to be first among you shall be your slave; just as the Son of Man did not come to be served, but to serve, and to give His life a ransom for many" *(Matthew 20:25-28, NASB).*

Dedication

You've probably heard it said that "Christianity is the only army that shoots its wounded." It's an aphorism that is right on target. The following story is dedicated to the victims of that army—those who have been used, abused, and discarded—all in the name of Christianity. It is for those who have become casualties—people of faith wounded by fellow Christians but certainly not by Almighty God—that I have written this novel.

Table of Contents

Preface 9

1 Dark Eyes 11

2 A Casserole in the Refrigerator 17

3 You Tried to Feel Her Up 24

4 Her Hair Was Blond—Except for the Roots 32

5 My Mannerisms Were as Defiant as a Boxer 40

6 Self-Serving, Unscrupulous, and Unethical 46

7 He's Mr. Fumblethumbs 54

8 Like a Frog in a Pot 63

9 A Wrinkled, Old Nun 73

10 Jesus Stuck to the Roof of My Mouth 80

11 It Gives Her a Little Buzz 88

12 My Face Began to Throb 96

13 They Were Gone Weeks at a Time 102

14 Out of the Dreck of My Failed Marriage 111

15 God Did Love Me After All 118

16 He Sported a Haughty, Imperious Look 126

17 They Became Embittered—Often Blaming God 132

18 Lifting Up Christ Works—Pushing Jesus Does Not 141

19 An Asset I Might Need on a Rainy Day 150

20 With Little Light and Less Saltiness. 157

21 A Bite of the Forbidden Fruit 162

22 Two FBI Agents Knocked on My Front Door 168

23 Driving Evangelicals to Their Knees 175

24 Pray for Fluffy 182

25 A Funeral Atmosphere Permeated 189

26 A Ten-Inch Stack of Paper 194

27 I Will Be the Next Commander-in-Chief 199

28 Do You Know Who I Am? 206

29 Entry into My Soul 212

30 I Started Planning Our Escape 218

31 Of Course, I Did—Duh! 226

32 What Happened in Vegas Stay in Vegas 235

33 An Unspoken Irrelevancy 243

34 A Myriad of Wounded Believers 251

35 To Live in That Much Fear 259

36 He's Not Going Anywhere. 266

37 We All Have to Start Someplace 272

Conclusion: The Lords and Ladies of Evangelicalism 282

Preface

Feet of Clay is a work of fiction—a story set during the heyday of mega television ministries. To some, it may seem like it's too detailed to be fictional. I suppose that's because the characters and storyline are so plausible. Nevertheless, it is fiction.

The story is uplifting and purposeful, but it certainly isn't sappy or trivial. As you get into it, you will probably experience conflicting emotions, which is my intention. The novel is purposeful, but it is not to save the lost or to reach seekers. Instead, it's to help wounded Christians understand they are not alone. Their painful experiences are common. There are nearly 40 million believers in America who have abandoned their Christian faith, or at least put it on the shelf.

Feet of Clay is for them—the used, abused, and discarded. I want these rejected Christians to know God still loves them and continues to reach out to them. To accomplish my purpose, I may have stepped on the toes of the sanctimonious and the self-righteous. Am I sorry I have done that? No, I am not.

Feet of Clay is about the dark side of Christian ministry. It calls out those who speak for God, while pursuing their self-serving purposes. The story is very interesting. By reading it, you will learn a great deal about the business side of evangelicalism in large ministries, and I suspect you will have fun doing so. There is nothing like *Feet of Clay*.

In our society, we are consumed with reality TV, but most of what you see isn't authentic—not really. *Feet of Clay* is. Although a work of fiction, the story depicts what commonly occurs in ministries across the fruited plain. Although set primarily in the 1980s, nothing has changed. If the timeframe was today, the stories of spiritual abuse would be no different.

Let me thank several people for helping me with this project, which includes John and Patty Fitts, Anne Alexander, Dwayne Bassett, Colin Hawk, Paul Shepherd, Penny Bruner, and Dan Wright. Your work and encouragement were essential to completing the book. Gracias.

Jack Watts
Atlanta, Georgia

1

Dark Eyes

It was a magnificent, warm evening in New York City as I left the Hilton on the Avenue of the Americas in late June 1993—the kind pictured on brochures to show the city's charm. Although nearly midnight, the streets were bustling with thousands who came and went amid a cacophony of laughter, shouts, engines, and distant sirens.

I've always loved the sounds and sights of New York, nearly as much as the city's vibrancy. My name is Cole Cassidy; and I was reared in Wellesley, Massachusetts—not far from the Big Apple by plane or by train. As my name suggests, I'm Irish and proud of it. I'm the only one in my family who moved away from the Boston area. Although I left decades ago, I still root for the Celtics, Red Sox, Patriots, and Bruins—in that order. If you're from the Bay State, you'll understand my undying allegiance. If not, you probably can't comprehend the depth of loyalty New Englanders feel toward their pro sports teams.

I've lost my accent—at least for the most part—except for when I'm driving. If someone cuts me off, I tell them what I think of them in my native language—Bostonian. Sometimes, I'll let a guy know he's number one with the finger God provided me with to convey that message. This part of my personality hasn't changed much, but I would never flip off a woman. My mom, who we called Midge because of her diminutive stature, taught me well. She was a master at telling people they were number one with her crooked, arthritic middle finger. She flipped off men and women alike, but she always told me it was wrong for a man to flip off a woman. So, I never have—not once. I wouldn't even consider it.

During my business trip in '93, I was with my best friend Pete Chalmette, a Cajun from Bayou Bijoux in the Mississippi Delta—not far from Napoleonville, Louisiana. His parish was mostly swamp. The folks down there liked to joke that the population of gators and snakes exceeded that of humans. The high school football team was nicknamed the Moccasins, but they were more commonly referred to as the Mosquitoes because of their swarming defense. The first time Pete mentioned the Mosquitoes, I thought the nickname was humorously appropriate—a fitting tribute to what life must be like on the Bayou.

Like many from "The Swamp," Pete could spin a mesmerizing tale. I loved to listen, never tiring of the way he talked—mostly English garnished with a little Cajun, which folks in the Delta called pidgin-French. Pete always cussed in Cajun—much to my delight. He was a short, dark-complexioned guy who could talk about football for hours, especially about his alma mater, LSU—Geaux Tigers!

Having become a born-again Christian less than ten years earlier, Pete was serious about Christianity, making a determined effort to practice what he preached. Earlier in life, he had been a hard drinker—a guy you never wanted to mess with after he had more than three drinks or a couple of tokes. As a college student, he sold drugs to pay for his schooling—with little care about the devastating impact his product had on its recipients. That was the addict's problem—not his. He took no responsibility for the lives his drugs destroyed. What drug dealer does?

All of this changed the day he invited Christ to come into his life. His transformation was dramatic and lasting—much to the relief of his mother and girlfriend, who fretted about his behavior, terrified he would end up in prison, which seemed like a pretty legitimate concern.

By the time Pete and I met, he had become a first-rate human being; bearing little resemblance to the guy he had been a decade earlier. He worked on one bad habit after the other in his relentless quest to improve his character. He was successful in most areas, but one made virtually no progress—his cussing. He tried valiantly to curtail his profanity but with little success. One reason was largely responsible for Pete's inability to curb this vice—Alvin Dettler Carter.

Pete's boss and mine, Carter was the Senior Vice President at Ludlow Randolph Publishers in Orlando, one of the largest producers of Christian literature in America. Dett, which is pronounced like being in debt, was what everybody called him; and he loved it, thinking it provided him with a negotiating advantage. He hated his given name, Alvin, which was what Pete and I called him, especially when he wasn't around.

Dett was the same age as Pete and five years my junior. Although Dett had no formal education beyond high school, it wasn't his lack of erudition that made accepting his leadership a challenge. It was his character—or should I say, lack of character. Although charming and engaging, Dett was not even close to the person he appeared to be. His warmth and compassion were nothing but a façade, masking his true purpose, which was to use and manipulate others to further his ambitions, especially his clients and subordinates.

Consistently feigning altruism, Dett was the most self-serving person I had. He was handsome and charming—the kind of guy you loved to trust.

Possessing an engaging smile and superior listening skills, he was a little over six feet tall. Exuding a winsome way, he was trim and well groomed. He had dark eyes and a warm look that could penetrate a person's soul effortlessly. His cheeks were a little pudgy. When he had food in his mouth, he resembled a chipmunk. Pete and I used to mimic "Alvin and the Chipmunks," mocking our boss, laughing heartily each time we did. Obviously, Dett brought out the worst, most childish aspects of our personalities.

Unlike Pete and me, Dett was never profane. He wouldn't even consider it. Instead, he loved to recite mellifluous prayers with those who came to see him, especially authors and ministry leaders—people who were renowned. His prayers sounded so genuine and authentic they made him appear to be an upright guy—someone completely trustworthy. Because his entire demeanor encouraged people to pour out their hearts, they did just that. After revealing their deepest, most intimate secrets, misgivings, moral lapses, and personal failures, these ministry leaders and other notable figures felt relieved.

For them, it was like a remorseful Catholic going to confession. Being candid with Dett lifted a tremendous burden of guilt from their shoulders. When they left the confines of their seemingly sacred meeting with Dett, like penitents receiving absolution, they felt better about themselves and about what had been troubling them.

As they drove away, with a serene smile to uplift their spirits, they were blissfully unaware they had just taken a huge bite from a forbidden fruit—a delicacy that would act like poison to their souls. Eventually, each confessor would live to regret being candid with Alvin Dettler Carter.

Why they chose to unburden their hearts was simple. They needed a wise, godly counselor—someone to share their misgivings, guilt and remorse—and Dett seemed like he had been divinely appointed to fulfill this function.

For reasons most troubled people can grasp, the need for a trusted confidant is essential. Life can be stressful and difficult, grinding men and women down, robbing them of their joy, leaving them drained and defeated, producing debilitating, desperate anxiety and fear. When this happens, even the strongest, most confident person will become tentative and apprehensive, revealing insecurities in subtle and not-so-subtle ways.

Dett's special gift was detecting lack of confidence in others. When he was on his game, no veneer of "having it all together" was effective at masquerading a person's troubled heart. Dett had a discerning spirit—a gift he used to manipulate and exploit others, rather than serve them. Nevertheless, he acted as if he was being helpful. Once Dett discovered a person's flaws or closely held secrets, he would encourage this person to disclose every intimate detail about what had been troubling them.

Feeling safe, men and women alike would expose their souls, certain they were confiding in a trustworthy, compassionate listener—a genuine Christian. Dett would empathize with them consolingly, indicating he had been through something similar, regardless of what it happened to be. Occasionally, he would create wild, lurid tales, having no basis in reality; while at other times, he would shamelessly exaggerate the truth.

I marveled at his ability to keep his stories straight, which neither Pete nor I could possibly do. There was just too much deviation from the truth to remember, but that was never a problem for Dett. Instead, it was a challenge, and he always seemed up to the task, rarely getting caught in his web of prevarication.

Having such an understanding way about him was one of Dett's most distinguishable characteristics. Nevertheless, promising confidentiality with his lips, in his cunning heart, he routinely calculated how to use the information to further his ambitions—all at the expense of his unsuspecting supplicant.

For Dett, penetrating the weakened boundaries of another person's soul was recreational sport—like jogging for an athlete. He did it regularly, wounding many in the process. Outwardly, his supportiveness was so complete it bordered on being sycophantic. Inwardly, he was a coiled serpent, planning to strike at his victim's most vulnerable spot—all to further his personal and corporate aspirations.

For those of us who were around Dett—those who witnessed his emotional rape of another's soul—we chose profanity as the outlet to vent our indignation. Although childish and ineffective, it was an act of defiance we found deeply cathartic. It was also our only option.

When we watched people leave Dett's office, we could tell when he had hit his mark. Dett's smile became syrupy. He would actually rub his hands together, reminiscent of Uriah Heep in *David Copperfield*, after accomplishing some nefarious goal. Most were incapable of recognizing how disingenuous Dett actually was, but not Pete and me. Because we witnessed him in action routinely, we knew exactly what was happening.

Coupled with his covetous smirk, Dett would use fawning gesticulations to mask his glee at having trapped another fly in his web of deception. As we watched the charade being acted out, either Pete or I would say reproachfully, "Dett has that 'F.F. look' about him, doesn't he?"

"He sure does," the other would respond, reminiscent of a liturgical response. With that, we would laugh reproachfully. By the way, an "F.F. look" is a "freshly 'you-know-what' look;" and at Ludlow Randolph, Dett sported it as often as a groom on a long anticipated honeymoon.

2

A Casserole in the Refrigerator

We witnessed Dett in action regularly. His behavior was galling, and his manipulations were so blatant and provocative our sense of fairness was constantly being assaulted. Regardless of how upset he made us, we were helpless to alter the outcome of his ethical breaches, which pleased him. Affronting our sense of justice added joy to his conquest; I'm sure of it. I could see the glint of triumph in his devious eyes, which were tauntingly defiant.

Being so powerless was exasperating. It was like watching a movie; when the hero or heroine was about to walk into a room, where Dracula was rapaciously lurking, ready to assault his hapless prey. We knew what was about to happen, but there was nothing we could do to prevent the vampire from ravaging his victim—not and maintain our livelihood.

Neither of us could afford to lose our job. We had kids to feed. That's why having each other's encouragement and support was so important. It helped us maintain our sense of equilibrium, as well as our sanity. Working for a guy like Dett didn't help my problem with profanity—that's for sure.

If anything, my cussing was worse than Pete's. Being reared Irish-Catholic in the suburbs of Boston, where profanity is proudly considered to be an art form, I swore as much as I did when I was in high school.

Pete and I meshed at Ludlow Randolph, becoming fast friends immediately. There were others who worked with us in our department as well. We were a tight bunch of guys, each sharing numerous experiences while working for Dett—experiences, which were often interesting but, just as often, disturbing.

One guy joined the team toward the end of my tenure at Ludlow Randolph. His name was Jeremiah Doucette. Pete nicknamed him, Acy, as in Acy—Doucy. He was younger and had recently married a bright, pretty, and vivacious young lady. Being open, honest, and friendly, Pete and I liked Acy immediately.

He was a handsome, gregarious guy, who was already losing his hair while still in his mid-twenties. Acy grew up on the mission field. He spent his entire youth abroad with his parents and twin sisters. All three siblings had significant family of origin issues, originating from Pastor Doucette's obsession with reaching "the lost." His outward goal to help others was so consuming, Pastor Doucette paid little attention to his wife and three children. Focusing on the needs of those who were without faith, at the expense of his family, Pastor Doucette pursued his obsession relentlessly, almost compulsively.

Because his children didn't seem to be as important as his calling, his kids, Acy and the twin girls, felt unloved. They resented their father's consistent inattentiveness. Being less important than strangers hurt the Doucette children's sense of self-worth, producing pain in their young hearts, which turned to acrimony, adversely impacting their development. Because of the role they were expected to play in their father's ministry, they were forced to suppress their feelings and control their outward behavior. Reared in this rigidly repressive environment, where outward conformity was required, they had no alternative but to comply.

Among other things, they were forbidden to be honest about their feelings—not to anyone—especially to those in their father's congregation. Instead, they were tasked with maintaining the appearance of familial perfection. They were mandated to uphold the illusion that their family represented a replicate-able example of what Christ intended for a family to be. To accomplish this, they routinely wore plastic smiles of contentment, which were disingenuous, routinely fooling others. Their mandate was to act the part of a submissive child flawlessly, and that's precisely what they did. They maintained this illusion, despite what was really happening behind the closed doors of the parsonage.

Rigidly admonished to maintain this facade of perfection, their home life was close to the exact opposite of what they portrayed it to be. Dutifully, the young children did precisely as their father instructed, despite the rebelliousness that smoldered just beneath the surface of their troubled hearts.

Being consumed with the never-ending needs of the lost, while being an absentee parent, is frequently a problem for missionary families—one their kids come to understand all too well. The Doucette children were taught that sacrificing their own desires for the "greater good" of God's work was their expected duty. It was relentlessly ground into them. If they didn't measure up to their father's unyielding expectations, they were scolded and punished.

Because they were required to maintain this illusion of perfection, the children's formative years were filled with repressed hostility. They obeyed their father's rules outwardly, although it became increasingly difficult to do so. That they were being sacrificed for the sake of their dad's ministry, while being emotionally deprived, was easier to accept when they were young and voiceless. As they matured, their rebelliousness began to manifest itself in ways that were not always pretty. By their mid-teens, their repressed hostility had begun to surface, exposing a dark side within each of them.

Predictably, Pastor Doucette's entire house of cards eventually collapsed, leaving familial waste that was anything but a model of what Christ desired. By the time Pastor Doucette became aware of the gravity of the situation, it was too late. There was no salvaging the emotional carnage he had created.

He had lost his children—all three of them—and his wife had become a dithering shell of what she had once been. As early as the time her children reached school age, Mrs. Doucette realized what was happening and tried to alter the dynamics within the family, but her husband paid no heed to her complaints. Instead, he rigidly demanded conformity from the children and her. Despite her valiant efforts to create a harmonious environment, it never materialized. Knowing what the future would hold for her children, as well as for her, broke her spirit.

Once a strong, capable woman, Mrs. Doucette's countenance and mental capacity atrophied appreciably. Her vision of what life would be like serving the Lord on the mission field wasn't her reality. It wasn't even a close approximation. She wasn't her husband's partner, neither in life nor in his ministry. She was little more than a useful appendage—someone to cook, clean, mind the kids, and satisfy her husband's frequent carnal urges.

She worked dutifully to fulfill each role. With little satisfaction, she eventually became less accommodating. Finally succumbing to depression, while maintaining the same superficial smile as her children, she stopped playing the game. Instead of becoming defiant on the inside like her offspring, however, Mrs. Doucette simply gave up. Inwardly, she abandoned her faith and became unwilling to participate in life. Blaming God for not correcting the situation, she abandoned her trust in Him, further embittering her soul in the process.

Being set in his ways, she knew her husband would never change. Seeing nothing positive on the horizon, she discarded further attempts to express her concerns. Her husband never listened anyway, and the backlash from being confrontational ceased to be worth the effort.

Loathing the lot in life she had been forced to endure, she eventually lost the will to live. Having fought depression valiantly for several years, she finally abandoned her efforts to reverse what was happening. When she did, she sank into a black hole of despair. Once there, even routine grooming, like brushing her teeth and washing her hair, became difficult chores, as her desire to continue living evaporated. Believing she had failed her husband and her children—just as God had failed her—she convinced herself that her family would be better off without her. This is when she made the decision to exit this world, which felt freeing and liberating. Once she reached this conclusion, she actually became cheerful for nearly a month.

Heartened that she had turned the corner in her struggle with melancholia, her family became hopeful, but they misunderstood what was really happening. It's an easy mistake to make, especially for family members who constantly look for encouraging signs from a depressed loved one.

One afternoon, before the teens arrived home from school, Pastor Doucette walked into the living room of their parsonage to find his wife of nineteen years hanging from the center beam. Rushing to her, he realized immediately she had been dead for quite a while. Her color was already pasty gray, except for her face, which was dark purple. Horrified by what he witnessed, Pastor Doucette's knees buckled. He fell to the floor, sobbing and writhing in agony. Finding it difficult to breathe, his hands shook violently and his stomach heaved. Racing outside, he barely made it to the shrubs before vomiting.

Returning to her as soon as he was able to regain a measure of strength, he saw a note pinned to her dress. Opening it, he read her final words:

There's a casserole in the refrigerator for dinner. The freezer has enough meals to last until springtime.

That was it—nothing more. No explanation, no regret, and no farewell for either him or for her children. There was no warmth to the note, which was as disturbing as it was surprising. Pastor Doucette reread its contents in his mind a thousand times. It haunted him, especially when he would awaken in the middle of the night, which he did routinely for many months following her death. He never came to terms with what she had written. Its coldness was crushing. He never recovered from what he witnessed that afternoon either. How could he?

As he thought about it, her last act had been similar to the role she played each day of her life. She had provided for the physical needs of her husband and children—nothing more. Since her life was devoid of passion, she chose her parting to be emotionless as well. As repressed as she had been for years, she exited life defiantly—at least as defiantly as she was capable of being.

Her death burst the bubble of familial perfection her husband had meticulously cultivated. As a result, Pastor Doucette's ministry faltered, atrophied, and finally collapsed. With no alternative, he and his children left Europe to return to the states, leaving Mrs. Doucette behind in a graveyard not far from the Normandy burial site reserved for World War II American GIs. Her family never even ate the meals she had laboriously prepared before taking her life. Just the thought of doing so made the widower's stomach feel queasy.

Once back in the States, Pastor Doucette began teaching evangelism at a small Bible college in Western Kentucky, where he finished the job of raising his children the best he could. At first, the three Doucette children, having lost their mom the way they did, blamed themselves—a typical teenage response. Once they began talking to each other, however, their perspective changed. Instead, they came to blame their father, abandoning any semblance of respect they ever held for him. Without realizing it, by repudiating him for the loss of their mother, they discarded the benefits of having a second parent, becoming emotional orphans in the process.

Their smoldering, repressed anger became deeply entrenched, never healing, producing bitterness toward Christianity in all three. Acy's two sisters abandoned their faith completely. Many wounded believers do, but Acy knew better than to make this mistake. He knew Christ was the Son of God. In spite of his anger, he maintained his firm conviction about the validity of the Gospel.

Neither girl fared as well as Acy. He was able to hold things together much better than his sisters, both of whom were institutionalized numerous times for drug abuse and alcoholism. Sadly, their inability to control their addictions made their adult life more miserable than their childhood. Acy looked like he had escaped the scarring of his dysfunctional upbringing, but he hadn't. His issues were there, effectively camouflaged beneath the surface of his charming personality.

In many ways, Acy was a remarkable young man. Despite spending his entire youth on the mission field, Acy spoke English without an accent. Living most of his formative years in France, he was bilingual, which the ladies in New Orleans loved, when he matriculated at Tulane University after graduating high school. In fact, he actually considered French to be his native tongue. He actually calculated math in French, translating his thoughts into English before providing the answer. This might seem like a handicap, but Acy was so smart he could still come up with the answer faster than most, including Pete and me. Extremely capable, we recognized Acy had potential for great things at Ludlow Randolph, and perhaps beyond.

3

You Tried to Feel Her Up

Although I worked for Dett as a full-time consultant for two years, I left Ludlow Randolph three years before my trip to New York in '93 to pursue my career as an independent consultant, working for various Christian ministries. Like Pete, I loathed working for Dett and had difficulty concealing my disdain. My antipathy began subtlety but intensified as I observed his dark side more frequently. Keeping my mouth shut, when I witnessed injustice, was never my strong suit. It still isn't.

The more I watched Dett, the less I became willing to remain silent about his manipulative behavior. Having to keep quiet made me feel like an unwilling accomplice, but an accomplice, nonetheless. This definitely wasn't within my nature to accept voluntarily.

Realizing I discerned his dark purposes made me Dett's enemy. Narcissists are like that. If you don't agree with their version of reality, which is always twisted, there is something wrong with you—never with them. Dett didn't consider himself to be at fault about anything. It was always the other person's problem—not just most of the time, always.

Because I wouldn't allow myself to be his accomplice, Dett finally made the decision to terminate me. Seeing the handwriting on the wall, when that fateful day arrived—as I knew it would—I was completely prepared. Having developed a client base from people I had met while working for Ludlow Randolph, I had everything in place to step into my new career as an independent contractor—never missing a payday.

Because we continued to work for many of the same clients, and because of our long-standing friendship, Pete and I maintained regular contact after I left Ludlow Randolph—Acy too. Pete and I talked on the phone nearly every day. For him, I was a sounding board—someone he could speak to candidly, with no holds barred. It was the same for me. We became very close during this period. Necessity bonds guys together tightly—far better than anything else.

It's funny because many people thought we were lucky to be working with Christian ministries. Routinely, people would tell us how blessed we were. They envied us because we travelled across America, helping ministries achieve their lofty goals. In theory, I understood how they would come to this conclusion. Sometimes, our jobs did have inspiring moments, but when it comes to the nuts and bolts of working with Christian ministries, there is a world of difference between appearance and reality. They are actually polar opposites.

This is why Pete and I felt it necessary to talk to each other so often. It was essential for our emotional wellbeing. By verbalizing about what was really happening, versus what was portrayed to the public, we were able to maintain our equilibrium in a subculture filled with Christian leaders who appeared outwardly to be enlightened servants of God but who were, in fact, anything but. Similar to Acy's upbringing, perception and reality were worlds apart, but few could discern the difference. Working on the inside, we saw rampant deceit, manipulation, and an absence of ethical behavior at a level and frequency few could imagine. Because each self-serving act was positioned to promote altruistic purposes, it was difficult for most to discern these situations accurately.

A great example of the difference was what was revealed to me on that fateful night in 1993, when Pete and I were in New York. We were in the city for the eightieth birthday party of Jake Smithson, the founder and president of Cherished Life Ministries. Jake developed a wonderful program to bring impoverished kids from the city ghettos in the Northeast to the pristine, bucolic surroundings of the majestic Adirondacks. While there, Cherished Life taught these kids how to swim, while at the same time witnessing to them about how Christ could transform their lives, if permitted to do so. During each summer, Jake's ministry instilled hope into neglected, impoverished children by the thousands.

Jake Smithson was a regal, distinguished older gentleman—handsome, with a full head of silvery white hair. His demeanor had been energetic and full of life since he returned from World War II with the intent of saving people rather than shooting them. He always had a broad, inviting smile that made even his worst detractors like him. Because his health had been failing for several years, his eightieth birthday became a celebration of his nearly fifty-year ministry. Everybody came. It was a Who's Who of the evangelical Christian world at the Hilton that night in New York.

Pete and I, who were relative nobodies among the luminaries, were placed at a table about half a football field away from the head table. Dett and the president of Ludlow Randolph, Benny Lessner, were seated with Jake Smithson at the head table—along with many other dignitaries. It was an affair to remember.

Before the large gathering was seated, there was an hour-long, alcohol-free reception. I said hello to Benny and his wife—as well as to Dett, who was always outwardly friendly. In fact, he continued to send business my way occasionally after he terminated me. He did this, knowing he could count on me to get the job done on time and within budget. As you can imagine, I was grateful for his referrals.

The celebration was very long and quite involved. When it was over, Pete said, "Be sure to say hello to Benny before leaving."

"I already talked to him, Pete."

"I know; but just do it again." After a long moment, he added, "It's important."

Looking at him quizzically, I replied, "Sure, if you think I should. I'll do it right now." With this, I made my way through the milling crowd and found Benny talking to a New York Congressman.

When they finished, I walked up and spoke to Benny for a few minutes. He seemed puzzled and a little annoyed, which made the conversation stilted, awkward and disjointed. Excusing myself soon thereafter, I walked through the thinning crowd until I found Pete. He and I were staying at a much less expensive hotel in Newark. Since Pete had a rental car, which was charged to Ludlow Randolph, I drove with him to save a little money. Those are the kind of corners you cut whenever possible, if you want to survive while developing your own business.

Before returning to Newark, we passed through Times Square—just like two yokels from down on the farm. We didn't care; it was a lot of fun. About 12:45 a.m., we headed out of the city. As we entered Lincoln Tunnel, I turned to Pete and said, "Why did you insist that I go back and talk to Benny?"

Pete just shrugged his shoulders.

"It was uncomfortable for both of us, Pete. I don't know why, but it was."

"I know it was, Cole; but believe me, it was important. Trust me on this," Pete said, with a little more emphasis in his delivery than I had anticipated, piquing my curiosity. I looked at him as he continued to drive, wondering what in the world was really going on.

I didn't say anything for a minute, as we both listened to an old Eagles' song on the radio. Driving deeper into the tunnel, the static became annoying; so I turned the radio off. When I did, my curiosity began to get the better of me, so I asked, "What is this all about, Pete?"

"Nothing," he replied dismissively.

Staring at him intensely, I replied, "That's not true. I can tell, and I want to know." By now, I had a hint of irritation in my voice that let him know I wouldn't drop the subject without a candid response.

Because of my persistence, he finally replied. "When you spoke to Benny the first time at the reception, he said your demeanor was 'a little unusual—a little peculiar.' That's all."

Pete offered this explanation in a lame effort to terminate my questions without further inquiry, but it had the opposite effect. I wasn't about to allow this to happen.

"What?" I queried, obviously confused. "I have no idea what you're talking about or what's really happening." After a few awkward seconds—with the tension mounting, I became insistent. "Tell me what this is all about. Just spit it out!"

Nodding in compliance, he replied, "Alright, Cole. You've got a right to know, and I guess I'm the one who has to tell you. It's because of the way you left the company—the thing about Crystal Moss. That's what it's about."

"What in the world are you talking about?" I replied—completely confused, obviously bewildered.

"Why do you think Ludlow Randolph let you go, Cole?" Pete asked in a lame attempt at Socratic questioning.

"Because Dett phased me out—just like we knew he would," I answered. "That and his realization I wasn't going to continue keeping quiet about his deceptions; that's why I was dismissed. You know that."

"You think that's the real reason?" he asked. "What about Crystal Moss?"

"What does Crystal Moss have to do with this?"

"A lot," he replied. "Benny and Dett don't see your termination the same way you do—not even close. They say you were fired because of what happened with Crystal. That's their version."

It felt like two conversations were occurring at the same time, and I was completely lost. "Pete, I'm confused. Just tell me exactly what you mean."

Sheepishly, he replied, "They're telling everybody they got rid of you because you put your hand up Crystal Moss' skirt. They said you tried to feel her up at the office. She was offended and told Dett. He took it to Benny; and Benny said, 'Get rid of him right away.'"

"What?" I exploded, as I tried to internalize the magnitude of what had just been said. "They fired me for groping Crystal—for trying to put my hand up her skirt? You're kidding?"

Pete just shook his head and repeated, "No, I'm not kidding, Cole. She said you were inappropriate. When she told Dett, he went straight to Benny, and they fired you three days later."

I was stunned. What he said had been so unexpected I couldn't assimilate it effectively. As the reality of the situation began to replace my initial shock, I became furious, barely able to contain my rage. Letting my emotions get the better of me, I bellowed at the top of my lungs, "That's the biggest bunch of bull I've ever heard. It's a lie—a damned lie!" Because my window was open, I could hear my words reverberate off the tunnel wall—despite the heavy traffic. My agitation made me that loud.

Continuing to vent, I added, "I never did anything like that. Nothing like that ever happened—not even close." I barely knew Crystal, and there was never anything between us. After a brief silence, I asked, "Do you think she really said that?"

"I know she said it, Cole."

When he responded with complete certainty, almost immediately, my rage evaporated, being replaced by despair. I felt defeated, deflated, and completely overwhelmed by what I heard, as I considered its ramifications. Pete glanced at me with compassion, knowing this revelation had wounded me to the core.

By the time we emerged from the tunnel a few minutes later, I had regained my equilibrium. "I won't stand for this, Pete—no way." I added, "The hell with them—all of them; I'm not going to let them get away with this."

After that, neither of us spoke for quite a while. My heart was pounding, as hundreds of thoughts passed through my mind. Turning to Pete, I finally broke the silence. "How did you find out?" I asked.

"Dett told me a long time ago," Pete responded. "A year ago—maybe more. Everybody at Ludlow Randolph knows about it; and Dett told some of the ministries you've worked for. It's why the ministry in South Florida isn't your client any more. Dett had a little talk with them about you."

Indignantly, I asked, "Why haven't you said anything about this before?"

"I knew it wasn't true; and your business has really been prospering." He added, "I didn't want it to be a distraction to what you've been accomplishing."

"But everybody at Ludlow Randolph thinks I did it, don't they?"

Pete nodded affirmatively. "Yeah, they do."

When I heard this, a chill passed through my body, as I realized that many of my old friends believed this false report. I asked, "Since I've never tried to defend myself and have kept quiet, they assume it's true, don't they?"

Pete hadn't thought about this. When he did, it made him wince.

It forced him to question the wisdom of his prolonged silence. In his simplicity, he thought he had done me a favor by not telling me what happened behind my back. Now that I had challenged this assumption, he was forced to reevaluate his position.

Sheepishly, he replied, “All of this happened three years ago, Cole. Maybe you should just let it go.”

“No way,” I said in a manner that left no doubt I would address the false witness against me. Looking at him, I asked, “If you were accused of something like this, would you just let it slide?”

“No, I wouldn’t,” he agreed.

“Neither will I. You can count on it.”

4

Her Hair Was Blond—Except for the Roots

After we reached our hotel in New Jersey and walked to our separate rooms, I began to reconstruct the events of my dismissal three years earlier. Dett had called me on a Thursday evening, telling me he and another executive from the company, Brandon Wolfe, needed to meet with me at the downtown Marriott in Atlanta at 7:30 a.m. the following morning. Because I worked out of my home, meeting at a restaurant was common—even on short notice. Since I had just spent two days at the home office, an urgent meeting this quickly seemed unusual—especially since the two of them were required to fly from Orlando to attend. I began to suspect what was about to happen.

Upon arrival the following morning, we ordered coffee. After talking pleasantries for ten minutes, Dett became serious. "Cole," he announced, "we've made a decision. We will not be requiring your services any longer. We're moving in another direction."

Because I knew this day was coming, I wasn't surprised, angry, or in the least bit upset. After Dett made his announcement, we talked amiably for several minutes before I left. Brandon barely spoke but, throughout the entire meeting, his expression was somber, almost morose. I assumed it was because he was sad to see me leave or uncomfortable about being part of the termination process, but that wasn't it at all. As I reflected, sitting in my hotel room three years later, I realized his expression wasn't out of concern for me. Instead, it was masked contempt—perhaps even loathing. Believing this false report, he had lost all respect for me.

As I continued to revisit the meeting in my mind, which I was destined to do repeatedly, I became increasingly infuriated. The more I thought about it, the angrier I became. It didn't just feel unfair; it definitely was.

During my exit interview, Crystal Moss' name was never mentioned—not once. I would have been surprised if it had been. Neither Dett nor Brandon gave me the slightest indication my termination was for any reason other than what they had indicated—a change in direction. Because I was a full-time consultant and not an employee, they weren't even required to document justifiable grounds for my dismissal. They had every right to release me without cause or notice, which is precisely what they did.

As I pondered the events from my enlightened perspective, I couldn't shake my anger. Nor could I stop thinking about it, especially when I would awaken in the middle of the night, which occurred frequently for quite a while. At the time, I didn't want justice; I wanted revenge. I felt used, abused, betrayed, and discarded—having no more value than an odious piece of trash. Reliving this outrage repeatedly, my anger increased rather than diminished.

Incensed at being disgraced on false grounds, I had numerous vengeful thoughts. They consumed my emotions, keeping me awake for long periods before I would finally fall asleep again. In the morning I would be exhausted and had difficulty focusing on the day's activities.

Knowing I had been treated unfairly produced disquietude that threatened to become debilitating.

The more I thought about my situation, the more I recognized how this was a perfect opportunity for Dett to exercise his gifted dark side, with the bonus that it would destroy my reputation in the process. For him, this was high drama—a successful sporting event that brought pleasure to his twisted existence. The prize was my termination, accompanied by my character assassination, which he considered to be the appropriate punishment for my revulsion at his manipulations and deceptions.

When exacting revenge, narcissists are routinely petty and vindictive, but Dett's maliciousness was nearly peerless. Best of all, from his perspective, I was as clueless about what had transpired as the victim from an old episode of *Mission Impossible*. Dett made me look like a nitwit—a clueless buffoon.

Knowing I had been soundly defeated by my nemesis exacerbated my bitterness by a factor of ten.

Crystal was at the heart of it all—or in this case, a little lower. At the time I was fired, both Dett and Crystal were married—but not to each other. He was a major corporate executive; and she was a fairly cute, diminutive, mid-level administrative assistant. Her hair was blond—except for the roots; and she wore her skirts short, accentuating her thighs, which were far too meaty to produce the enticing look she desired. The thing I remembered most about her though, other than her twangy Tennessee accent and slightly buckteeth, was her perfume. It was strong, pungent, and offensive. I'm not sure what the name of it was, but I think it might have been Jungle Gardenia. It had a rancid smell—like rotting flowers several days after a funeral. When she gave Dett a hug, he had her smell on him for the rest of the day.

Candidly, I had trouble being in the same room with Crystal—let alone touch her. When I came too close, her fragrance made me feel like sneezing. I wondered if she preferred adding layers of perfume to bathing. To me, she wasn't attractive. She reminded me of the type of woman Bill Clinton always liked—someone who would choose Waffle House as her preferred restaurant and Conway Twitty for her jukebox selection.

About the time I allegedly put my hand up Crystal's skirt, Dett's conflict with me became so acute it affected our ability to work together. To try and force me to resign, he became petulant, cruel, and vindictive. During sales meetings, for instance, he booked everybody to stay at the Marriott—everyone except for me. I was forced to stay at the Budgetel four blocks away. He did this to belittle me, hoping it would offend me enough to quit. I had to walk back and forth from meetings, even when it was raining.

With a family to support, I had to maintain a smile and endure his petty humiliations. I did this for the sake of my daughters, picturing how vulnerable and dependent they were upon me to be their provider. I kept them in my mind, as I walked back and forth, but his mean-spiritedness produced a lump in my throat with each step I took.

Not overreacting was difficult, especially knowing that making my life miserable brought him a twisted sense of satisfaction. Everything in me wanted to beat the crap out of him, which I could have done easily, but that wasn't an option. Instead, I was forced to laugh it off, as if it was no big deal—but it was. Dett's purpose was to hurt my feelings and grind down my self-worth, which he did repeatedly. He hoped I would overreact by lashing out, so that he could fire me on the spot, but I never did. Often, I felt like crying, but I couldn't. Guys can't do that. Frankly, it's embarrassing to admit this is how I felt back then, but it was.

Guys are forced to play a cavalier role at work frequently, for the sake of their families, smiling through the pain of being subjugated to mean-spirited, spiteful bosses like Dett. It nearly kills them on the inside, but they do it to fulfill their role as the family breadwinner.

Wives rarely understand how difficult situations like these can be. Because they are not as supportive as needed, many husbands turn to booze or another woman for comfort. Both are effective—a reprieve from the pain—a day off from the pressure. It works for a while—sometimes for quite a while—that is, until alcoholism or adultery becomes a greater problem than the original one, which inevitably happens.

Dett's spitefulness brought him deep satisfaction. Being constantly humiliated also diminished my confidence. If I had valued my sanity and serenity more highly, I would have left earlier, but I couldn't afford to miss a paycheck. Too many people were dependent on me. Every time I considered quitting in anger, I would see the smiling faces of my two daughters, Brittany and Briana, looking up at me, which effectively kept my emotions in check. Because I knew Dett's mistreatment would continue, all I could do was escalate my plans to establish my own business.

This is why I was able to play it cool the day I was terminated. I had planned for this scenario and had everything in place to make a swift, smooth transition. I'm sure Dett hoped I would fall apart, begging him to reconsider, but I didn't. I refused to give him the satisfaction of thinking he could grind me into the ground one more time.

Being fired wasn't what bothered me. What did bother me was knowing Dett could get away with such egregious conduct. The problem was none of the executives at Ludlow Randolph were willing to make an issue of his despicable behavior, which was something I never anticipated. Nobody who works for a Christian organization ever does. Like me, those who choose to work in this industry believe "Christian businesses" are above validating such vileness. Unfortunately, they soon discover their perceptions do not match reality.

Ludlow Randolph was Christian in name only, although senior

management would vehemently deny such an assessment. The corporate culture reminded me of a dysfunctional family more than anything else—one that was as far outside of God's will as Acy's missionary family. There was always an emotional price to be paid for the check I received twice a month.

Benny Lessner, Ludlow Randolph's owner, preferred to operate this way. His leadership style, which was to pit one man against another or one division against another, ensured that each would connive to outdo the other in Benny's never-ending mandate to maximize corporate profits. Ludlow Randolph produced Christian material, including leadership books—all founded on operating successful businesses based on Christian principles. Most of the books espoused the high values of teamwork and a win-win work ethic—none of which were operational at Ludlow Randolph. Although the work environment appeared ethical and wholesome to an outside observer—just like Acy's missionary family appeared to be—on the inside, it was an entirely different situation. Working at Ludlow Randolph was more like trying to function, while in a pit of hissing demons. Dett thrived in this hostile work environment, which championed mean-spiritedness, coupled with a healthy dose of obsequious God-talk.

I knew he was capable of being cunning, but I never considered that he would use Crystal to destroy me. Stooping to this level of duplicity never even entered my mind. Not being malicious by nature, I was at a disadvantage in dealing with the chain of command at Ludlow Randolph. I could never put myself in a frame of mind to think like my bosses, and it cost me—at least in the short term.

Although Dett had wanted to dismiss me for quite a while, he couldn't. Benny liked me and wanted to groom me to remain with the company long-term—just like he was doing with my friends, Pete and Acy. But the accusation by Crystal Moss changed all of that. Benny no longer looked upon me favorably—quite the opposite. This is why Pete insisted I talk to him a second time at Jake Smithson's birthday celebration. Pete hoped I could repair the relationship. He considered the chitchat between Benny and me to be damage control, but it wasn't. Instead, I was on a fool's errand that actually made things worse.

Not knowing what was really happening, I stumbled badly during our brief conversation. Now, all of that made sense. Benny's coolness towards me also made sense.

* * *

After Dett successfully dismissed me, he deserted his wife and daughter within a few months, obtaining a divorce shortly thereafter. Because the break up came out of the blue, his wife was devastated—as was their young daughter. Coincidentally, Crystal did precisely the same thing to her husband, dumping him and her children, practically at the same time. She just up and left her spouse and kids, citing irreconcilable differences with her mate.

Shortly thereafter, Crystal moved in with Dett. They lived together for several years but never married. Apparently, neither was willing to trust the other well enough to make a lasting commitment. This certainly didn't surprise me, especially after I discovered the circumstances that instigated their romance.

As I thought about it, I concluded somebody must have had a hand up Crystal's skirt; but it certainly wasn't me. Realizing that Dett's daughter and former wife were more badly hurt than I was made me feel guilty for indulging in self-pity, but that's exactly what I did. I ended up behaving the way most falsely accused people do.

After my dismissal, both Crystal and Dett continued to work for Ludlow Randolph—never missing a paycheck. Neither was even challenged about their perfectly executed plan to have me terminated, besmirching my reputation in the process. Their scheme was successful—a perfect surgical strike. Like their clandestine sex, it must have been deeply gratifying. When Evil triumphs, it's deliciously satisfying to its initiators—at least for a while.

5

My Mannerisms Were as Defiant as a Boxer

The convention for the Christian Booksellers Association was held in Atlanta a month-and-a-half after I learned about being falsely accused. I could hardly wait to attend. As the president of Ludlow Randolph, Benny Lessner was certain to be present. I was committed to finding him and exposing Dett's shenanigans—as well as Crystal's complicity. Practically salivating at the opportunity, I was determined to confront Benny the moment I spotted him.

Benny was a Christian. What Dett and Crystal had done broke at least two of the Ten Commandments—adultery and bearing false witness. Because of this, I convinced myself Benny would never allow them to get away with such sinful and duplicitous behavior. What Christian, especially one who was the president of a faith-based publishing house, would?

The convention was huge, and I was concerned I would be unable to find Benny. When I walked onto the exhibit floor the opening day, however, Benny was nearly the first person I saw. He was engaged in a conversation, so I waited for him to become available—just like I had in New York. This time, I wasn't sheepish about approaching him though. Sensing this, Benny ended his discussion quickly and turned to me.

With a circumspect look, he said, "Hi, Cole. How are you doing?"

"I'm doing well, Benny. How about you?"

"I'm fine," he responded crisply. "What can I do for you?"

This was my moment, and I knew it. Seizing the opportunity, I said, "I've just learned the real reason I was terminated three years ago." Looking at Benny intently, I stated, "I never touched Crystal Moss, Benny—let alone put my hand up her dress. It didn't happen. This false accusation is a complete fabrication. There isn't an ounce of truth to it."

He didn't respond, which surprised me. His face was nonplussed. I'm not sure what I expected, but it certainly wasn't stoic silence. He did give me his full attention though, which I took as permission to continue.

I was very nervous—terrified actually—but I was also resolute. I hated confrontations like this. I avoided them like the plague, but I was also determined to have my say. In this situation, my sense of righteous indignation trumped my inclination to be non-confrontational. Holding my ground—not retreating an inch—I continued. "When Dett and Brandon met with me, neither said a word about Crystal's accusation—not one. I finally heard about it, when we were in New York, nearly three years later!"

Again, he didn't respond. He just maintained his inscrutable demeanor, but he did continue to listen. Proceeding, I added, "It didn't happen, Benny—nothing even close to it happened. This is why I'm here. I came specifically to talk to you. I wanted to look you straight in the eye—man to man—and tell you it didn't happen. I want you to see for yourself that I'm telling the truth."

Benny finally responded by simply nodding his head, but he continued to remain silent. I had no idea what he was thinking; but since

I was already past the point of no return, I pressed forward, playing my ace of trumps. "Don't you think it's a little odd this accusation came just a few months before Crystal left her husband and started shacking up with Dett? Think about it, Benny. Dett left his wife at practically the same time. Doesn't this coincidence seem a little too convenient?"

Benny didn't respond, but he did flinch—just a little—and I saw it. If we had been playing poker, I would have doubled my wager. Finally having worked myself up to be more assertive, I pressed my advantage. "Dett wanted to fire me, but he knew you liked me." After a moment to allow this to sink in, I added, "He had to find a way to bring me down in your eyes, and he found one. But it's a lie, Benny—every word of it."

After hearing me out, Benny's nod seemed to be more genuine. I thought he had begun to look at things from my perspective. In fact, I was certain of it, although he didn't say so. I could see he was measuring my words, giving them great weight.

Finally, I made my pitch. "I'm leaving this in your hands, Benny. I'm not retaining a lawyer or anything like that, but I do need your help to right this wrong. Dett and Crystal have accused me of being sexually inappropriate, destroying my reputation with everybody at Ludlow Randolph and with several ministries. But it's not true, and it's not fair. I'm appealing to you, as the President of Ludlow Randolph and as my brother in Christ, to right this wrong."

As I was finishing, I saw Dett, who witnessed the intensity of our conversation from about five display booths away. Sensing danger, Dett practically sprinted toward us, implanting himself between Benny and me immediately. I just stood there, while Dett tried to make pleasantries—with his eyes darting back and forth between Benny and me. Dett knew something was badly amiss, which made him as nervous as a spotted cockroach.

I didn't say a word, but my mannerisms were as defiant as a boxer immediately before a fight. I looked at my nemesis, Alvin Dettler Carter, menacingly, nonverbally taunting him to be confrontational, but he wouldn't pick up the gauntlet—coward that he was. The tenseness only lasted a moment; but it seemed much longer, making all three of us feel uncomfortable.

Benny finally spoke. "Cole thanks for saying hello. We'll talk about this later. *I promise we will.* Now, I need to go to another meeting. Is that okay with you?"

"Certainly, Benny," I said graciously, as the tension between Dett and me dissipated. A moment later, we all shook hands, including Dett and me. Then, I turned and walked away confidently. I knew Benny would deal with the matter, and I would be vindicated. Undoubtedly, Dett would get fired—Crystal too, which is exactly what the two of them deserved. Being summarily discharged would be a befitting consequence for what they had done—one that would certainly be soul satisfying for me.

As I walked out of the convention hall to get a much-needed cup of coffee, I smiled, savoring my triumph. Justice would prevail, and I would be vindicated. Best of all, I would be able stop chafing and start sleeping through the night—free from the bitter recriminations that robbed me of my serenity, ever since I learned the truth about what happened.

Dett and Crystal's dismissal from Ludlow-Randolph is what you would expect, isn't it, especially from a Christian publisher who promotes God's Kingdom by selling millions of Bibles? That's certainly what I thought would happen. What other outcome could there be?

Well, that's not what happened. That's not even close to what happened.

I waited for several weeks before contacting Benny again. I wanted to give him every opportunity to address the situation at the office—as he promised he would. When I finally phoned, he wouldn't take any of my repeated calls. Neither would anybody else at Ludlow Randolph—except for Pete, Acy, and the corporate attorney. The company had closed ranks, shunning me and my plea for justice. It was obvious they were unwilling to address Dett's unethical behavior, which both Pete and Acy verified in subsequent conversations.

Benny didn't keep his word. He broke his promise and considered it prudent business to do so. From a financial perspective, perhaps it was—but not from a moral, ethical standpoint. There is never a right way to do a wrong thing, regardless of the consequences. Benny knew this, but he chose the expedient path, ignoring my situation completely. Doing the right thing might have made the company look bad, and Benny certainly wasn't willing to do that.

When I finally realized what had happened, my feelings were hurt more than anything else. I had been falsely accused, convicted in absentia, condemned, and discarded with the trash. Because it was so unfair, I felt the sting of my wounds deeply. I didn't deserve my fate and wondered why God would allow such a miscarriage of justice to occur in the first place.

Initially, it made me think He didn't care, which added to the bitter recriminations churning within me. I couldn't get past the unfairness of what had happened, especially how Benny's Christian principles were dismissed in favor of covering up Dett's misconduct. This added to my acrimony appreciably. In my resentment, I replayed the event in my mind over and over, especially in the middle of the night, as I continued to be robbed of sleep.

Emotionally, this was a very difficult time for me, as I suspect it would be for just about anybody. Perhaps I should have handled my feelings better, but I couldn't. Being human, the disillusionment I experienced exacted a significant toll on my soul. Being falsely accused was a bitter pill to swallow.

In my attempt to have the situation rectified, I made an appeal to a Christian brother to address a significant wrong suffered while in his employment. This certainly seemed like the appropriate thing to do, and I was certain it would work; but it didn't.

At first, I was frustrated, but my emotions soon turned to bitterness. I became angry about everything concerning Christianity—just like Acy and his sisters had done, when their father failed to nurture their emotional wellbeing. Like them, I was also powerless to do anything about it. Benny and Dett had all the power. I was as voiceless as Acy and his sisters had been before their mother's suicide. All I could do was chafe and become resentful, which is precisely what I did.

6

Self-Serving, Unscrupulous, and Unethical

Being one of the most influential leaders in evangelical Christianity, Benny Lessner was an important man—no question about it. Close to a billionaire—just like the old E. F. Hutton commercial used to attest—when Benny spoke, people listened.

My situation was a clear hindrance to his grand vision, which was to maximize his Christian business interests, regardless of what it required to accomplish his seemingly altruistic objective. He didn't want my situation to rock the boat at Ludlow Randolph. Consequently, like so many instances requiring principled leadership from him over the years, he swept the episode under the rug, disregarding it as if it never happened, defying me to prove differently.

When doing the right thing interfered with the company's profitability, financial considerations always took precedence. Benny would deny this, saying the company operated on biblical principles; but his actions consistently contradicted his Christian testimony, which was essentially a sham. Several decades later, I'm sure Benny still believes he did the right thing—that is, if he even remembers the event or who I am. You see, I wasn't that important. I was a minor player, a peon—someone who just happened to get in the way of his goal to create a giant Christian conglomerate, anchored by his publishing company.

In his mind, building his Christian empire was God's purpose for his life. Like so many others before and after him, Benny deceived himself into believing he was pursuing God's will, regardless of the methods he used to achieve it. This kind of thinking came naturally to Benny. Grandiosity was hardwired into his DNA. So was victory, which he played like a zero-sum game. Smart and talented, along with being as driven as he was, Benny was destined to achieve enormous success.

When it served his purpose, he could be generous and noble—just like he had been at Jake Smithson's birthday celebration in New York. When it didn't, he could be as ruthless as the hero of Machiavelli's *Prince*. Anybody who interfered with his divine mandate was removed by whatever means necessary—whether ethically or unethically. It didn't matter which, just as long as the result furthered Benny's single-minded purpose. From my vantage point, once my eyes became opened, more people were treated ruthlessly than fairly, which made these unfortunates as bitter toward God as they were toward Benny and Ludlow Randolph.

Benny's obsession with success, which he equated with God's will, was what made Dett more valuable than Pete, Acy, or I. Benny depended on Dett to do whatever was necessary to get the job done. Whenever there was an unsavory task, Dett was always there—ready, eager, and willing to do his master's bidding. Benny empowered Dett to be a bully—a role the latter relished. Benny came to count on Dett in the same way Vito Corleone counted on Luca Brasi to "take care of business" in *The Godfather*.

Correcting my situation would have been a minor detour—a slight bump in the road—but Benny wouldn't permit this. He never deviated from what he considered to be his objective—not even a smidgen.

He preferred to do the right thing—make no mistake about it. This is how he differed from being a true tyrant, but doing the right thing in the right way was never a requirement. If being honorable and selfless hindered the furtherance of his objective, it ceased to be a consideration. This is just the way Benny was.

For him, like Vito Corleone, it was never personal. It was always business. Although Benny could be equally ruthless, it was never in a violent way. Unlike the Godfather, carnage is where Benny drew the line.

If Benny was the only Christian leader who operated this way, it would be one thing, but he wasn't. Among the elites of evangelicalism, such self-serving, unscrupulous, and unethical behavior was common. In fact, for many, it was more than common. It was their standard operating procedure. When doing the right thing interfered with their inflated vision of what God called them to do, heaven help those who got in their way.

This is what happened to me. I got in the way. It wasn't personal; it was business. At least for Benny it was business. From his perspective, that I took it personally was regrettable but insignificant.

When I discovered the truth about my dismissal and had the audacity to bring it to his attention, I became a bit of a nuisance. Rectifying my situation, however, certainly wasn't important enough for Benny to deviate from his course. To my surprise and dismay, when I finally realized who he really was, it was too late. The damage had already been done, and I was destined to reap the negative consequences. He continued moving relentlessly forward, while the false witness against me remained intact, adding to my embitterment.

If my story was an isolated incidence, it would be one thing, but it wasn't. I wasn't alone. Similar things happened to others at Ludlow Randolph. In each case, those victimized slinked away wounded and defeated, but none of this seemed to phase either Benny or Dett—not one iota.

Because Benny—like numerous other evangelical leaders—was striving to achieve God's will, Benny believed he was justified in doing whatever was necessary to accomplish the task set before him. Dett, sycophantically idolizing his mentor, was uniquely gifted to be his boss's enforcer, creating mayhem in the lives of others—all to aid Benny's obsession with fulfilling his "divine mandate."

For Benny, like so many of the superstars of Christendom, the ends justified the means. Achieving success, at any price, became coterminous with God's will. With this overarching conviction, which differed from the New Testament ethic Benny espoused as foundational to his belief system, it's no wonder the false witness against me was never addressed.

That I believed he would do the right thing is a clear indication of exactly how naïve I was. Like so many of life's lessons, I learned the hard way. Being clueless is never what God intends for a grown man or woman to be. I was equally unaware that many of the other lords and ladies of evangelicalism embraced Benny's success-at-any-cost value system. Where they were concerned, I had to learn my lessons through trial and error, but I did learn them.

During this period, I lacked the insight and discernment to see things as they really were. Lacking wisdom, I foolishly believed in Benny and trusted him completely. I also trusted the other great evangelical leaders—those whose ministries were being blessed by God. I actually believed what these luminaries wrote about themselves in their brochures. I mistakenly assumed it was the true report, which it rarely was.

Because of my naïveté, I put myself in a position to be exploited. Benny and Dett used my innocence to their advantage—just like they did with so many others. Because I worked with him on a daily basis, I learned what Dett was like quickly, but Benny had me completely fooled.

Trusting Benny to be who he said he was, which others seemed to validate as the true report, made me vulnerable to exploitation. It also made me expendable when my presence no longer served his purpose. Knowing what I know now, I wouldn't allow such abuse to impact me adversely. Like so many born-again believers, however, I was gullible, even though it never occurred to me that I was. I guess this is what the definition of being gullible is, isn't it?

After spending a substantial period thinking about the injustice of my experience, I came to realize how limited Benny actually was—just like Pastor Doucette was. Both were blinded by self-exalting ambition. Thinking they were working for the Lord, building His Kingdom and not their own, they had the perfect excuse to treat others as objects, rather than as God's beloved children, effectively dehumanizing them.

My wounding—just like the Doucette children's—occurred because I got in the way of "God's will." My purpose, like Acy and his twin sisters, was to serve those with a higher calling than I had—nothing more. People like me were there to help and not to hinder, to believe and not to question, to serve and never to be served. Our purpose was to enhance our master's efforts, while never deviating from our belief in his benevolence. We were mandated to accept the lofty goals and ambitions of our leaders as our own, embracing them as God's will for our lives.

To go against either Pastor Doucette or Benny was depicted as rebelling against Almighty God Himself. Being crossed was all the rationalization that either needed to crush the spirit of a child or an underling—something both considered to be the just punishment for those who got in their way.

Looking back, it's hard to believe these men were the spiritual envy of others, but they were, particularly Benny. When he was in his sixties, Ludlow Randolph published a book about how God had favored

Benny's dramatic climb to the top. It focused on his business practices and Christian ethics, which were lauded to the world as exemplary.

When Pete, Acy, and I heard about the project, we joked that the book was anything but an accurate biography. Instead, it was a work of fiction—an attempt by a character resembling Shylock, from *The Merchant of Venice*, to be lauded as praiseworthy. To those on the outside, who saw nothing but the veneer, Benny looked gracious, principled, and altruistic. To those of us who got in his way, however, we experienced an entirely different person.

We knew who he really was. The only difference between Shylock and Benny was the latter routinely obtained his pound of flesh. Praised as a great Christian, Benny was far more Machiavellian than Christ-like.

* * *

After being stonewalled at Ludlow Randolph for several months about Crystal-gate, as I came to call it, I became weary of beating my head against the wall and eventually dropped the matter, as Benny predicted I would.

Through my ordeal, I didn't gain wisdom immediately or easily but, as the years passed, many things became quite clear. To help deal with my pain, I spent quite a bit of time in counseling. This helped me process my bitterness, which was so consuming it left me nearly immobilized for a while. I'm not sure I would have been able to heal without talking about my painful grievances numerous times.

Once I was able to vent, addressing my painful experiences openly and candidly, the poison from the sting was alleviated. This is when things started to become clear. At first, I was obviously too wounded and upset to develop discernment. Initially, all I could do was emote. I didn't deserve what happened. The false witness, coupled with the ensuing character assassination, hurt me deeply, but my discomfort didn't concern those responsible for causing it—not in the least. This is what bothered me the most.

My reputation and career were expendable—acceptable collateral damage. Exposing what happened might adversely impact the reputation of the company, and Benny would never allow that to happen—not for anything. Repudiating Dett's wrongdoing wasn't even a consideration. Glossing over it and hiding it became standard operating procedure at Ludlow Randolph.

I came to realize the perception of *being seen as righteous* was more important than actually *doing the right thing*. Once I understood this and accepted it, I actually began to heal from my abuse.

The results of my mistreatment followed me for years. I'm sure there are still people who believe I groped Dett's slattern nearly a quarter-of-a-century ago. If I allowed myself to dwell on the downside though, I never would have healed. This is why I had to let it go—all of it. Staying angry and unforgiving was like saying; "I'll get even with you by hurting me." I couldn't continue to move forward by remaining stuck in the past, which counseling helped me resolve.

Nurturing bitterness isn't a strategy that works, nor will it make you the kind of person others want to be around. When you are consumed by resentment, especially when it's justified, your sense of entitled wounded-ness engulfs your entire being. You become a joy sponge, sucking the life out of everybody around you. I didn't want to live like this. Neither did I want to subject others to a person who acted this way, especially my family.

At first, letting go was extremely difficult. I wondered why I should be the one whose life was filled with pain and not theirs? Why should the negative consequences fall on me and not on Dett, Crystal, and Benny? I even blamed God for my situation but, in my heart, like Acy, I knew God could never be the author of abuse.

Letting go of my entitled sense of victimization was definitely the most difficult part of healing. I couldn't discard it all at once; but I did one day at a time. Instead of allowing anger, frustration and outrage to settle, becoming unshakeable—exercising all-consuming dominion over me—I released these debilitating emotions. It was the only option that would restore serenity to my soul and allow me to move forward, unencumbered by the chains of my past.

Learning acceptance and forgiveness wasn't all I gained. I wanted more than that. I wanted to understand the dynamics of what happened. I wanted to abandon my naïveté and develop discernment. I wanted to be able to help others who had been wounded by people like Dett, Benny, and other self-serving Christian leaders.

To do this, I began asking myself some hard questions—questions about what was really happening at Ludlow Randolph, as well as with the other Christian ministries I served. I didn't obtain the answers immediately. In fact, discovering the truth about this perplexing problem became an essential part of my life for the next twenty-five years.

7

He's Mr. Fumblethumbs

Dett meant my dismissal for evil. Crystal too. With Benny's support, Dett's ruthless scheme produced an overwhelming success for him. Best of all, it was accomplished with no negative consequences for Benny, the company, or for my former boss. Dett also used the incident to solidify his affair with Crystal. By divorcing his wife and having his paramour move in with him, Dett's victory also produced lascivious benefits.

By getting rid of her Redneck husband, Crystal also upgraded her situation. That is, if sleeping with Dett could be considered an upgrade. She was certainly better off financially than she had been, which was a plus. Perhaps this was her real motivation.

From Dett's perspective, I had been completely vanquished—surgically removed—leaving nothing but the slightest scar. Being so successful in his ploy, Dett must have smiled with satisfaction, as he savored his triumph—the undisputed winner in our little war.

To me, it certainly seemed like Evil had prevailed. Although this is how the results were viewed at the time, in subsequent years—as is so often the case—life changed the outcome. It's what makes the stories of our lives so interesting. What Dett intended for Evil, God used for Good, creating something worthwhile out of the emotional devastation that came close to destroying me.

New life and purpose came from the carnage, making me a much better person. God used this experience for my growth, as well as for the elucidation of others. At first, I didn't believe this could be possible. In fact, I was certain it couldn't, but experience demonstrated how mistaken I was. God had a purpose for all of it. I'm not overstating this conclusion, as you will come to recognize.

* * *

My mistreatment at Ludlow Randolph wasn't an isolated occurrence. Others were also used, abused, and discarded. Dett got away with devious, unethical behavior repeatedly—actions for which anybody else would have been fired on the spot. Nearly everybody suspected it was because he had something on Benny. Most thought it was an extramarital affair. A few thought it might be worse than that. Nobody knew for certain and probably never will. What I do know is Benny never addressed Dett's false witness against me—as he promised he would. Instead, he dismissed it, as he did so many other ethical issues concerning Dett.

For instance, several years later, Dett entered the corporate offices of Ludlow Randolph at 3 a.m., on Christmas morning, when nobody but Santa was supposed to be awake. When the security team noticed someone had entered the building at such an unusual hour, during the holidays, they became immediately suspicious. Reviewing the security tapes, they saw Dett in the mailroom, rifling through people's mail. While there, he even had the audacity to throw away a letter placed in Benny's mailbox, which could be construed as tampering with the US Mail. After spending an hour perusing the correspondence of every important executive, Dett opened a tin of popcorn, which was a Christmas present for the men in the warehouse. He began eating the caramel corn, sporting a smile of satisfaction when he did. Obviously, he thought it was delicious. That it belonged to someone else probably enhanced its flavor. When he finished the task of ferreting through everybody's correspondence, Dett picked up the tin of popcorn, placed it under his arm, and left the building.

The alarmed security guard brought the tape to human resources who, in turn, informed Benny about Dett's activities. Because this was a serious infraction of corporate policy and a potential federal crime, the incident was held in the strictest confidence, which meant it became office gossip immediately, spreading through corporate headquarters more quickly than a California wildfire.

Because Dett's behavior was obviously unethical, everyone assumed Benny would be forced to dismiss him. When the tape was reviewed, Benny said he wasn't certain it was really Dett. The resolution wasn't good enough to be sure, so Benny ordered the inquiry to be closed. From that moment forward, nobody suspected Dett had something on Benny—they were certain of it.

Benny admired Dett's cunning ruthlessness. If you're extremely rich, having someone like Dett, who is devoid of scruples and fundamental decency can be very advantageous, especially because Dett maintained a credible pietistic facade. To say the least, Dett's unique set of skills was useful to Benny in the Christian publishing business. Dett was a wolf resembling a lamb, which few had the ability to discern. It made him invaluable in assuring that efforts to further God's Kingdom also produced substantial profits for Ludlow Randolph.

Benny was no fool. He knew what ministries were really like. Most were so self-serving they would do practically anything to achieve their goals. Dett knew this as well, and he was up to the task of protecting Ludlow Randolph's interests, guaranteeing Benny would come out on top.

Dett's fierce loyalty to Benny made their relationship more than tight; it was unassailable. More than any other variable, this was the reason why Dett was able to terminate me with impunity—without even receiving a reprimand. He continued to run his division for years after "Crystal-gate."

Pete, Acy, and I witnessed similar episodes of Dett's misconduct frequently. His ploy to get rid of me was so successful he tried it twice more with other employees he wanted to dismiss without cause, each time using Crystal Moss to assert she had been sexually harassed. It worked the first time but not the second. By then, nearly five years later, Crystal had gained an additional thirty pounds of comfort weight, making her derriere larger than Oprah's.

Nobody bought her story, but neither did they reevaluate what had happened to me years earlier, which was disheartening. It shouldn't have been, I suppose, but it was. Like anybody who has been treated unjustly, in the back of my mind, I longed for vindication, hoping it would come one day. That it never did hurt my feelings—especially after people realized who Crystal really was and the level of harm she was capable of inflicting. It's difficult to accept being considered so unimportant that nobody would care enough to set the record straight, but this is precisely what happened. It made me feel like a used teabag—no longer having any worthwhile value.

I'm gratified the third guy was vindicated, but like Crystal's second victim, I lamented; "What about her false witness against me? Can't anybody see what really happened? Doesn't anybody care?"

Apparently, nobody did. They didn't seem to realize this is a pattern of abuse—not an isolated incident. When Crystal's accusation about the third man was dismissed summarily, she felt the sting of being disrespected. Never a favorite at the office, the staff no longer wanted anything to do with her. When she passed, they began casting contemptuous glances her way. This made her feel uncomfortable, but more than anything, she was miffed that people would have the audacity to question her word. No one had ever mustered the courage to do that before.

In her fury, Crystal lashed out at the only safe person she could—her lover, Dett. He may not have been safe for anyone else, but he was definitely safe for her. As many sexually intimate couples are, Crystal and Dett were verbally abusive toward one another. Behavior like this is what happens when paramours don't respect one another, which neither Crystal nor Dett could, obviously.

Their sex may have been pleasing in the carnal sense, but it wasn't fulfilling—not in a soul-satisfying way. Because unconditional love wasn't foundational to their relationship, neither were kindness, compassion, or acceptance. These desirable qualities were replaced by strife, contempt, and disrespect, which are never characteristics of a lasting relationship. Surprisingly, both had fooled themselves into believing they would always stay together.

Angry that her accusation had been rebuffed at the office, which also evaporated the tenuous respect she maintained as Dett's paramour, she lashed out. In her pique, she spitefully sent an email to one of her girlfriends. In it, Crystal lamented, "Dett is a terrible lover. He may be a bigwig at the office, but he's Mr. Fumblethumbs in bed. I never get off with him, and I definitely need to. I fake it all the time. I'm so bored I can't stand it."

Laughing heartily when she read the email, Crystal's girlfriend forwarded it to a couple others, one of whom happened to work at Ludlow

Randolph. Unbeknownst to Crystal, while she was outside smoking a cigarette to calm her nerves, the recipient went to Crystal's cubicle, sat in front of her computer, pulled up the email from the sent box, and forwarded it to everybody in Crystal's address book, which included nearly all of the employees at Ludlow Randolph. By the end of the day, everybody had a good laugh—all at the expense of Mr. Fumblethumbs.

Dett became the laughing stock of the entire building. Both Pete and Acy forwarded the email to me. Loathing my former boss, I roared with delight. It wasn't one of my better moments, but I couldn't help myself.

When Dett confronted Crystal that evening in the privacy of their living room, the conversation that ensued certainly wasn't a laughing matter—far from it. Knowing she was on thin ice, Crystal tried to be coquettish and alluring, which had always worked with Mr. Fumblethumbs, but this time she couldn't seduce him. He would never again be captivated by her fraudulent charms or her fake orgasms.

Neither would he be forgiving; he couldn't be. For a narcissist like Dett, the one thing he could never tolerate was an affront to his person. His ego structure was far too fragile to allow that. He believed he was a great lover, and that was all there was to it. Crystal's denunciation was a personal betrayal, which meant she had to be purged from his life—the sooner the better.

Since the house was his and not hers, she was forced to leave that evening. With nothing other than the clothes on her back and all she could fit into her car, she went to a Hampton Inn. While driving there, crying bitter tears, she tried to formulate a plan to salvage her situation, but she couldn't come up with anything.

With Dett, you were either on his side, or you were his enemy. There was no middle ground. With him, everything was black and white. There were no shades of gray. Having shown her true colors, Crystal became public enemy number one—a woman to be scorned. Reconciliation was out of the question. She had hurt him, but nothing about her departure generated sorrow for Dett. It's not like this for a narcissist.

With her gone, there was a void in his life, a position that needed to be filled, but he didn't grieve her absence—not like a normal person would. Acting on his decision to rid himself of her, the following day Dett had his locks changed, as well as the password for each of his accounts. This ensured Crystal couldn't pull a fast one and pirate away any of his earthly belongings. He also removed every picture of her from his house, as well as the ones from his office. For Dett, Crystal had become a non-person.

She ceased to exist. Incapable of genuine emotions over their failed relationship, he wasn't hurt. He was angry, bitter, and vengeful. Although Mr. Fumblethumbs may have been incapable of selfless love, or of being an adequate lover, he was definitely capable of settling a score.

That same afternoon, Crystal's supervisor asked to meet with her. When she walked into his office, the head of human resources was also present. Directing her to be seated, her supervisor, Percy Atwater, came straight to the point. "Crystal, we are very concerned about the defamatory email you sent to nearly every employee of the company. Being a Christian publisher, maintaining the high standard of our image is essential, which your email has tarnished badly."

Interrupting him, Crystal retorted defensively. "Mr. Atwater, I didn't send that email. Someone else sent it from my computer, but it wasn't me. I promise it wasn't. I would never do something like that. I'm very embarrassed by what happened. Please accept my apology; it will never happen again."

Atwater paid no attention to her protestation of innocence or to her impassioned plea for mercy. Neither interested him in the least. Continuing, as if she hadn't responded, he added, "You have violated the ethical clause of your contract. Consequently, we are exercising our right to terminate your employment immediately. This will be your last day at Ludlow Randolph."

"But Mr. Atwater, I can't lose my job. Dett threw me out last night. I don't have a place to live, and now this. You can't do this to me. It's not fair," she lamented.

Nonplussed, Atwater continued. "Yes, we can, Ms. Moss. You should have thought about the consequences of your actions before you sent that email."

"But I didn't send it," she whined.

Unsympathetic, Atwater announced. "This is what is going to happen. When you leave this meeting, security will escort you to your cubicle, where you will have ten minutes to clear out your desk. While there, you may not send an email, use your company computer, or place a telephone call. Are my directives perfectly clear, Ms. Moss?"

On the verge of tears, she just nodded that she understood.

"Good," Atwater replied. With finality, he announced, "When you've gathered your things, you will surrender your key to the building. Then, you will be escorted to the front door. When you leave, you will never be allowed to enter the offices of Ludlow Randolph again."

He waited for her to respond, but she didn't. Continuing, he said, "One more thing: there will be no severance pay for you. When an ethical violation is involved, severance is never provided. Do you understand everything I have explained, Ms. Moss?" he asked matter-of-factly.

She definitely understood, but she wasn't willing to accept complete defeat—not that easily. Regaining her composure, while successfully fighting back tears, she went on the offensive. She pitched a fit, screaming at her boss and the vice president of HR for two minutes. When she finished, she realized neither Atwater nor the head of HR had been moved, swayed, or intimidated in the least by her recriminating tirade.

Narrowing his eyes, Atwater became confrontational. "Ms. Moss, your time at Ludlow Randolph is over—so is this meeting. You can either go peacefully—right this minute—or I will instruct security to call the

Orlando Police Department and have you forcibly removed from the premises. Now, which will it be?"

Having no alternative, with quivering lips, glistening eyes, and a runny nose, she gave both men a dark, menacing look, rose from her chair, and left the meeting, without saying another word.

As she walked to her cubicle, trailed by the two security guards, she began to cry once again. Her punishment seemed so unfair. She hadn't forwarded that email, so she didn't deserve getting fired—and certainly not like this. After gathering her things and placing them in a small box, she was escorted to the front door by the two guards. While walking the "green mile," her co-workers stepped out of their cubicles to watch her pass. Being Dett's concubine, Crystal wasn't popular, especially with the women. Most of them bitterly resented her. As Crystal walked by, in her diminished state, out of the corner of her eye she could see the contemptuous sneers of those who were her enemies. Their satisfied smirks exacerbated her humiliation significantly.

It never occurred to Crystal that she was receiving the just recompense for her past behavior. Being as shallow and self-serving as she was, such a realization was beyond her ability to either compute or accept. Instead, she chose to dwell on the unfairness of how she had been treated, never accepting the slightest responsibility for her actions, which ended up costing her everything her connivance had produced.

The following day, when Pete called to inform me about Crystal's fate, I suspect the look on my face resembled that of her co-workers. It was difficult not to take pleasure in her demise. It was an outcome she richly deserved. As Pete and I discussed the events surrounding her dismissal, we hoped this would be the last we would hear from her. Like a bad penny though, women like Crystal seem to resurface, creating havoc. When you least expected it, she could appear, reeking of Jungle Gardenia, but she never did—thank God.

8

Like a Frog in a Pot

Once absent, the dysfunction resulting from Crystal's shenanigans quickly became a distant memory, as Ludlow Randolph returned to its goal of maximizing profitability. Promoting Christianity was good business, especially within Dett's division of the company. As Benny's faithful vassal, Dett always "made his numbers."

Dett knew every television evangelist and influential church leader in America. Because Ludlow Randolph was a major player, he was welcomed with open arms wherever he went. Because Benny could be philanthropic whenever it suited him, cash strapped ministries were constantly jockeying for position, relentlessly seeking a substantial donation. Few were given, but just the possibility that it might happen ensured Dett's visits were ballyhooed as special occasions.

Being Benny's surrogate made Dett's job much easier and far more prestigious. His stature was inflated so disproportionately that, when he arrived at a ministry, he was treated as deferentially as a Presidential Ambassador. Such treatment was intoxicating to Ludlow Randolph's high school graduate. Dett came to expect accolades, craving the attention like an addict needing a fix. He convinced himself such attention and accouterments were appropriate and warranted—something akin to being his destiny.

Ministries hoped to use their relationship with Dett to influence Benny, but they had no idea with whom they were dealing. Once Dett ingratiated himself into a ministry's inner circle, which required little effort, he began his search for like-minded people—those motivated by the lust of the flesh, the lust of the eye, and the boastful pride of life. And he always found them—lots of them. It was his special gift. When he did, he would focus on gaining that person's trust—his long established and predictable pattern. As soon as this happened, he found a way to compromise the person.

This is when circumstances would begin to change. Once he owned a piece of some unfortunate person's soul, Dett would start exerting his influence, tilting the scales in his favor, creating an economic advantage for Ludlow Randolph, Benny, and himself—much to the delight of his benefactor in Orlando.

Having been compromised in one way or the other, coupled with the fear of public exposure, followed by ridicule, the ministry representative would never be able to hold his or her ground in dealing with Dett again. Weakened, this person would be emotionally coerced into agreeing to terms that were clearly not in the ministry's best interests.

Knowing that people—whose souls were owned by him—could never negotiate from strength, Dett leveraged the compromised person's trust to maximize his advantage. This was his purpose all along. In these situations, Dett was routinely the victor.

Despite the power differential between the abuser and his victim, Dett was never heavy-handed. Instead, he remained deferential, which kept his prey constantly off balance. Dett was smooth. He was never an outward bully; he wouldn't even consider being one. His methods were far too subtle for that. Being overtly confrontational was never his style. Instead, his influence was always exerted in smooth, calculating, and shrewd ways.

When he was at a ministry, Dett was consistently obsequious. His malice, which he carefully concealed, remained hidden just below the surface, camouflaged perfectly by a syrupy, disingenuous smile. To nearly everybody, he seemed like a benevolent, competent, and trustworthy servant of the Lord.

Dett knew what was happening, as did his victim. The person didn't realize it at first, of course, but eventually his or her compromised position became painfully clear. Other people in the ministry never comprehended what was happening. They were usually clueless. Their knowledge of negotiations remained superficial at best. They only knew what Dett wanted them to know—nothing more. Because they were oblivious, their approving smiles were genuine—never forced or coerced.

Being certain things were copacetic, ministry workers effectively convinced those who might have doubts that things were progressing smoothly. Dett counted on this and used it to his advantage. Keeping people in the dark was essential.

Just as he had done with me, he never allowed lesser mortals to see the situation for what it was. His ability to accomplish this effortlessly is what made his serpentine ways so effective. It's also why Benny consistently overlooked his devious misconduct.

People trusted Dett until his one-sided deal became a reality. This is when they realized how unfair it actually was. By then, however, there was nothing they could do to alter the situation. Like Faust, who struck a deal with Mephistopheles, those compromised by Dett came to regret their candor, as their worst nightmares came to fruition.

To avoid exposure, and perhaps even the loss of their positions, these unfortunates—people who trusted Dett—agreed to terms that were disadvantageous to their ministry, effectively making their side the vanquished for the duration of the deal. Others—the rank and file workers in the ministry—who were oblivious throughout the negotiations, simply accepted their fate like good victims. They bemoaned their reversal of fortune, as they came to realize their efforts were building Benny's empire at Ludlow Randolph rather than the Lord's or their own.

Seeing how this unfolded numerous times is how I came to realize who Dett really was. When I began working for him, he fooled me—just like he fooled everybody else. This didn't change until I began to piece together exactly how he operated, which required time, since he was so cunning.

While I was still working at Ludlow Randolph, either Pete, Acy, or I would set things up for Dett—just like we were the warm-up team, getting the crowd ready for the star's appearance. This was our job. We would make the preliminary effort, working out a book deal or a marketing venture between the ministry and Ludlow Randolph. We would provide the product; the ministry would provide the audience—either from TV viewers or from radio listeners. In theory, such an arrangement should have worked well, with everybody winning.

When we had every facet of the agreement worked out, Dett would make his entrance to seal the deal. If it was large enough, Benny might even make an appearance, but his presence was rare. He preferred to allow Dett to be the bad cop. As president of Ludlow Randolph, it allowed him to maintain plausible deniability if things fell apart.

More often than not, when Dett arrived, having compromised someone within the ministry, he would change the specifics of the agreement. This certainly wasn't what we wanted or expected, but it is what happened. It made us liars by proxy, which was deeply disturbing, especially since we were powerless to rectify the situation. I can't tell you how many times Dett embarrassed me by changing key points of an agreement I thought had already been finalized.

It got to the place where I would ask Dett hard, direct questions about what to expect before I would even made the initial proposal. I wanted to be certain everything was as I had communicated it would be. Dett would promise the deal was straightforward and true, and his assurances were very convincing.

Then, at the last minute, he would announce changes that had been made behind my back. He did the same thing to Pete and Acy. It occurred repeatedly. I felt like Charlie Brown, trusting that Lucy would not pull the football away when he tried to kick it, but she always did—just like Dett did. Metaphorically, I landed on my derriere more often than not.

* * *

Being in such a situation became increasingly untenable, but I also knew the problem was greater than what was happening at Ludlow Randolph. Pete and Acy recognized this as well. Nothing was as it seemed to be at nearly every ministry we served. What we saw was a disturbing trend that was occurring across the fruited plane—a trend that required addressing—a pattern of darkness that needed to be exposed to the light. It's a problem that most people don't even realize exists. If they did, they would be appalled.

In America, some people are so skeptical of religious leaders they refuse to give them a chance, choosing instead to ascribe ulterior motives to everything they do. Such people don't seem to be able to help themselves. Cynical by nature, they reject having faith in anything. I suppose it's just a part of their natures to be that way. There are many people like this—those who refuse to believe in anything other than themselves. They are the doubtful, the dubious, the distrustful, and the jaded. They refuse to be fooled, but by doing so, they also miss out on much of life's richness. Choosing to be cautious and suspicious, they never lower their guard about anything involving faith.

There is another type of person—those whose natures allow them to believe freely and easily, perhaps too easily. It's why people refer to them as "believers." Because it's in their nature to trust, they can also be easily hoodwinked—fooled by those they come to trust, by those who claim to speak for God. Unfortunately, their open-heartedness, which is a positive character quality, can be used against them; and it often is. The world is full of such people, and I'm one of them.

Frequently, people like me choose to bury our heads in the sand, when our leaders fail to meet acceptable standards of behavior. We refuse to call a spade a spade. When we finally recognize something is amiss, we don't speak out—not at first anyway.

Most of the time, we don't make a conscious decision to behave this way. Instead, we simply drift along, trying to make the best out of a difficult situation, without overtly admitting how destructive it has become. Always thinking positively—trying to "look at the glass half full"—we accept behavior from our spiritual leaders we shouldn't. We make excuses for them to everybody, including ourselves. We behave like a frog in a pot of water. Before we realize how hot it has become, the water is boiling.

Nefarious Christian ministries thrive on people like us because we routinely give our leaders a pass for conduct we would never tolerate in others. This is especially true when we work for them. As part of our unspoken job description, we are expected to hide the truth, to camouflage what is really happening "behind the curtain," and to put a positive spin on questionable ethical behavior. Occasionally, we are even required to turn a blind eye to various forms of sexual deviancy.

We do this to protect the religious leader and the ministry from suffering the natural consequences of inappropriate behavior. Without thinking through the ramifications, we tell ourselves we are protecting God's Kingdom, but this is a mistake. We are deceiving ourselves. When we operate like this, our loyalty becomes our weakness rather than our strength. Even worse, we rarely perceive reality, as we should. Not wanting to hurt the work of the Lord, we maintain a stiff upper lip, while keeping our mouths shut, particularly about the aberrant behavior of our leaders behind closed doors.

We act like a woman who believes it's her responsibility to protect her alcoholic husband from facing the legitimate consequences of his drunkenness. Our behavior could also be compared to that of a longsuffering wife of a scandalized politician—a woman who stands by her spouse at a news conference, while he admits to being involved in adultery, homosexuality, or graft and corruption. By so doing, like these women, we believe we are validating the person but not the behavior. Again, this is a mistake because the problem is usually much deeper than simply acting out. Essentially, we end up enabling the fox to return to the henhouse, once minor penance has been satisfied.

I know this is true. I'm not guessing. What I've witnessed over the years is not an isolated problem with a few ministries. It's much worse than that. What I came to realize is there is a "cover-up mindset" in America that is fully operational in numerous ministries, mega-churches, and Christian publishing houses. For more than a quarter of a century, I have watched ministry staff go to elaborate lengths to shield duplicitous leaders, protecting them from being exposed to the light, sheltering them from facing the appropriate penalty for misbehaving. Recognizing the enormity of the problem required years for me to grasp. Once I did though, it became far easier to understand the causal factors behind the problem.

When I was younger, I couldn't understand why solid Christian people would participate in such conduct. It was a real mystery. That is, I didn't understand it until I realized I had become one of these people, when I began working for Alvin Dettler Carter.

Like others, I never made a conscious decision to do anything wrong or misleading. It just happened. Not knowing what else to do, I simply kept my mouth shut about Dett's unethical escapades instead of speaking out, which was a mistake. Dett knew this was what I would do—at least for a while. Knowing I had to support my family, he used my vulnerability to his advantage. This was my weak spot—the place that provided him the leverage he needed to exploit me.

By knuckling under to his deviousness, knowing I couldn't miss a paycheck, I sold a piece of my soul. It's something I never intended to do, and I deeply regret my complicity. By the time I became fully aware of what was happening, the water in the pot was already boiling. I had become part of the problem, which as you can imagine, is a painful admission for me to make.

As I think about my situation, it reminds me of a commercial that aired many years ago. It hit the mark perfectly with its witty, profound message. Slightly dark, satirical, and irreverent, the commercial was thought provoking, while also being entertaining.

It starts with half-a-dozen clean-cut, all-American grade-schoolers announcing to us, the listening audience, what they want to be when they grow up—what their lifetime goals and aspirations are. Expecting them to say they want to become doctors, teachers, engineers, or professional athletes, I was surprised by what they actually said. One nine-year-old girl proudly announced: "When I grow up, I want to be the office gossip." A ten-year-old followed with boyish bravado, "When I grow up, I want to be a brownnoser." The other kids made similar ignominious assertions. It was hysterical. I can't remember the product these kids were peddling, but I grinned from ear-to-ear each time I watched the commercial.

The satire was obvious. Nobody sets his or her career goal to be cowardly, devious, or ingratiating. Nor does anyone want to end up being a brownnoser. When young people enter the workplace, they have praiseworthy, high-minded goals. You can see it in their eyes when they graduate from high school and college. During nearly every commencement ceremony, those graduating listen to a successful businessman or politician pontificate about how the current generation has the unique ability to change the world, making it a better place for each of us, while at the same time, accumulating substantial wealth to enjoy "the good life."

During commencement, when you look from one smiling face to the next, you can see hope radiating from these young people. Coupled with their enthusiastic smiles, each graduate anticipates the future, believing he or she will produce noble, praiseworthy accomplishments. They are convinced their dreams will soon become a reality. All that is required to achieve their dream is hard work—performed honestly and honorably.

Unfortunately, for most, that's all it ever becomes—a dream. Reality is far different than what they believe it will be, making the commercial as poignant as it was funny. The "real world" produces far more brownnosers than men and women who stand by their convictions—especially if negative consequences are certain to follow.

This is no surprise; but if this dichotomy is true in the world of politics and business, the difference between aspirations and reality is even more pronounced for those who choose to serve Christ by working for ministries. Nearly all who pursue this path—the road less traveled—do so for altruistic reasons, sacrificing material gain as part of their noble calling. It just goes with the territory. They decide that fulfilling their dreams can best be accomplished by working for the Lord, which is a praiseworthy ambition.

Serving Christ, however, also means being employed by the

ministries, mega-churches, and publishers that champion His name. This is where a huge disconnect occurs. Working for Christian leaders has little resemblance to what most envision life would be like serving the Lord. It's different—worlds apart really—but not in a healthy way.

The stars of Christendom—those whose faces and voices are easily recognized by millions—bear little resemblance to the biblical version of Christ or the principles He taught. Somewhere along the way, the career path for many who have been "chosen to lead" takes a sharp turn from the biblical standard, producing an entitled mentality, elitist behavior, and a consumptive lifestyle most would consider antithetical to the desires of a servant of God. It was a lifestyle Benny enjoyed regularly and one Dett convinced himself he should possess as well.

There is a story behind all of this that needs to be told, but my purpose is more than just to curse the darkness. Rather, I intend to offer hope to the millions who have been used, abused, and discarded—all in the name of God.

To accomplish this, I will need to tell you a good bit about who I am. Like everybody, my story begins the day I was born. From day one, my challenge was about whether to accept authority or to challenge it—whether to speak out against abusiveness or simply keep my mouth shut. Obviously, I've landed on the side of speaking my mind, but becoming that person has required a lifetime of battling adversity.

9

A Wrinkled, Old Nun

I came into the world on a hot, sultry day in early June 1944 at Mercy Hospital in downtown Des Moines, Iowa, the day of the Normandy Invasion, which is commonly referred to as D-day. The focus of the entire world was on the coast of France for nearly everybody other than my parents. I was Mom's second child. My dad, Bill Cassidy, was one of the few men not serving in the Armed Forces in some capacity.

During the war, Dad traveled the state of Iowa and northern Missouri for his company; while Mom stayed at home, mostly alone, as she reared my older brother, Amnon. My parents married in 1935 at the height of the Great Depression. Eight years later, they still couldn't afford a telephone.

Once, when my dad had been on the road for nearly a fortnight, he received a telegram from my mom. In those days—at the height of the war—telegrams nearly always contained bad news; so Dad opened it quickly. Filled with apprehension, he read:

Not getting any better STOP

Come home soon STOP

Immediately canceling the remainder of his trip, Dad raced home from Sioux City. He had no idea Midge was ill—let alone *not getting any better*. He was concerned it might be serious—especially since she went to the expense of sending a telegram, which she had never done before. When he pulled up to their tiny second-story apartment building on the south side of the city, he practically bolted up the stairs to get to her, leaving his suitcase unattended in the back seat of his Packard.

When he opened the door, Midge was reading the latest issue of *Life* magazine, while Amnon was playing in his room. She looked perfectly fine. In fact, she looked good. Surprised, but relieved, he asked what had been wrong with her. Puzzled, she said she hadn't been sick at all. Confused, Dad showed her the telegram. When he did, Midge giggled and said the punctuation was off. It should have read:

Not getting any STOP

Better come home soon STOP

I was born nine months later. In those days, dads weren't permitted in the delivery room. Instead, they were required to keep their distance, spending hours in the waiting room, listening to war reports and music on the radio. As soon as I was delivered, an octogenarian nun brought me into the waiting room so that my dad could take a good look at me. When she did, he smiled and began to laugh. From that day forward, Dad told anybody who would listen, "The first time I saw Cole; he was trying to nurse a wrinkled, old nun."

Everybody loved the story and laughed heartily. After the laughter subsided, Dad would add, "When I saw this—*Cole taking his first taste of religion*—I knew he was going to love the church." Seven days later, I was baptized into the Holy Roman Catholic Church, and it became the center of my universe.

My dad loved to tell the story of my birth, as well as others about when I was a little boy. His audience always seemed to get a good laugh from them. These Norman Rockwell moments notwithstanding, my formative years were less than pleasant. My dad yelled at me all the time—my brother too—for the slightest provocation. Dad wasn't vicious, but he wasn't kind either. Because his humor was sharp, sarcastic, and cutting, I felt unloved. It seemed like my existence was a nuisance. I can't remember a time when he validated me. Instead, my feelings were constantly being hurt. I wanted to love him—all kids want to love their dads—but I never felt safe when he was around. I actually preferred it when he went away on one of his long business trips.

My situation became so difficult I decided to run away from home shortly after my fifth birthday. By this time, we had moved to Wellesley, Massachusetts. As I remember the incident, my dad had spanked me very hard for something, and I didn't want to live at home anymore. After my spanking, I was sent to my room. While there, I quietly packed my things in a knapsack and crept outside to the car, which was parked in front of the house going down a steep hill. With no well-thought-out plan, I got in the vehicle and sat in the driver's seat. As I looked around, I saw the little, beige plastic statue of the Blessed Virgin on the dashboard and put my life in her hands—just like we all did every time my dad was driving.

I figured the family car, a 1949 Studebaker—the Packard long gone—was as much mine as theirs. So, I felt justified in taking it. I didn't know how to get it started, but I had seen my dad release the handbrake. So I twisted and released it—just like he did. To my surprise and astonishment, the car started rolling. I knew the steering wheel guided the vehicle, so I grabbed it as the car gained momentum going downhill. Back then, steering wheels didn't have locks, and there was no such thing as power steering. By the time my parents realized what was happening, I was headed out of town. Turning my head to look back, I saw my dad racing frantically after the car, but it was moving just a little bit faster than he was able to run—fat as he was.

The hill was steep, so the car gained momentum, rolling along—perhaps eight-to-ten miles per hour. I was scared—really scared—and decided to stop it by going into my friend's driveway, which was a right-hand turn and further downhill. Steering into the driveway and down the hill, I brought the Studebaker to an abrupt halt as it hit the car parked in the driveway with a loud bang, throwing me into the steering wheel and dashboard.

There were half a dozen people sitting on the porch. All of them jumped out of their seats shouting, "Jesus, Mary, and Joseph! What in the hell was that?"

My dad arrived a few seconds later with his belt already doubled to spank me. Once he determined that I wasn't hurt, his face darkened with a look of fury I'll never forget. The collision caused substantial damage to both cars. My father informed me I would have to pay for it, when I was old enough to start earning money.

When all was said and done, I got spanked again, which my father referred to as a "beating within an inch" of my life. I'm sure this was one of the truest statements he ever made. When he finished, I was sent back to my room without supper. As I left the scene of my chastisement, I turned to my father and said, "The next time, I'll drive it around the block." From that time forward, Dad kept the car locked for years.

Being the second son, I was always the rebel. Even as a kid, I bristled whenever I saw or experienced injustice. This is why I ran away. I couldn't stand the unfairness of my father's constant scolding. That I recognized this at five might be a little unusual, but I definitely did. Even from such an early age, I stood up to injustice, refusing to acknowledge it as being acceptable. Back then, I neither had power nor a voice. I still may not have much power, but I definitely have a voice. I guess it's what has always made me a rebel—just like I was, when I began working for

Dett at Ludlow Randolph.

Although my story about running away may seem cute, if you think about it, it's also unusual. For a preschooler to be determined to run away from home can't be normal. I wanted to get away from the family dysfunction that made me feel unloved all of the time. My earliest memories were about living in a family where there was little affection, especially coming from my dad. He was physically and emotionally abusive, especially after he had been drinking, which was a routine part of his lifestyle.

I was mischievous—no doubt about it—but I was just a little boy. Dad found my playful disruptiveness particularly annoying, and everything in our family revolved around Dad's petulant and peevish ways. He was always right and never admitted being wrong about anything. It didn't matter what it was; he was right, and everybody else was wrong. Neither did he apologize—not for anything. It wasn't in his nature to do so. If he were clearly wrong, he would redefine events to make it appear as if he was right. If any of us balked at his revisionism, he would shout us down.

My dad's denial of reality was astounding—even about trivial things. He actually denied being bald, which was obvious to even a casual observer. He tried to hide this shortcoming by combing his hair from the side of his head to the bald spot on top in a sweep-over motion. Once he did this, he plastered it solidly in place with Spray Net. When the wind blew in the opposite direction, this clump of hair, which was solidly matted together and looked like a Sam Snead divot, would flap around like a screen door left ajar. It made my father look ridiculous—something Midge pointed out every time it was windy. Unloved wives are excellent at making pointed, biting criticisms like this, and she was definitely unloved.

Like his favorite character on TV—Ralph Kramden—my dad had a huge potbelly, at least three chins, and a cigarette in one hand with a beer can in the other, nearly all the time. Nevertheless, he was the kind of guy who would walk down the street—with these obvious imperfections—and believe that every woman who saw him wanted him. Some women actually did, which I found absolutely astonishing.

Sadly, I was forced to deal with narcissistic behavior like this at an early age. Back then, I had no idea what it was, of course, but I did know what it felt like to be subjected to my dad's self-serving leadership.

When we moved to Wellesley, we lived in a neighborhood where there were more Jewish people than Gentiles. On Rosh Hashanah, there were only four or five kids who came to school—all *goys*. Shortly after my sixth birthday, a seven-year-old Jewish boy named Arthur Goldstein told me testily there was no such thing as Santa Claus.

"He isn't real," Arthur taunted, sporting a snide, mean-spirited grin.

Infuriated by his lack of respect for the institutions of Christendom, I knocked the grin off his face. He cried and tattled, but I didn't care. I was doing something right—something for God. Santa was real, and God was on my side. I was sure of it. To this day, I can still remember feeling justified about beating up Arthur.

Predictably, my dad didn't see things the same way. He said, "There's no such thing as Santa Claus, son. What kind of idiot are you?"

By the look on my face, it was obvious I was a complete idiot. This revelation—and the condescending way in which it was delivered—shattered the foundation of my little-boy world. Additionally, I got spanked for punching Arthur with a closed fist, which not only surprised me but also seemed particularly unfair. I was crushed, disillusioned, and furious. I began to wonder if my parents had also lied to me about God being real.

They say you learn half of what you will ever know in your first five years of life. If this is true, and I suspect that it is, I learned adults couldn't be counted on or trusted. Because I was voiceless, I just wanted to be in a place where I was loved—free to be safe and secure—just like the other little boys I knew. But that never happened.

I felt certain there had to be something better than the angry, hostile world of my early childhood. At least, I thought there must be, but I didn't have a clue about where to find it. In my young, troubled heart, this is what I longed for.

10

Jesus Stuck to the Roof of My Mouth

My formal indoctrination into Catholicism began when I was six. Learning the catechism was difficult. There was constant criticism from the nuns for not remembering the answers to the questions flawlessly. Their censure didn't differ much from the reprimands I received at home from my mother. She would have made a perfect Mother Superior. Because of her scolding, I became a poster boy for Catholicism.

I went to church every Sunday and each Holy Day of Obligation, which meant I attended Mass at least sixty times a year. Many of my earliest memories were of things that happened while there. Part of my education was parochial, which was challenging academically but good for me. Dealing with the priests, however, who positioned themselves as intermediaries between God and me, was difficult.

Their reproachful demeanor, which I rarely found to be encouraging, was the basis upon which I formed my foundational impression of God's nature. Based on what I learned, I never considered God to be loving. The concept never even entered my mind. How could it?

I certainly wasn't alone in my thinking. There are millions of disillusioned Catholic kids who had a similar perspective. For us—those whose experiences preceded Vatican II—Catholicism has produced permanent, lifelong emotional scars. I'm not exaggerating. It's why there was a massive exodus from the Catholic Church in my generation. Nearly all of us have war stories about the clergy's abusiveness.

There was one incident, in particular, I'll never forget. It was on the day of my First Holy Communion, which occurred when I was just seven years old. For months, the girls and boys from my class practiced going to the altar rail, kneeling down, holding our heads back, opening our mouths, and sticking out our tongues. When we did, the priest would place the Eucharist on our tongues, say something in Latin—which none of us could understand—and then move to the next kid. There was also an altar boy who dutifully accompanied the priest. Attentively, the boy placed a gold plate with an elongated handle under our chins to make certain the Host didn't drop on the floor.

Doing as we had been instructed, which was to swallow the communion wafer, sounds simple enough, but its execution on that fateful day was anything but simple. We were told repeatedly—and in no uncertain terms—that we were to close our mouths immediately after the Host had been placed on our tongues.

The priest said, "You don't want to drop Jesus on the floor, do you?" He added that this was a sacrilege, a mortal sin, and it would send us to hell. This was terrifying, of course, as it would be to any seven-year-old child. I can still feel the cold chill of fear from his stinging admonition more than half a century later. What he said wasn't accurate Catholic doctrine but, as a seven-year-old, I assumed his warning was the truth.

I remember trying to look at the wafer when the priest held it up. I wanted to see Jesus' face on it, but I never could. It didn't look like Him, and it didn't look like any part of a human body I had ever seen before either, but the priest was adamant that it was Christ's body. Accepting what the priest said at face value—along with my fear of going to hell—was what made me determined to swallow Jesus and not drop Him on the floor.

When the day arrived, each girl was dressed in white, as were the boys. We wore white suits, white shirts, white clip-on ties, and white gloves. Everything we wore that day was white, symbolizing our purity. There were at least fifty kids taking communion, which excited our parents far more than it did any of us.

We sat up front—away from our families—the boys on the right side, the girls on the left. Sitting immediately to my right was Cary Sullivan, who was a little goofy on his best day and slightly retarded on his worst. Because of where he sat, he was in line to receive communion immediately before me.

As scheduled, we were ushered to the alter rail by a nun. Each of us knelt down dutifully, precisely as we had been told. When the priest came to Cary, he didn't open his mouth as widely as he had been repeatedly instructed to do. This irritated the priest, who spoke to him sternly.

Scared, Cary started to whimper. Exasperated, the priest put the Host on Cary's partially protruding tongue, hoping that all would go well. Then the unthinkable happened; Cary let the wafer drop from his mouth. It bounced off of the altar boy's plate, and Jesus landed on the floor—right before my eyes. Aghast, the priest hurriedly grabbed the wafer, scraped up all of the crumbs and surrounding dust, and put all of it in his own mouth—slobber and all. After that, he rose quickly, gave Cary a look of pure hate, and slapped him right across the face. It was a hard slap. Terrified, Cary screamed from surprise, shock, embarrassment, and pain.

As the drama was unfolding, Cary's mother rushed forward to retrieve her son, who had become hysterical, screaming at the top of his lungs. When she arrived, she looked up at the priest and said, "I'm so sorry, Father." With that, she clutched her boy, put a protective arm around him, and led him out of the church. I can still remember his receding sobs, as adults looked at Cary and his mom, sneering at them with disapproval, mixed with self-righteous contempt.

Immediately afterward, the priest turned his focus on me. With defiant eyes, he dared me to make a mistake. Shaking, I came close to wetting my pants, but I didn't. Instead, I sucked it up and did exactly as I had been instructed. But because I was so afraid, my mouth was bone dry, and Jesus stuck to the roof of my mouth. He wouldn't dissolve and might as well have been peanut butter. We weren't allowed to talk with Jesus in our mouths either, nor were we allowed to chew Him up. Both were sins. It took at least thirty minutes for Jesus to dissolve, and the Mass was long over before I could finally open my mouth to speak, making my first formal experience with Christ dry, punitive, and distasteful.

Even worse, the next year Cary died from a brain aneurysm. Because he became so traumatized by the priest's actions, he was never allowed to make his First Holy Communion. This meant he couldn't go to heaven, which saddened me. Everybody said he went to limbo—wherever that was. The harshness of this incident is why I have such a vivid memory of it so many years later.

It solidified my fear of God or, more accurately, my terror of Him. I saw God as cold, exacting, impersonal, petty, vindictive, and mean-spirited. This experience, along with numerous others, colored much of my beliefs about God throughout my formative years.

Everybody believed the priest had a right to do what he did. Nobody protested—not even Cary's mother. Catholics were terrified of the clergy—priests who wielded unquestioned authority over the congregants in their parishes. Catholicism was not a loving, warm, or nurturing religion. It was dogmatic and unapologetically severe. The priests and nuns were authority figures whose words and actions went unquestioned. Nobody in their right mind would mess with them.

What I learned from this and from hundreds of other less dramatic examples was to never question the authority of those who were my spiritual superiors—not if I wanted to go to heaven. To question a priest was to rebel against God's one, true, holy and apostolic church. It was a sin that would jeopardize my standing with the Almighty and might send me to hell.

When I was ten, I was walking up the church steps on a cold, winter morning when an old man in front of me stumbled and fell. I grabbed him before his head could hit the brick stairs. He gasped once, clutched his chest, and died in my arms of a massive coronary, as his horrified family watched helplessly. Fittingly, that morning the priest spoke about the importance of being in "Sanctifying Grace" because, if you weren't, you would go to hell. The priest added, "And you never know when your time is up."

His warning, as you can imagine, terrified me. I suspect this was the most vivid sermon illustration he ever had.

Two years later, Cardinal Cushing, who was to become famous when John F. Kennedy became President a few years later, confirmed me. After the ceremony, with the entire class of kids standing at attention in bleachers erected for a photo, my dog ruined the shot when he came into focus, copulating with a bitch in heat. Back then dogs were rarely leashed.

My mother, full of righteous indignation, yelled at the dog as if he had knowingly committed a social *faux pas*. Wagging her finger menacingly, Midge said, "Just wait 'til I get you home!" My dog, having his own agenda, continued with the task at hand until he was finished.

The Cardinal gave my mom a cold, menacing look I'll never forget. To him, she was responsible for ruining Confirmation for everyone. The parents were aghast too—as were the girls; but the boys thought it was cool—really cool. Afterwards, many of them petted my dog.

This incident horrified my mother, who thought she might go to hell for it. This is how irrational many Catholics were during this era. Hundreds of things would send you to hell. If you didn't go to church every Sunday and each Holy Day of Obligation, which were numerous, you would go to hell. I had no trouble with this because Mom was like a drill sergeant. She made certain my brother and I went to Mass whenever required.

The list of mortal sins was endless—each of which would send you to hell. Like everybody else, I lived in terror of eternal damnation. By thirteen, I didn't have trouble with most of the rules; but there was one sin that stymied me repeatedly—masturbation. To Catholics, masturbation was a mortal sin that—if you committed it just once—would send you to hell. When I was thirteen, I tried to hold the line at five or six times a day—just like nearly every other adolescent my age. It was a sin I confessed repeatedly, a wrongdoing I could never control—not completely anyway.

Every Saturday, I would hitchhike to Waltham, Needham, Newton, or Framingham to find a church where nobody knew me. Then, I would confess the terrible sin that would send me to hell—beating my meat. If you think it's embarrassing for me to write about it now, just imagine what it must have been like when I was thirteen and had to confess it to a priest—with nothing separating us but a thin screen behind a sliding door.

As I entered the confessional, I would kneel, cross myself, and wait in terror for the priest to slide open the connecting screen window. Sometimes, I had to wait a long time. When it finally opened, I would say, "Bless me, Father, for I have sinned."

Answering, the priest would respond, "How long has it been since your last confession, my son?"

"It's been one week, Father."

"And what are your sins?"

"I was disrespectful to my mother, cussed, and masturbated."

"How many times were you disrespectful?"

"Once."

"How often did you cuss?"

"A lot—several times a day, at least."

"And how many times did you masturbate?"

"Forty times, Father."

"That much!"

"Ummm, yes Father. That much," I admitted, filled with shame, fear, and remorse. Sometimes I would lie and only admit to twenty or thirty times a week. I had to. I was mortified. During confession, I always held my head down—fearful of being scolded or mocked. It was awful—far worse than you can possibly imagine.

After a long pause, the priest would reply, "Your sins are forgiven, my son. For your penance, say one Act of Contrition, five Our Fathers, and fifty Hail Mary's."

"Yes, Father."

Once, he added, "Try to put your hands to better use. Will you do that?"

"Yes, Father," I responded. I considered telling the priest it only required one hand, but I wisely refrained.

When I left the confessional—absolved and relieved—I would say my prayers hurriedly and leave, nervous that someone might discover my dark secret. I remember wishing a car would hit me on a Saturday night, when I was in a state of Sanctifying Grace, before the urge to whack off would overwhelm me on Sunday. If a car hit me on Sunday or after, I was destined for hell—no question about it.

This was exactly what Catholicism was like for kids like me before Vatican II. The guilt imposed upon us by arbitrary medieval rules, which have no basis in the Scriptures, made fidelity to Catholicism irrational and unappealing. I used the example of masturbation because it demonstrates how the church kept kids like me in line by shaming us. Being young, it worked, but the backlash from this repressive strategy was considerable when we got older. It's why there are more lapsed Catholics than those who attend church. I've heard it said the largest religious group in America is lapsed Catholics. I believe it; it's easy to see why.

Tragically, my perspective of God came from these experiences as well. To me, He was scary and impersonal. To be in His good graces, I had to follow a multitude of rules that made no sense and took all of the joy out of life.

Interestingly, drinking was never considered to be sinful—nor was smoking. My dad smoked so much that every room in the house was decorated with an ashtray. In grade school, an ashtray was what I made my parents for Christmas in arts & crafts.

When a priest from the church would come over for dinner, which happened three or four times a year, he always smoked. Additionally, my dad served the priest Scotch; and they drank and smoked until the priest was so drunk he staggered to his car and drove off, weaving his way down the road. None of this was considered to be a mortal sin, but jerking off, which I eventually discovered was normal adolescent behavior, was.

I wanted to run away and never think about God or Catholicism again, but I couldn't. Not only was I too young, but once you're a Catholic, you're always a Catholic—even if you leave the church. For better or worse, it's the voice in your head. You can't get away from it—not completely. It was foundational in forming my worldview—whether I liked it or not. Loyola once said, "Give me a child until he is five, and I'll give you a Catholic for life." Loyola was right.

11

It Gives Her a Little Buzz

By the time I reached high school, Catholicism wasn't nearly as influential as it had been just a few years earlier, but it was still there, robbing me of the carefree life I desired. To counteract its castigation, I became cocky and impious, which kept me in trouble constantly. I thought that since I was incapable of being a good Catholic, I would do my best to be irreverent. Going to parochial school provided me with ample opportunity to do so.

As a ninth grader, I can remember boarding the bus on the first day at my new school with my best friend, Billy Crenshaw. Both of us were wearing blue blazers adorned with the school's crest, white shirts, gray slacks, and bright red ties. It was our school uniform. Our Catholic high school was nearly nine miles across town, making the long trek back and forth tedious and boring.

By that time, I had a girlfriend. Melissa went to public school, where I used to attend. I was despondent at the thought of not seeing her and my other friends after the long summer. I felt a lump in my throat and balked at going to Marist High School in Natick. All I could think about was how I was missing out on all of the wild tales of real and imagined bacchanalia—a ritual following every summer vacation. Most of the stories were wildly exaggerated, including mine—but fascinating nonetheless. I loved listening to them. I wondered if Melissa missed me as much as I missed her. *Probably not,* I thought, which deepened my misery.

Billy, on the other hand, eagerly embraced our new adventure. For him, it was a fresh start; and best of all, I was sitting right beside him. We were the Cisco Kid and Poncho—best friends through thick and thin.

Billy couldn't have been happier. For Poncho, life was rich and rewarding but not for Cisco. Looking out of the bus window, our prospects for the future couldn't have been further apart. As we headed toward school, I saw the glass half empty; Billy saw the glass half full.

When we arrived, our new school looked spotlessly clean. It also smelled like fresh paint, which brought a smile to my face, despite my commitment to detest every minute I was there.

When I looked at the girls, which was priority one, I was shocked. There wasn't a cute one in the bunch. Those who didn't have acne had mustaches—or both. For whatever reason, many were unaware that two eyebrows were preferable to one. None wore makeup other than dark red lipstick. Not one girl was blond, and most wore their mousy brown hair long, with bangs to hide their pimpled foreheads. It was as if the school had a sign—*Preparatory School for Slatterns.* My misery turned to despair.

At Marist High, the teachers were nuns, which by the look of them, was because they couldn't "get none." I had never seen such a grotesquely ugly bunch of women in my entire life. What they lacked in appearance, they made up for in mean-spiritedness. Always peevish, the nuns never smiled and seemed to enjoy inflicting minor corporal punishment on the students. Pinching was by far their favorite sporting event, and I quickly became one of their favorite targets. The nuns were from the Sisters of Mercy, which was certainly an oxymoron because they were a vindictive lot. They were *furbissimas*—a Yiddish term for old women who have become sour on life. It seemed as if every nun was a bitter, misanthropic, hateful, old hag.

The most vindictive, by far, was Sister Anna Catherine—my English and Latin teacher. She was a particularly malevolent crone. From the moment students entered her class until the period ended, no talking was permitted—not even a whisper. If some poor, unfortunate ninth grader breached protocol, Sister Anna Catherine would swoop down from her desk like a spider cornering a hapless fly caught in its web. With a gleam of delight in her mean-spirited eyes, she would grab the kid's cheek with her thumb and forefinger and lead the unfortunate miscreant to the office to speak to the principal, Father Dunnigan.

Father Dunnigan was a broad-shouldered, handsome priest, who looked like a Hollywood producer had cast him for the part. He even had a charming Irish accent, which endeared him to everyone. He was extremely intelligent and very fair. Everybody liked Father Dunnigan, but he was nobody to mess with—that's for sure.

I felt like an outsider from the moment I arrived and never acclimated to Marist. I hated it and remained aloof from everybody except for Billy. My way of protesting my forced incarceration was to sit in the back of the class, do as little as possible, and secretly hope I would get kicked out. If I did, I would be able to go to public high school with Melissa and my friends, leaving the trappings of Catholicism far behind.

At Marist, they loved to give homework—the more, the better. Sister Anna Catherine delighted in piling on assignments. When she did, at the end of every class, the students would groan audibly in unison, which was the only time she allowed a sound to pass without painful repercussions.

Secretly, she loved this corporate, plaintive cry; I was certain of it.

Billy said it gave her an "A. O.," which he defined as an Auditory Orgasm. Billy would add, "She gets off when she hears us whine—I'm sure of it. It gives her a little buzz—you know where." I concurred and smiled every time Billy said it, which was practically daily.

By October, I was performing at a low C level, doing as little as I could to get by. Billy worked feverishly, which meant our grades were about the same.

There was one girl in class I absolutely loathed. Her name was Mildred Tedeschi—the smartest person in class and a world-class "brownnoser." She always had her hand raised to give the correct answer. Even Sister Anna Catherine, who wore a perpetual scowl, as if she had just bitten into a quince, smiled approvingly every time she looked at her pet student.

Mildred was a little heavier than most of the other girls—none of whom were svelte; and she had a pencil-thin black mustache—like Rhett Butler in *Gone with the Wind*. It made her the brunt of many jokes from the boys—all deserved in my opinion. Teenagers, as you know, look for any flaw in a girl to criticize. Mildred had many, including an overly developed sphincter.

In Catholic school, each ninth grader was given an I.Q. test, which was administered by an outside agency hired for this purpose. Finding no reason to sandbag, I answered each question with ease, precision, and confidence. I was curious—like everyone else—to see if I was as dumb as my dad and the nuns said I was. Truthfully, I had no idea if I was smart or not. I didn't have a clue. In those days, the best form of validation a kid ever received was to be left alone, which didn't happen often. The process of discovering the results was long, however, with the results left in limbo, where Cary Sullivan resided. So, like all the other kids, I quickly forgot about it.

One day, about a month after the test was given, I was sitting in Latin class, paying as little attention to Sister Anna Catherine as I could. This was standard operating procedure for me. Suddenly, and for no apparent reason, Sister called on me, saying, “Cole, are you awake back there?”

“Yes, Sister,” I answered, sitting up in my chair. I didn’t have my eyes closed; I was sure of it. My focus became heightened the instant she called my name though.

“Are you paying attention, Cole?”

“Yes, Sister,” I said, standing up promptly—as my apprehension mounted. “I’ve heard every word you’ve said,” which was more-or-less accurate.

“Really, Cole. Is that true?”

“Yes, Sister,” I said—now genuinely alarmed. All the kids in the room turned to look at me, knowing that something more interesting than conjugating Latin verbs was about to transpire.

Mildred Tedeschi smirked, hoping I was about to get in trouble. Sensing her malice, I looked directly at her, sitting in the front row. Recognizing she had been caught, she changed her look of glee to concern; but it was too late. I saw how happy she was that I was about to get in trouble—the little kiss ass. This really irked me.

“Cole,” Sister Anna Catherine continued—unaware of the silent exchange that had just transpired between Mildred and me. “I’ve just received the results of the I.Q. test given last month. Do you know what your I.Q. is?”

“No, Sister.”

“You have no idea of how high your I.Q. is?”

“No, Sister,” I said. By the apprehension in my voice, it was clear I was clueless. Frankly, I was worried I might start drooling at any moment—imbecile that I considered myself to be.

“Alright, Cole. Maybe you don’t. Let me ask you this: Your I.Q. is exactly the same as someone else in this class.” Looking from one student to the next for dramatic effect, she continued. "Tell me who you think that might be?"

I just shrugged my shoulders—genuinely mystified.

Miffed, Sister pressed me for an answer. "This isn't rhetorical, Cole. Give me an answer. To whom do you compare in intelligence? Answer me right now," she said in her most insistent tone.

"I don't know; Billy, I guess," I answered reluctantly—anxious for her inquisition to cease.

"Oh no, Cole. You won't get off that lightly. You're much smarter than Billy," she said with a mirthless, wry grin. When she did, I cast a furtive glance at Poncho, who seemed to have no cognizance that his teacher had just verified his stupidity in front of the entire class.

This bothered me. Sister Anna Catherine had no right to be cruel and condescending to Billy—without reason or instigation, I might add. My sense of fairness had been offended; and I became determined to never allow this mean, old woman to get the best of me again—even if she was a nun and a servant of God. I concluded that if my attitude would send me to Purgatory, or maybe even to hell, then so be it. I'd rather be there than where Sister Anna Catherine was anyway. If heaven was reserved for people like her, I didn't want to go.

"Give me another answer, Cole," she insisted. "Pick another person. Look around the class, and give me an answer."

"I don't know, Sister, I really don't. I'm sorry, but I can't answer your question."

Raising herself up to her full height of 5 feet, 2 inches, she barked, "Then, I'll tell you; and I want everybody to listen. Your I.Q. is the same as Mildred's. That's right, Mildred Tedeschi. But she's a straight A student, Cole, and you're a low C student. Can you tell me why that is?"

I just shrugged my shoulders and said nothing, but I was no longer passive in this exchange. Sister Anna Catherine had cornered me and embarrassed me badly. Even worse, my sense of fairness had been offended. A quiet storm was mounting deep within me, and I knew I was close to defying Roman Catholic authority for the first time.

Unwilling to drop the subject or leave me alone, Sister pressed her point in an obvious attempt to humiliate me further. "Tell me, Cole—and all of your classmates—why is Mildred a straight A student and you're inches away from being a D student? No more stalling. Tell me, Cole. Tell me right now."

Looking directly at Sister, I said, "Because I don't want to have her brown nose or her black mustache."

The entire class froze. Even Mildred, who I had ridiculed mercilessly, had a look of fear on her face. Stunned by my effrontery, Sister Anna Catherine hesitated—but just for an instant, regaining her composure quickly. Without saying another word, she gave me a look of malice that made me quiver with fear. Then, she turned so quickly her habit swished like a full skirt, as she left the room headed straight for the principal's office.

In the two minutes she was absent, nobody spoke—not even Poncho who was quietly whimpering. A sense of foreboding engulfed the entire class. Those courageous enough to venture a glance in my direction looked at me like I was a prisoner on death row, awaiting imminent execution. Even Mildred felt bad for me. I just stood there, while my classmates sat watching, as a feeling of pure dread overwhelmed me.

Father Dunnigan walked into the room with Sister right behind him. Without saying a word, he simply pointed at me with a motion to follow him, which I did instantly. When we entered his office, Father sat down with me to have "a little talk." Patiently, and with no malice, Father Dunnigan tried to reason with me, imploring me to perform to the high standard of my mental capacity.

"God gave you an outstanding brain, Cole. It's your responsibility to put it to good use." Trying to exhort me, he added, "If you do, you'll be able to serve Him your entire life."

"Yes, Father," I said—as if I actually knew what he was talking about.

I had no idea I was smart. This was the first I had ever heard that I was. My father routinely called me, "*Dum Kopf*," which is German for "stupid." By using this term, it made people think he was bilingual—with the added assumption that he must have served in the European theatre, during World War II, rather than being a salesman in Iowa. If I hadn't been so frightened, I would have been confused. It never occurred to me I was smart, and nobody had ever suggested that I was either.

After he finished his exhortation for me to excel for God's glory, Father Dunnigan became confrontational for a brief moment. "No disrespect for a teacher will be tolerated, Cole—not as long as I'm in charge. Do you understand me?"

"Yes, Father."

But that was it. No further punishment was administered, which absolutely astounded me. I thought, *If you're going to be bad, be really bad. You can get away with it much easier.*

I had escaped punishment of any kind. I had been disrespectful to Sister Anna Catherine with impunity, which felt surprisingly good. Smiling, I said to myself, *Way to go, Cisco! Things are looking up.*

Best of all, Sister Anna Catherine couldn't question Father Dunnigan's authority under any circumstance. Nuns weren't allowed to do that. There were some good things about Medieval Catholicism after all. As I left the principal's office, I was grateful I didn't get detention, which I expected and deserved. I was also secretly pleased I had said exactly what I wanted to say. Once again, Cisco was back in the saddle—the heroic cowboy who was always victorious. It was a wonderful feeling, but it didn't last long.

12

My Face Began to Throb

From that moment forward, Sister Anna Catherine had it in for me, which wasn't entirely unfair. She was on my case daily. If I didn't do my homework precisely the way she wanted, I paid dearly. She would embarrass me routinely by saying things like, "Cole, someone with an I.Q. like yours should be able to answer that question. You're not stupid, you know."

She never let up—never. She made a derisive comment about my I.Q. every day—without exception—which made me feel dumber than I had in the first place. I hated going to school and faked being sick routinely. Like most teens, I put off doing my homework until the last minute. Because I liked the TV programs on Sunday night, I skipped doing my homework, which was voluminous, preferring to be agonizingly sick on Monday morning instead.

One Monday, my plan failed—even when I writhed in pain from a near fatal stomachache, completely contrived, of course.

Midge said, "I don't care how sick you say you are. I don't believe you.

You're going to school."

I hadn't counted on this. Grudgingly, I went to school that day totally unprepared, which did give me a stomachache—a real one. That's the day "the you-know-what" hit the fan in Sister Anna Catherine's Latin class.

I walked in without having finished my Latin homework, cursing myself for choosing to watch *Gunsmoke* and *Lawman* instead of translating three paragraphs from *Caesar's Commentaries on the Gallic War*. As soon as class started, Sister Anna Catherine asked for my homework, which I reluctantly admitted I hadn't done.

Without saying a word, she went to her desk and retrieved a white tennis ball, which she held out for the entire class to see. Instantly, everybody paid attention. My classmates couldn't wait to see what was about to happen.

"Cole, come up here right now," Sister demanded. She could barely contain her glee, which would have given away her true goal—my complete humiliation. When I reached the front of the class, she said, "Cole, I want you to bounce the ball. Each time you bounce it, recite the Latin declensions—singular and plural—for all five persons. Do it now, and do it without making a mistake. With an I.Q. like yours, that should be easy enough."

Everybody in class was on the edge of their seats, knowing what a daunting task this was. There were a total of fifty answers, and I had to give them in fifty bounces. I wasn't sure I could get them right in English, which only has three declensions and three persons, totaling nine answers. But Sister Anna Catherine handed me the ball—intent on mortifying me in front of everybody.

Without complaint, which I knew would be futile; I took the ball and started bouncing it. As I did, I said, "A . . . ae . . . ae . . . am . . . ae; ae . . . orum . . . is . . . as . . . is." Then, I stopped, having completed the first declension correctly in ten bounces. With a victorious smile, I handed the ball back to Sister.

"That's just the feminine declension, Cole. I expect you to do the masculine, neutral, and other two declensions as well. Bounce the ball and start over."

With that, she handed the ball back to me. Once again, I started with the feminine declension. Midway through the masculine declension, a boy in the back row started to laugh. Another followed. Finally Sister Anna Catherine let out a small giggle. When she did, the entire class erupted with laughter that a comedian like Jackie Gleason or Milton Berle would have envied.

The laughter was so loud my recitation couldn't be heard by anyone, which allowed me to cover up several mistakes. Nobody cared; they were having too much fun—all at my expense. I was so embarrassed I wanted to cry, but that certainly wasn't an option. Suddenly, and without forethought, I caught the ball, raised my arm, and threw it out of the open window. Nobody thought I would do something that crazy, including me. I regretted my decision before the ball was out of sight; but since it couldn't be retrieved; I had no choice but to hold my ground.

Instantly, the laughter ceased as every kid switched his or her gaze from the window to Sister Anna Catherine. They wanted to see what she would do. Once again, she didn't say a word. She simply turned and glided out of the room at a pace worthy of a marathoner—with her habit shuffling in the breeze. I just stood there stiff-necked in righteous indignation, not even bothering to return the timid looks of my incredulous classmates.

Although terrified, I tried not to panic. I hoped Father Dunnigan would just give me another reprimand. If that was all that happened, it would be worth it. By throwing the ball, I had put Sister Anna Catherine in her place. When I talked to Father Dunnigan, I intended to let him know how out of line Sister had been to humiliate me like that. He was fair. Unlike her, he would understand.

Once again, Father came to the classroom and motioned for me to follow, which I obediently did. As I passed Sister Anna Catherine, she had a triumphant smirk on her face, which was quite intimidating. For an instant, I wondered if I had misread the situation—badly misread it.

When we reached Father's office, I walked in as confidently as I could under the circumstances. As I turned to plead my case, Father Dunnigan hit me on the left side of my face with a right hook that knocked me off my feet—flat on my back. Lying there—stunned and confused, I managed to prop myself up on my left elbow. Not yet cognizant of my surroundings, the left side of my face was completely numb, and my left ear was ringing. Stunned, I couldn't fathom what had just occurred. Life seemed to be moving in slow motion. Dazed and disoriented, I began to regain my senses—as the numb feeling gave way to throbbing pain.

Before I could utter a word, Father knelt down beside me inches from my face and said, "Do I have your attention, Cole—your complete attention?"

In stark terror, I nodded vigorously. Father Dunnigan did have my undivided attention.

"That's good, Cole. I'm going to talk to you man to man. May I do that?"

Again, I nodded vigorously—far too frightened to speak. I was terrified and couldn't even cry.

"That's good, Cole. Thank you for that." In a clear, calm voice, Father Dunnigan said, "I'm tired of your disrespect. You've got a piss-poor attitude, Cole; and I want it to change. I want it to change right now—this very minute. Do you understand me, Cole?"

I nodded affirmatively; I did understand. By now, I was nodding vigorously—without stop.

"Good. I'm glad you do," Father concluded.

Changing tone and moving away from his confrontational position, Father Dunnigan said, "Now sit here for the rest of the afternoon and say the Rosary five times. When you come back tomorrow, I want to see a completely new attitude from you. This is your last chance. If your attitude doesn't change—not improve but change, I'll throw you out of here on your ass. Do you understand me, Cole? Do you know I mean what I say?"

"Yes, Father," I answered contritely while continuing to nod—just in case. By this time, the entire left side of my face had begun to swell, and it ached badly.

"That's good, Cole. Now let me get you some ice." With that, the altercation ended. I sat in his office whimpering from pain, fear, and embarrassment for the remainder of the school day, which passed uneventfully.

On the bus ride home, nobody spoke to me or sat beside me—not even Billy. Poncho had abandoned Cisco and chose to sit next to another boy from our class. The kids were curious, but this was far too serious for any of them to stick their necks out. I was on my own with this one, and most of them thought I got what I deserved anyway, including me.

Arriving home, as I opened the front door, Midge took one look at me and said, "Cole, have you been in a fight?"

"No, Mom."

She just looked at me with a puzzled expression.

I said, "Father Dunnigan hit me," bursting into tears as I did. Although I could tell Mom had been drinking, it didn't matter. She was my mother, and I was just fourteen. I cried like a little boy—her little boy.

Once her brief consolation was complete, Midge's nostrils flared. Emboldened by drink, she picked up the phone and called Marist High School. As she did, I listened intently, trying to control my whimpering at the same time.

She said, "Hello, this is Midge Cassidy. I want to speak to Father Dunnigan."

As the receptionist spoke, I couldn't hear what she said; but I did see Midge's face become resolute. She was furious.

After listening to the receptionist for a minute, Mom interrupted, "I don't care what kind of meeting he's in. He has hit my son—with a closed fist, and I demand to speak to him immediately. Get him right now!" she insisted in her don't-mess-with-me voice.

After a wait of several minutes, Father Dunnigan finally picked up the phone. When he did, Midge lit into him. "Father, my son's face is swollen; and he says it's because you hit him. Is this . . ." she started to ask but never finished. Being interrupted, I could hear Father's muffled voice speaking very fast, very loudly, and very authoritatively.

"But, Father, hitting a . . ."—again, he interrupted her.

After listening for another minute, Mom's demeanor changed. No longer furious, she listened to every word Father Dunnigan spoke, nodding in agreement with him, which I could see but the priest could only sense, as he continued to speak nonstop for several more minutes.

Finally, she successfully interrupted him. With equal authority, she pronounced, "Father, I have something to say." Looking directly at me in her slightly intoxicated state, Midge proclaimed, "If he ever does anything like that again, you have my permission to beat the crap out of him."

13

They Were Gone Weeks at a Time

Things settled down for me appreciably after Father Dunnigan "knocked a little sense into my head." My attitude did change. It wasn't that I necessarily became compliant. That didn't happen. My will had not been broken—not completely—but I definitely learned when to pick my fights, or more importantly, when not to pick them. From their perspective, Sister Anna Catherine and Father Dunnigan were convinced they had done the right thing—my mom too. Maybe they did, but that certainly wasn't how I viewed it.

For me, being slugged by Father Dunnigan was the last straw for Catholicism. I didn't abandon my faith outwardly, but inwardly, where it really counts, God ceased to be important. I just stopped caring, knowing that I could never live up to the standards Catholicism demanded. So, I discarded it—chucked it all—which was freeing, except for the feelings of guilt I couldn't shake, despite my steadfast determination to do so.

Like Acy and his sisters, while on the mission field, with no alternative I learned to sit down on the outside while standing up on the inside—

remaining defiant. In some ways, I was more rebellious than ever, but I did learn to curb my tongue.

Regardless of what others thought, I knew I had been treated unjustly—just like Cary Sullivan had been. Being sucker punched never settled well with me. I didn't want anything to do with the clergy, Catholicism, or God, who I actually blamed for what had happened. I knew I didn't deserve to be struck with a closed fist by a grown man—no kid does. I had been disrespectful and deserved to be punished, but what I received certainly didn't befit my misbehavior.

It wasn't that I became bitter or cynical; I didn't. It wasn't like that. It was more like there was a whole world out there waiting to be explored, and I intended to delve into it, without the constraints of my archaic religion. If I kowtowed to Catholicism's many rules, I was certain that most of life's unique adventures would pass me by. I wanted more than to be controlled by people who didn't even like me, let alone have my best interest at heart.

I refused to be imprisoned by the confines of Medieval Catholicism, so I stopped going to confession and to mass. When asked, I lied to Midge about it. She was suspicious, of course, but just like most teens, I learned how to manipulate my mom. My dad didn't care. He was far too busy with other things.

To achieve all that I desired from life, I had to bide my time until I could discover what my future would be—*que sera, sera*. I had numerous grandiose aspirations—like all teenagers—but I had no idea what would eventuate.

Despite my emotional withdrawal from Catholicism, I actually did much better in school—not out of fear of Sister Anna Catherine—but because numerous subjects actually started to interest me. My natural inquisitiveness kicked in. Perhaps it was just my time to grow up. Because I ceased being confrontational, my grades improved substantially. By my senior year, I was a better student than Mildred Tedeschi, but unlike her, I was never a brownnoser. I was no longer interested in pubescent games like Cisco and Poncho either.

Nor was I interested in continuing to be best friends with Billy. I had outgrown him. We didn't quarrel or anything like that. We just drifted apart. I don't even know what happened to him. I lost track of his whereabouts decades ago, which makes me sad now. At the time, it didn't seem important.

Even thinking about Melissa ceased to consume me. Eventually, she lost interest and found someone else. Being dumped by her stung, but not for long. That's what is so fantastic about being a teenager. There are so many options available—so many interests from which to choose. Life was like a smorgasbord of possibilities just waiting for guys like me to make our selections. Indeed, those were the wonder years.

When I graduated from Marist, I was accepted at the University of Massachusetts in Amherst. I loved it there, especially being free from the confines of Catholicism—except for the feelings of guilt I couldn't shake. No Catholic ever does.

The girls were much prettier, and I found one in my sophomore year I really liked. Her name was Barbara DiNapoli. She was a knockout, and I fell for her hook, line, and sinker. Even better, she was equally smitten. She had a wonderful singing voice and planned to entertain professionally once we graduated. I could sit for hours and listen to her sing, and often did. Best of all, masturbation ceased to be an issue, being replaced by something far more fulfilling.

Spending a great deal of time together, we drifted into a serious relationship without ever actually planning to do so. In April of our senior year, Barbara became pregnant, so we eloped just a week after graduation. When Barbara walked across the stage to receive her degree, she nearly threw up from morning sickness but managed to keep it down, smiling and waving to her parents who had no idea about her compromised situation.

I graduated that day as well, with a degree in English literature, specializing in the Victorian era. Once we were married, we settled in Alston so that Barbara would be close to nightclubs, where she could potentially find work singing in downtown Boston.

Just before Christmas, our first daughter was born, followed by our second daughter fourteen months later—Irish twins according to my mom. Brittany and Brianna were both beautiful and healthy.

Being a schoolteacher, we needed for Barbara to work to supplement my income, especially with two young daughters. She was an outstanding vocalist. Unfortunately, there were very few engagements for her, even in a city the size of Boston. As we were to learn, the performing arts can be a very tough business. So was teaching. My students found Dickens, Thackeray, Yeats, and Bronte to be boring, much to my dismay. It actually made me appreciate Sister Anna Catherine's efforts.

While the girls were still toddlers, Barbara got her big break. She landed a job at Disneyworld, which necessitated us moving to Florida. Having shoveled snow my entire life, I embraced the idea as much as she did. At Disneyworld, Barbara was teamed with an extremely handsome guy, and the two of them sang romantic duets. Looking like a real life Ken and Barbie, with my wife being extremely beautiful, even after having two children, they became a smashing success. Everybody loved them. They even cut an album that did moderately well.

Teaming with Jeffrey Varner, Barbara achieved a measure of success she was never able to achieve on her own. Occasionally, the two were booked on a cruise ship, which meant they were gone for a week at a time, sometimes two. This was very difficult for Brittany, Brianna, and me. Our lives were definitely not the same when Barbara was gone. My wife and I understood sacrifices needed to be made, but it was still tough.

Because her partner was gay, I never felt insecure about them being together for extended periods, including traveling together. Besides, Barbara was completely trustworthy. She and I were both genuinely grateful for the added income, which was substantial. For the first time in our marriage, we were making more than we spent. The fulfillment of the American dream was just beyond the horizon—an outcome we both greatly desired.

While she was at sea in the Caribbean, I wasn't even able speak to her on the phone, which was a real hardship. I felt like a single parent most of the time, but like always, I sucked it up and did the best I could. I became both mother and father to our two girls, while also having to teach high school in Altamonte Springs.

Even when Barbara was home, when the girls were hungry, they would ask me what was for dinner. So did Barbara. Needless to say, my hands were full.

As Barbara and Jeffrey's career flourished, she seemed to be gone more often and for longer periods, putting a strain on our family that became increasingly difficult. When she was home, she was often distant, aloof, and rarely amorous. I noticed this, of course, but when you are raising two rambunctious kids, the focus of marriage is consumed with meeting their needs and not your own. Other young families we knew seemed to have similar problems.

Barbara and I just kept drifting apart, which both of us noticed, but did little to remedy. After four years of living this way, with our daughters now in kindergarten and first grade, Barbara came home from a two-week cruise with something on her mind. When she walked in, she wasn't smiling. I knew instantly something was amiss.

After feeding the girls and getting them settled for the night, Barbara and I sat in the living room with a glass of wine to talk about what was bothering her. Without mincing words—not even trivial chitchat—she announced that she wanted a divorce. She added that she wasn't interested in counseling, a trial separation, or anything that was aimed at restoring our relationship. She wanted out—period.

Because this was so unexpected, I probed for a reason, asking repeated questions about why she wouldn't even consider reconciliation? Obviously upset by her announcement, my mouth became as dry as it had been on the day of my First Holy Communion. Even worse, I felt just as frightened. As I sat there, my insides froze, and my hands trembled so badly I was forced to keep them clasped firmly together. This is how shaken I was, but I didn't accept her decision passively. I needed to know what was behind it.

After probing for about thirty minutes, with her trying to deflect each of my questions, she finally decided to come clean. She told me Jeffrey wasn't gay after all—far from it. In fact, they had been lovers from the beginning and had actually sought out gigs on cruise ships so they could be together more consistently. When she confessed this, I was stunned.

At first, I couldn't accept that it was true. I had no idea—none whatsoever. Blindsided, I had been completely fooled. I never suspected a thing. My dad used to call me "*Dum Kopf*," and this is exactly how I felt—like a complete fool.

By being absent so often, while being on cruise liners, it made it easier for Barbara and Jeffrey to enjoy their time together. While on board, they just pretended to be married and slept together regularly. Essentially, they had been living duplicitous, non-overlapping lives and planned to keep it that way, especially while our daughters remained so young. They had hoped to continue this self-indulgent pattern so that "nobody would get hurt," but Fate forced them to alter their plans.

Breaking eye contact, Barbara looked aside, and her face reddened. Finally, she divulged her secret. She said, "Cole, I'm pregnant. The child is Jeffrey's—not yours. It couldn't be yours. There, I've said it. Now, you know everything."

The way she announced this—so matter-of-factly—floored me. Although we had been together close to thirteen years and married nearly ten, I never expected anything like this. Looking at her, I realized I didn't know this woman at all—didn't even recognize her. She was a completely different person than the one I married. She wasn't trustworthy and never had been. As I began to fathom the level of her duplicity, I felt the foundation of my world being rocked. Her revelation, delivered the way she had, made me feel queasy.

As she finished repudiating our marriage, and me she said, "I love Jeffrey—not you. I'm not sure I ever loved you, Cole. I'm sorry but that's the truth."

When she said this, it was more than I could take. My body shook from head to toe, and my skin became cold and clammy. Feeling sick, my stomach began to lurch. Suddenly, I jumped to my feet and raced to the bathroom. I needed to vomit, but I didn't reach the commode in time, despite making a valiant effort to do so. Instead, I threw up all over everything, leaving a foul, sour smelling mess. As I sat on the edge of the bathtub sweating and breathing heavily, waiting to throw up a second time, I wondered if this was actually happening. I hoped it was just a bad dream, but I knew it wasn't.

In my misery, I thought Barbara should be the one who was experiencing morning sickness, not me. When I returned to the living room, she continued talking, as if I was perfectly fine and hadn't even been sick. In a stoic, detached voice, she informed me about the plans she and Jeffrey had made. It was like she was describing a casual weekend event, rather than the dismantling of our family. Everything seemed surreal. When she was finished, she stood, smiled, and walked out of the house to begin her new life, symbolically washing her hands of me and even of our daughters, who she didn't even kiss goodbye. She needed to meet Jeffrey, who was waiting for her, and I needed to clean up my vomit.

Watching how she walked out reminded me of an old Proverb. "This is the way of an adulteress. She eats, wipes her mouth, and says, 'I have done no wrong.'"

* * *

Unbeknownst to me, Barbara had already retained a lawyer. She filed for divorce earlier in the day. Because of her situation, she pushed for an immediate dissolution to our marriage. It was difficult to process everything, especially her four years of un-confessed infidelity. In her desire to distance herself from the three of us, neither my desires nor those of our daughters were taken into consideration. As difficult as this was for me to accept, we simply ceased to matter. Jeffrey's life had become hers, so what was best for us ceased to matter.

As part of the settlement, we decided to co-parent, but the lion's share of the work fell upon me, as I knew it would. This didn't bother me in the least. I was grateful. It was what I wanted.

There was a part of Barbara that balked at having so little to do with her daughters, but Jeffrey wanted a fresh start, so he insisted upon this arrangement. He wanted Barbara and their child completely to himself, so he continuously found ways to keep our daughters away from their mother. Consequently, our co-parenting was in name only. I became the de facto custodial parent—just like I had been for the past four years.

Eventually, Barbara and Jeffrey moved to Las Vegas, where the work was plentiful. Once there, they didn't have the burden of our daughters being around their mom. By the time they settled, Barbara had become a new mother for the third time.

When the divorce papers were finally presented to me for my signature—no longer crushed by her rejection or her infidelity—I signed them gladly. By that time, I was relieved to see the end of her.

Our daughters weren't, but I certainly was. Badly deceived, I didn't want anything to do with Barbara or with any other woman for that matter. This was probably a good thing, as bitter as I had become about the way our marriage ended.

14

Out of the Dreck of My Failed Marriage

Because Barbara and I had similar abusive experiences in our Catholic upbringing, in our courtship and subsequent marriage, we became completely secular. We were married by a magistrate and never went to confession or mass—not once. To have done so wasn't even a consideration. Nor did we discuss spiritual matters—not that I can remember anyway.

This wasn't a conscious decision we made—quite the contrary. It was simply the lifestyle we chose—one devoid of the trappings of meaningless sacramental religion, but it also meant we abandoned our sense of right and wrong. At least, she did—clearly.

It may seem strange that two people with deep roots in Catholicism would choose to live this way—by repudiating and disregarding our heritage—but that's what we did. Our entire focus was to achieve the American dream, which shifted our focus away from our foundational values. We relinquished everything except for our work ethic, which was so deeply ingrained in us; we didn't consider it to be Catholic anyway.

Our "religion" was getting ahead, becoming rich, and making the American dream work for us. We didn't even have our daughters baptized, which crushed my mom, who fretted that if anything should happen to either of them, her granddaughters would end up in limbo or hell. By this time, Midge's concern seemed so ridiculous I refused to even address it. If anything, Barbara was less patient with her mother-in-law than I was, which made things tense whenever my mom came to visit.

With my dad having died two years earlier, mom liked to visit often, but it was generally more convenient when Barbara was absent—away on one of her cruises. From my enlightened perspective, this now made sense. Never a fan of Barbara's, Midge would have been far more difficult to deceive than I was. Women can't be fooled about such matters as easily as men.

I liked it when my mom came. From the moment she walked through the front door, she assumed the role of caregiver for Brittany and Brianna, which was the only time I ever enjoyed a break.

By the time Barbara moved to Las Vegas, our divorce had become final, and things started to settled down quite a bit. From the moment of her unexpected confession until her departure, my life had been filled with drama—none of which was instigated by me. My goal was to be civil, as was Barbara's, but that's not the way terminating our marriage played out.

When going through a divorce, being gracious is rare, despite people's best intentions. I had to deal with one distasteful episode after another, as the fabric of our family was ripped apart, leaving all parties emotionally wounded, especially our daughters.

When people go through a divorce, their lives are never the same, although many pretend differently. If nothing else, innocence is lost and can never be restored. Divorce takes emotional chunks out of a person's soul that can never be replaced. Very few realize this while it's happening, including me, but most come to realize it—if they are willing to be honest with themselves. It's why so many divorced people experience deep-seated bitterness.

Even a bad marriage is difficult to end. To deal with the pain of being rejected, many medicate their pain with alcohol, drugs, and promiscuity. They don't make a conscious decision to become self-destructive. They just drift into it, taking the easy way out, fooling themselves into believing it's just for a short time. Some medicate with anti-depressants or tranquilizers, while others overeat or over-spend in a desperate effort to regain a sense of normality.

I didn't do any of these things. Instead, I worked out compulsively. It was the only thing that seemed to calm my nerves. My energy level was so high, because of internal stress and disquietude, that I ran, lifted weights, and played basketball at the YMCA, nearly every day after I finishing teaching school. I had to. Rigorous physical activity seemed to mollify the painful emotions that were eating me up on the inside. I worked out so much I got in the best shape of my life, but looking good and developing a chiseled body was a byproduct of exercising—not my primary purpose.

Battling my anger with excessive training was the only way my mind found peace from the bitterness that churned within me. I was hurt and deeply wounded, especially realizing how gullible I had been, but I didn't want to take out my anger on my daughters or on my students. That's why I went to the YMCA each day, pumped iron, and played basketball. It was very cathartic. While on the court, I fouled guys and cussed them out, but this was perfectly acceptable behavior. We all did it.

Many of them were there for the same reason. It was tremendously therapeutic for all of us—and a lot of fun. While running up and down the court, I never thought about my troubles. It was the only time I could be myself—a playful little boy without a care in the world. I've heard people grieve in different ways. Playing basketball was mine.

During this period, I actually considered going back to church, but I didn't. There wasn't anything there for me. I had already been beaten up emotionally, so I didn't need more of the same. Besides, returning to Catholicism would have been an admission of defeat, and I wasn't willing to do that. I needed to look forward—not backward. I understood this, but I also knew I was floundering badly.

While playing ball, I became friends with a bunch of great guys. On the court, we were very tight, but it was completely superficial. There is nothing deep about playing basketball, nothing philosophical, but it's what each of us needed—a mindless diversion. Fouling and getting fouled allowed us to emote on the court, but that's as far as our confrontational anger went. It was wonderful.

When the game was over, I left my aggression behind—just like everybody else. It provided me with a reprieve—a brief respite from my anxiety and feelings of despair. It was incredible. I can't imagine what my life would have been like without it, but I also realized it didn't solve any of the underlying issues that threatened to destroy my future. It provided a temporary fix—a once-a-day medication for pain—nothing more.

One of the guys I played with regularly asked if I would like to get a cup of coffee with him. I agreed and met Mark Wade one day after school at a Dunkin Donuts before heading to the Y. While driving to meet him, I wondered if he was going to pitch me about some multi-level marketing scheme, which certainly didn't interest me, but this wasn't what he wanted at all.

Instead, the conversation focused on what I was going through, especially about how badly I had been hurt by my divorce. Our little chat made me feel very uncomfortable. If I had known this was what Mark wanted, I wouldn't have agreed to come. Lapsed Catholics are very private about their feelings, especially guys. I didn't want to talk about my divorce or anything personal. It simply wasn't in my DNA to discuss such things. I wanted to keep a lid on the subject and told him so.

Mark backed off immediately, which I appreciated, but he also asked if we could meet again. When he made the suggestion, I was surprised, but I was even more surprised that I agreed to do it. I'm glad I did though.

We began to meet regularly and Mark became a first-rate friend. He was also a good basketball player. He dominated the boards and always made quick outlet passes that initiated fast breaks—a valuable skill in pick-up basketball. I loved being on the same team with him because his teams usually won. This meant I played more, instead of having to sit on the bench after losing, waiting for my next up.

On the court, he was a ferocious competitor, but off of the court he was entirely different. As we continued to meet, I realized he was a guy I could trust, which was exactly what I needed, although I wouldn't have sought out such a friendship.

After meeting for a month or two, he asked about my spiritual background a second time. No longer reluctant to discuss such matters with him, I opened up.

Once I got started, things just seemed to pour out—the pain, the anger, and the hurt from my upbringing, including my wife's four-year sexual betrayal. I'll bet I talked for nearly an hour, but he never interrupted—not once. He just sat there and listened, which must have been difficult, because I didn't hold back anything.

When I was finished, Mark and I talked about what I had divulged for quite a while. At one point in our conversation, he said, "Cole, you know that God loves you despite everything, right?"

I was flabbergasted. Once he said this, I don't remember anything else he said for the remainder of our conversation, but his off-handed statement pierced me to the core. I had never heard anything like it before—not once in my entire life. At first, I was startled and didn't believe what he said was true. Yet, something inside me kept telling me it was. I wanted it to be; that's for sure. When we left a few minutes later, his proclamation haunted my thoughts for the rest of the day. I couldn't shake that one statement. It kept replaying in my mind over-and-over.

The next time we met, before he could even take a sip of coffee or a bite out of his old-fashion donut, I challenged him about it. Admitting that I had never heard that God loved me before, I asked what made him think it was true.

"Because it's in the Bible, Cole, that's why," he answered matter-of-factly. "Do you want me to show you where?"

"Definitely," I replied, which surprised him a little—me too.

Without hesitation, he stood, grabbed his donut, and headed out to his car. Less than a minute later, he returned with his Bible in his left hand and his half eaten donut in his right. Sitting down, he took a sip of coffee and opened the Bible to show me the place where it said: "For God so loved the world He gave His only begotten son . . ."

Seeing these words on the page of Mark's Bible was all that was required. God *did* love me after all. It was right there in black and white and had been for nearly two thousand years, but nobody had ever informed me about this simple truth.

Mark wanted to continue, but he didn't. Once he saw the look on my face, he knew that he should let it rest, which was exactly what I needed.

A moment later, I began to cry and couldn't stop, but I wasn't embarrassed. Neither was he. I cried intermittently for a long time. I couldn't help it, but the catharsis it provided was the most soul-satisfying event I had experience I since my divorce.

After leaving our meeting to drive home and fix dinner for my daughters, I remember thinking that—out of the *dreck* of my failed marriage—I had found myself. Things were going to be different, and I knew it. From that moment forward, by accepting God's love rather than fighting it, I had a purpose that was greater than simply getting ahead in life, and it was more fulfilling than trying to achieve the elusive American dream.

* * *

Unlike many, I had no trouble believing in God's existence. I knew He was real. Because of my background, I simply didn't believe He cared. When I realized that He did—and always had—my hardhearted, protective shield evaporated. From that moment—from that precise instant—I never doubted God's love again. This was my transformational moment. This was when I started to seek God's will for my life, while simultaneously ceasing to be apathetic.

Because I had so many experiences in Catholicism with those who insisted they spoke for God, while altering His words and His intentions, I made a commitment from the day I invited Christ into my life to stand firmly against people who used God's name in vain. I'm not talking about profanity, which is trivial. I'm referring to those who ascribe characteristics to God that are not true, profiting from being deceptive, wounding innocent people in the process.

15

God Did Love Me After All

Before leaving Dunkin Donuts that afternoon, Mark made a second trip to his car. Returning, he handed me a copy of the New Testament, which I had never read—not once in my entire life. Catholics were never encouraged to read the Bible—not even the clergy are encouraged to read it.

When I arrived home, after getting the girls settled for the evening, I looked at the Scriptures Mark had quoted in our discussion. Reading each passage several times, I pondered the truth about what he had said. Not only did God love me but He also had a plan for the rest of my life—a plan for good things and not for bad. This really surprised me.

I had spent more than three decades being convinced God was real but indifferent at best. To learn of the depth of His caring was a welcomed surprise. Nevertheless, believing He didn't care about me for so long, I had difficulty internalizing this new reality as being accurate. Doing so felt awkward. I was much more comfortable believing a lie.

Over the course of the next several weeks, Mark and I met more frequently, which helped me transfer my head knowledge to internal conviction. We met at the same Dunkin Donuts so often—now initiated by me—the staff considered us to be regulars. I suppose we were.

Although Mark was no biblical scholar, he knew enough to guide me in the direction I needed to go. There were so many things I didn't understand—things that were clearly stated in the Scriptures but had little relevance with my ritualistic upbringing. It was obvious I had been effectively indoctrinated, while being badly misled at the same time. I doubt my teachers knew any better, which made me feel sad for them, but it didn't excuse them from teaching error.

Nevertheless, I didn't dwell on the negative. Being on an explosive learning curve that opened up a new world of possibilities for me, I released one misconception after the other. Life, once again, was becoming meaningful. Each day, I felt stronger and more empowered than the day before. Being a decisive person, although badly shaken by my divorce, I once again became strong.

I felt like Jean Valjean—the protagonist in *Les Miserables*. I realized my past had been more wasteful than productive, but this no longer mattered. Things were about to change. A new story was about to begin, and I was ready for it. Nurturing these purposeful thoughts, I looked forward to starting afresh at the tender age of thirty-five.

* * *

As part of my new life, Brittany, Brianna, and I started attending church. We went with Mark and his family a few times, but I was very uncomfortable with how each service seemed to drag on endlessly. Each time we went, they sang the chorus of "Just as I Am" at least a half dozen times, which I found irritating rather than uplifting. Besides, the alter call was just too emotional and demonstrative for me. Don't get me wrong. The people were warm and friendly. That part of Mark's church was wonderful, but I simply didn't feel at home.

Someone suggested I try an Episcopal church, which I did. I found one where the pastor taught from the Scriptures instead of from some well-meaning leftist political agenda, which definitely would have turned me off.

I wanted to learn from God's Word—nothing else. My head was already filled with indoctrination. All I desired was to study what the Bible taught. I knew I lacked depth, but just like my attitude changed at Marist, I was ready and eager to learn everything I could.

Apparently, others in the congregation felt the same way. The rector's teaching was always deep and solid, which is why the church service was packed every Sunday. For me, it was the best of both worlds. The teaching was consistently informative, while the service was liturgical and structured, making me feel much more comfortable than I did when I attended Mark's church.

During this period of enlightenment, I gained foundational faith, while I continued to teach literature in high school. I was also Mr. Mom for my girls, who were the delight of my life. Needless to say, I was busy and often felt overwhelmed. Despite this, I kept plugging along—just like millions of other single parents.

At church, there were several women who took notice of me, hoping I would respond, but I didn't. I went out with a few, but I was too gun-shy to get involved in a serious relationship. You know the old saying—once burned, twice cautious.

Despite how difficult things had been, I was fairing better than Barbara. A little less than two years after she divorced me, Jeffrey became involved with another woman. His dalliance split up their marriage, as well as their act. Moving out to spend more time with his new paramour, Jeffrey left Barbara and their infant to fend for themselves in Las Vegas, crushing his bride in the process.

Apparently, what Jeffrey liked the best about his affair with Barbara was its clandestine nature. He loved the excitement of being involved in a secret romance more than he actually loved her. Once they were married and she became his wife, with the added burden of caring for a newborn son, Barbara's appeal to him diminished, apparently dwindling to nothing.

Jeffrey felt trapped. He loathed the mundane lifestyle of being a husband and a father. He needed fawning adulation—not the thankless task of caring for an infant. Where was the fun in that? Where was the romance? Additionally, with their relationship being out in the open, it lacked the titillating intrigue he craved. Being clandestine was Jeffrey's aphrodisiac. He required it.

Being without it meant there was a role to be filled—the role of a secret lover who would provide sexual stimulation through adultery. Although feeling a little guilty about leaving Barbara and his son, marital fidelity wasn't for Jeffrey. Finally admitting to himself who he really was, he set out to fill the vacant role, which didn't take long—not for a handsome professional singer like him.

Barbara, of course, having given birth twice before, knew exactly what being a new mother entailed. Committed to making her second family a success, she looked forward to establishing a solid foundation with the man she really loved. Unfortunately, she fell in love with an illusion—a man whose character qualities were conjured out of thin air. She thought he was capable of selfless love, betting her future on it, but she had been mistaken.

Jeffrey was not the man she thought he was, which became crystal clear just as soon as the going got rough, which always happens with a newborn. The life they lived in Las Vegas was completely different from the one they enjoyed while traveling together. While on a cruise, everything was done for them, and they enjoyed a fairytale existence. As the ship's headline act, they were fawned upon constantly, but the real world doesn't resemble a Caribbean cruise, where everything is catered to your liking. Jeffrey loved their fairytale life but was unable to make the transition to reality. As Barbara discovered to her chagrin, he didn't even make much of an effort.

When she became aware of Jeffrey's infidelity, which was inevitable, she was crushed—exactly the way I had been by her. Hating the role of being victimized by adultery, Barbara began to understand how I felt, adding substantially to her regret about the way our marriage ended.

One evening, about six weeks after Jeffrey's abandonment, I received a surprise telephone call from her. Tearfully, Barbara described what her life had been like, which I hated for her. Without actually saying so, Barbara tried to square things with me. Because we had the responsibility for co-parenting our daughters, I was grateful to be able to speak candidly with her once again. It felt good to bridge the gap of estrangement and become friends—at least as friendly as recently divorced people can be.

As we talked, she made a veiled hint about returning, but I feigned obtuseness—never picking up on her offer. I was delighted for our relationship to be friendly, but there was no way I was going to get involved with her again. That ship had sailed. I had no interest in boarding it for another voyage, but it did feel good to know she had been considered reconciling. It might have been tacky for me to be delighted by her overture, but I was. It was validating.

* * *

By the time the girls were in the fourth and fifth grade, their hectic schedules made it nearly impossible for me to take care of everything. The amount of time I spent teaching made it difficult to accomplish my single-parent duties. Besides, having spent several years studying biblical truth, I wanted to use my life to further God's Kingdom. Although I loved English literature, having taught it for so many years, I wanted a new challenge—one that involved Kingdom building aspects.

Supplementing church, I also attended a men's Bible study, which met on Saturday mornings at Perkins Restaurant near Disney World. Mark brought me there and helped me get acquainted with numerous young Christian businessmen, including a guy I really liked—Alvin Dettler Carter. Dett and I hit it off the minute we met. He was interesting and went out of his way to get to know me, which I definitely appreciated. It let me know he was a genuine Christian and someone I could trust—just like I had learned to trust Mark Wade.

Confiding in Dett, I told him about my life and my difficult schedule, which had become overwhelming. He said he would keep his eyes open for an opportunity in his industry. As you can imagine, because he was in Christian publishing, his offer was an exciting prospect, but I doubted anything would come from it. Obviously, I was mistaken.

Several weeks later, when I arrived at 7 a.m. for the Saturday morning meeting, Dett approached me before I could even get a much-needed cup of coffee. He informed me about a prospective job with a Christian ministry in Atlanta that produced devotionals. He added that it would necessitate a move, but it might also be a great opportunity for me to do something worthwhile.

Encouraging me to apply, he said, "Cole, this could work out nicely for you. You would spend most of your time on the phone from your home office, which means you would be able to create your own schedule. This would make it easier to take Brittany and Brianna to ballet and gymnastics."

My interest being piqued, I asked, "Is it a sales job?"

"Yes, but it's not high pressure sales. You would be a natural." He added, "This is a great opportunity for you."

"Do you really think so?"

"I know it is," he affirmed.

"Then, I want to interview for it," I replied, without thinking of the ramifications of uprooting my daughters from their school and their friends.

Dett added, "With my recommendation, which will be a good one, I think you'll get the job."

"I guess this puts me in your debt, doesn't it?" I replied with a grin, congratulating myself for having made an excellent pun.

"Think nothing of it," Dett replied, with a warm smile, having heard similar puns many times before.

Humbly, I added, "Thanks, Dett," and I meant it.

"No problem. It's what I do," he said with a warm, ingratiating smile.

* * *

The following week, I was contacted by Living Water ministry in Atlanta about their position as a national sales representative—a job that had been open for nearly a year. They were as anxious to have it filled, as I was to make the transition. Nevertheless, the hiring process was long and arduous. There were times I nearly abandoned the effort, but it continued to pop up on my radar. After nearly three months of going back and forth, they made the decision to offer me the job, but there was one caveat. They wanted me to start immediately—the following week.

Being a teacher, I wasn't sure this was possible, but my department head understood my dilemma and made it easy for me to transition out of the classroom. Grateful for his help, I called Living Water and accepted the job.

Although I was nervous, I was also excited. A new phase in my life was about to begin—a welcomed one. My work would now further God's

Kingdom, and I couldn't wait to be surrounded by like-minded, selfless people—those who made the choice to take the road less traveled.

16

He Sported a Haughty, Imperious Look

Once I accepted the job, my transition to Living Water ministry occurred at lightning speed, which was difficult. I was used to a methodical routine and realized quickly that being flexible was a skill I would need to master.

I was required to be in Washington, D.C. the following week for a convention. Being in attendance was the reason I was asked to leave my teaching position with virtually no notice. It also meant I needed to get my mom on a plane so that she could take care of the girls. She agreed to help without hesitation, which I knew she would. I could always count on Midge and often did. Brittany and Brianna loved it when their granny came, which made it easier for me to leave. God bless my mom.

On my first day working for Living Water, I traveled with our founding president, Donald Duncan, to the National Religious Broadcasters Convention (NRB), which was held annually at the Washington Sheraton—not far from The White House. It was February 1983, and Ronald Reagan was beginning the second half of his first term—thanks in large part to a substantial effort put forth by hundreds of evangelical leaders, most of whom attended NRB. Flexing their newfound political muscle, nearly every person at the convention was ecstatic about Reagan's election, which repudiated Jimmy Carter's "born-again" candidacy, sending the "Peanut President" back to Georgia to pound nails for his favorite charity, Habitat for Humanity.

Evangelical Christians—infuriated by Carter's political positions, which they considered antithetical to God's will—came out of the woodwork to support Reagan. They detested Carter because he favored abortion, homosexual rights, the weakening of the military, and Arabs over Israel, while promoting an overall liberal agenda, which nearly everyone who attended the convention detested.

Reagan, who understood that the NRB was his crowd, was scheduled to speak, which he did each year of his presidency. Having the President at the convention added to its excitement, which was already high. I was there for each of his speeches, beginning in 1983. Every time he spoke, the enormous auditorium was packed. You needed to arrive at least two hours early if you wanted a seat, which I certainly did. After being uncomfortable during the duration of his first speech, I made certain to use the restroom just before I entered the auditorium in subsequent years.

This was the heyday of "electric Christianity"—several years before any of the scandals surfaced. Because of the separation of church and state, there was virtually no monitoring of the evangelical world, making it one of the last bastions of pure capitalism—the survival of the fittest. When I walked into the Mecca of broadcast Christianity the first day, I didn't have a clue about what to expect, which meant I was ill prepared for what I witnessed.

To me, Mark Wade's church—my basketball buddy—seemed too demonstrative, but it was subdued compare to what I saw from the minute I walked into the atrium at the Washington Sheraton.

To say I was psychologically unprepared for the spectacle would have been a substantial understatement. As I surveyed the hotel's cavernous atrium, which displayed NRB banners everywhere; I noticed there was a large section cordoned off for Jim and Tammy Faye Bakker to broadcast their TV program. As if on cue, less than a minute after I walked in, their band began to play, belting out music that filled the hall, adding to the enthusiasm. Each musician was a perfectly groomed professional. They all wore Las Vegas-style costumes, which reminded me of the times I watched Jeffrey and Barbara perform.

Bakker's band was just as talented as the musicians at Disney World and Las Vegas, which surprised me. Without warming up, they played one song after the other, making it difficult for people to carry on conversations. Nobody seemed to care. They loved it, but I certainly didn't.

Having spent the better part of my life being a participant in Catholicism's stayed ritualism, there was nothing in my background to prepare me for this glitzy, show-biz style, professional entertainment, which was touted as being sacred. Less than two years earlier, an emotional song like "Just as I Am" was too much for me to handle. Standing there, I was shocked, repulsed, and mesmerized simultaneously. It was a little scary, but it was also as tantalizing as the forbidden fruit that seduced Eve and her husband, Adam.

Several hours later, I walked into the exhibit hall, where more than a thousand vendors showcased their wares. Each booth displayed tinsel and plastic, as the eyes of the vendors sparkled with unbridled avarice. Walking through, I understood how the Lord must have felt when He cast out the moneychangers. Of course, this was a convention hall and not the Temple in Jerusalem, but I felt overwhelmed and uncomfortable, nonetheless.

Equally surprising, it seemed like everybody felt right at home. The facade of disingenuous religious fervor didn't seem to bother anybody but me, which was perplexing. Inwardly, I was repulsed—as appalled as I had ever been. I wanted to run, get back on a plane, and head home to my classroom, where I could teach *Great Expectations* in peace, but I didn't.

I couldn't. For better or worse, I had made my decision and needed to stick with it. So, instead of revealing my revulsion, I smiled and feigned enthusiasm, which made me as disingenuous as everybody else. Because I needed to fit in, I maintained my counterfeit approbation for the duration of the convention.

The following day—once again in the atrium—I noticed the bar was filled to capacity, but nobody was smoking or drinking. They were simply using the area for business meetings. I was surprised there was no alcohol—not even somebody having a beer. Later, I discovered that the bar did virtually no business during NRB. Instead, attendees chose to drink in private, where room service delivered more alcohol during that week than at any other time during the year.

Paying better attention my second time through, I saw my first celebrity—Jimmy Swaggart. He was wearing a cashmere camelhair topcoat, draped over his shoulders like it was a cape. Adding to his regal ambiance, he sported a haughty, imperious look, which let everybody know how important he was and how unimportant they were. His condescension was so obvious only a blind fool could miss it. Nevertheless, as he walked by, people parted, standing aside to allow him—as well as his entourage of a dozen smiling sycophants—to pass unimpeded. Looking like a medieval prince, people came close to bowing as he passed, which he relished, as if it was his divine right. This seemed comical and had a surreal aspect to it, reminding me of one of my daughter's favorite Saturday morning cartoon characters—a miscreant who loved lording it over his cringing underlings.

Not to be outdone, Jim Bakker passed by a minute later, sporting his trademark smile. The only difference between the two was Bakker was willing to make eye contact with people he passed, which the arrogance of Swaggart wouldn't allow. When I saw Bakker for the first time, wearing a custom-fit beige suit, I noticed that every hair on his head was perfectly coifed. When my ex-wife's hair was flawless, it was always because a makeup artist had just finished with her. Bakker had that same look. I noticed his small, dainty hands, which were perfectly manicured—just like the rest of him. Not much over five feet, three inches, he was diminutive in physical stature; but when he was making the rounds, he filled the room with his presence. His operation was a huge moneymaker, and everybody wanted to be in business with Bakker and his operation, PTL—the initials for Praise the Lord.

Jerry Falwell and Pat Robertson followed next. Each had a group of men and women trailing close behind. At NRB, self-importance was the name of the game. Adrian Rogers, who was President of the Southern Baptist Convention at one time, said that if God dropped a bomb on NRB, half of the egos in America would be destroyed. The more brownnosers a superstar employed, flattering on cue, the better. Notoriety, fame, and self-importance were magnified—each at the expense of humility, service, and godliness.

The last superstar I saw was Billy Graham, who just walked around like a normal guy, speaking to everyone who approached him. Although his clothes weren't shabby, they were not custom-made either. By far the best known of the bunch and certainly the most important, Graham appeared to be unpretentious, which was a relief. My respect for him, which was already high, increased.

Being the newest kid on the block at Living Water, I spent most of my time manning the booth, meeting people and telling them about our ministry's devotionals. As you can imagine, this was a challenge because I still didn't know much about the business. I had a huge learning curve ahead of me.

On the second day of the convention, Dett dropped by the booth to say hello. Accompanying him was one of his subordinates, Pete Chalmette. After initial introductions, we talked for nearly thirty minutes. Pete, who was nearly as new to the industry as I was, said very little. He was content to maintain an expression that resembled one of my students when asked a tough question. When they left, I concluded that Dett was the sharpest guy at NRB, but I wondered if someone as quiet as Pete could possibly make it in a business where being gregarious was required.

* * *

The next time I saw the two of them was a year later at the same convention. Again, I was manning the booth when both walked up—each sporting a genuine smile. Dett extended his hand to shake mine—as did Pete a moment later. Exchanging pleasantries for a few minutes, Pete finally took an appraising look at me and said, "Cole, you've gained a little weight, haven't you?" Not waiting for me to respond, he added, "Maybe ten pounds or so, right?"

He was correct. Not being able to play basketball very often, I had gained ten pounds. His astute observation made me bristle. Irritated, I never would have thought he would become my best friend and that Dett would become my enemy, but that is precisely what happened.

17

They Became Embittered —Often Blaming God

The girls and I made the transition from Orlando to Atlanta much more smoothly than I anticipated, thanks to my mom. She provided us with a down payment for a quaint house not far from Bobby Jones Golf Course in Buckhead. It was beautiful—our first real home—and it was located in one of the most fashionable areas of Atlanta. Even better, Brittany and Brianna made new friends easily. The house also had a mother-in-law suite over the garage for Midge, but she preferred to live in Massachusetts, saying it was "wicked hot" down south—a response nearly every Bostonian articulates.

Midge loved having her own place though. It afforded her the peace and quiet she needed, while also allowing her to be accessible whenever required. Although she was not completely settled with the girls and me attending St. Philips Episcopal Church, rather than Christ, the King Catholic Church, Midge was happy both girls had finally been baptized and confirmed.

Once, when Barbara had a solo gig at the Hyatt Regency in Atlanta, she brought her young son and stayed with us in Midge's mother-in-law suite. While Barbara was performing, Brittany and Brianna took care of their younger half-brother, treating him like he was a puppy. Watching this was both adorable and hysterical. He was a cute kid, had a sweet disposition, and adored his older sisters.

Since we had bridged the gap and become friendly, having Barbara around—even for a short time—wasn't unpleasant. By the second day of her stay, neither of us felt the least bit awkward or uncomfortable. Her new boyfriend, who remained in Las Vegas, didn't like it one bit though. He was nearly apoplectic with jealousy, which let me know she had not yet learned her lesson. I felt sad for her, knowing the outcome of her most recent, ill-suited relationship would prove to be as disastrous as her marriage had been.

Now in my third year of employment at Living Water—my first two being consumed with efforts to stop the attrition of clients from abandoning our devotionals—I knew what I was doing and had become fairly well known within the evangelical community. For better or worse, I had become the spokesperson for our ministry, other than Donald Duncan, who was an evangelical luminary.

My job was to bolster the sales of *Fruitful Living*, our premier devotional. Halting its decline was quite a job, but I accomplished it by finding a dozen new clients. Dett was right; I was a natural at the job and came to love it more than teaching. I especially liked the freedom it afforded me, which I could never have experienced as a schoolteacher.

In addition to *Fruitful Living*, I had the simultaneous responsibility of developing the client base for *Truthful Living* and launching *Family Values*—the ministry's third devotional. My duties were substantial. Since I wasn't wise enough to complain, I just worked diligently, with surprisingly successful results.

By far my greatest challenge was launching *Family Values*. Because it required the entire family to have devotions together, it was a very difficult sale to make. The primary place it was to be used was at the dinner table, where families were encouraged to spend fifteen minutes a day with their children. The idea was noble, but obtaining a commitment like this was easier said than done. Sustaining it was even more difficult. Everybody knows it's nearly impossible to keep kids at the table when they've finished eating for even a minute—let alone fifteen. I couldn't do it effectively with my girls more than once or twice a week. When I insisted we use *Family Values* every day, they whined, moaned, and balked; pitching such a fit that the reward wasn't worth the effort.

Nevertheless, it was my task to find several large ministries to customize this product, creating their own version of *Family Values*. I made my initial pitch to Your Family matters, the ministry started by my hero, Larry Boothe—the man whose book helped me come to terms with Barbara's infidelity. I flew to the home of their operations in the Los Angeles area to meet with Boothe's people at least ten times before they made the decision to use *Family Values*. By making the sale, we were able to launch the magazine.

To ensure there would be a large number of subscriptions, Donald Duncan appeared as the guest on Dr. Boothe's radio program for five consecutive days, explaining the virtues of having family devotions. Donald made it clear this would strengthen the foundation of each family, which was absolutely true. Duncan and Boothe hit it off well. They talked back and forth in a meaningful way, which meant listeners were intrigued by the value of the monthly devotional magazine.

The week *Family Values* was launched on Boothe's radio program, more than 35,000 people signed up for a year's subscription. Just before this happened, I made another sale to the Church of God in Cleveland, Tennessee. So, we printed an additional 75,000 magazines to send to many of the tithing families in this large denomination. This sale—added to my Your Family Matters sale and several smaller clients—made the magazine a success from day one. I became a hero at the ministry, which was very gratifying.

When we mailed our first issue, however, everything exploded in my face. To customize *Family Values,* we put a picture of Dr. Boothe on the back cover, along with a letter he wrote, encouraging families to begin using the devotional immediately. Unfortunately, our art department flopped his transparency, which meant the part in Boothe's hair was on the wrong side of his head. While this might seem like a trivial mistake—something that could easily be rectified in subsequent issues—it was an egregious, relationship threatening error, according to Dr. Boothe.

When I spoke to my primary contact at Focus, he was clearly shaken by how ghastly our mistake had been. Thoroughly rattled, he said, "Boothe's so furious he is considering canceling the entire project. He's threatening to refund everybody's money."

"What?" I said in astonishment, as my mouth became dry.

"He's livid, Cole. He doesn't want to use *Family Values* anymore, and I'm not sure I can change his mind." Nervously, he added, "I doubt there will be a second issue."

Trying to defuse the situation, which seemed to be a massive overreaction, I explained it was a simple error to correct, and we would guarantee the mistake would never be replicated. Additionally, I explained that canceling *Family Values* would deprive 35,000 families of a huge spiritual blessing—a benefit that would help parents and their children communicate at a much deeper level. I did everything I could to calm the troubled waters, trying to prevent Your Family Matters from making a knee-jerk reaction—a reaction that would do nothing other than assuage Dr. Boothe's ruffled feathers.

Booking a flight, I made an immediate trip to their headquarters, performing a *mea culpa* before Boothe's staff, assuring them that nothing like this would ever happen again. Dr. Boothe, who was either too busy or too miffed to meet with me, finally calmed down from his personal affront, which ended the crisis peacefully.

From my perspective, the problem was Dr. Boothe's huge ego. He was just as bald as my father. Like my dad, Boothe refused to acknowledge the truth about his male pattern baldness. Reminiscent of my father, Boothe also parted his hair right above his ear, allowing that area of his hair to grow very long, sweeping it over the top to cover his bald spot to pretend he had a full head of hair.

Boothe must have thought this fooled people, which was wishful thinking. To acknowledge he was bald was unacceptable to him—an admission he refused to declare. The way his image was depicted was more important than anything else, including helping the families who had purchased *Family Values*.

Later, I learned that pictures of his bald spot had caused problems on other occasions. Once, a candid picture had been taken of Dr. Boothe—with President Reagan placing his hand on the Christian leader's shoulder. Because Reagan was smiling fondly at Boothe, it became the Christian psychologist's prized possession. Unfortunately, because Boothe's back was to the camera, his bald spot was plainly evident, glistening in the sun. In an effort to cover it up, Boothe had one of his graphic artists fill in the spot with hair—long before Photoshop would have made this request easy to accomplish. When the artist was finished, it looked like Boothe was wearing a yarmulke—a Jewish skullcap. The altered photo looked far more ridiculous than the bald spot to everybody other than the man who refused to admit his shortcoming.

That Boothe would consider something this trivial, as a justification to cancel *Family Values,* was astounding to me. As I thought about it on my cross-country flight back to Atlanta, I couldn't believe how angry he became over something so inconsequential. Even more perplexing was reconciling his petty vanity with the person who had written such profound wisdom about marriage and families. It didn't seem possible for someone who was so insecure about his appearance to have such deep insight into the behavior of others, while being oblivious about his own. It was baffling but true.

I thought Dr. Boothe was a bigger man than this, but I was mistaken—a realization that saddened me greatly. Although he became a favorite of President Reagan and did some extraordinary work on family values, pornography, and other issues, I never viewed him with the same respect I previously held.

Although still new to the world of Christian ministries, this was the first time I witnessed such self-serving egotism; but it wouldn't be the last. As I came to realize, being petty, vain, and self-indulgent was common among the lords of evangelicalism.

Working for Christian leaders like him actually became toxic to my soul—an occupational hazard both spiritually and psychologically. It wasn't simply that many of the lords and ladies had feet of clay—just like everybody else. It was more significant than that.

For them, the rules were different. For Boothe, it was acceptable to be peevish and petulant. Normal behavior—that applies to everyone else—didn't apply to him or to others like him. Because of their calling, they didn't believe they were required to follow traditional rules—not really. In the deepest recesses of their hearts, they believed they were above the rules that applied to everyone else. This belief—this exalted perspective—which their words would deny but their behavior affirmed—is the root of the narcissism that has plagued Christian ministries in America for decades.

Routinely, the lords gave themselves permission to be trivial and mean-spirited. From their perspective, it was permissible to be this way. They deserved special consideration; they were justified in being irritable and grouchy.

Those around them learned to coddle their demanding and inconsiderate ways, rather than confront them. Constantly making excuses, those who worked for these superstars were rarely empowered to challenge their leader's inappropriate conduct. This is why the lords and ladies routinely surrounded themselves with people who were willing to placate their childishness. Their sycophants learn to tolerate conduct that would never be permitted from anyone else. In many ways, it's similar to a permissive mother indulging her spoiled child, rather than providing much-needed discipline.

As a de facto part of their jobs, ministry employees learn to pamper their bosses, telling them their weaknesses are excusable because of the great work they are accomplishing for the Lord. Often tolerance for sinful behavior is tacit—with no words spoken. In essence, a ministry-wide understanding about the boss' uniqueness evolves over time.

Although many ministry employees learn to look the other way, many cannot. This is why there is such high attrition in Christian ministries. Those who become fed up with unethical and aberrant behavior leave. When they do, they become embittered—routinely blaming God for their distasteful experience.

Dr. Boothe's staff nurtured his pettiness, castigating Living Water for making a mistake, while never challenging his surly behavior—the tantrum of a spoiled child. He never apologized for overreacting either. People like Boothe, who have difficulty admitting they are wrong, rarely do.

In the Roman Empire, when Caesar returned from war, leading his triumphant army through the streets of The Eternal City, the people cheered, telling him he was a god and not a man. Wisely, Caesar appointed a servant to follow closely behind. It was this man's responsibility to say, "You are not a god. You are a mere mortal." Caesar did this in an effort to maintain a sense of humility—a sense of humanity. Although not always successful, at least, the intent was there. It's a strategy the superstars of Christendom need to embrace.

Unfortunately, the problem with Boothe's photo wasn't the only fire I was required to put out when we printed the first issue of *Family Values*. The cover we chose for the Church of God, Cleveland, had a much more substantial issue. It showed a grandfather, holding his grandson in his left arm. The child was displaying a string of fish the two had just caught. Both the grandfather and the child beamed with delight at their bountiful catch.

It was a good family photo with great metaphorical overtones, but it had one problem: The grandfather was wearing a pinky ring on his right hand, which was clearly visible in the lower left quadrant of the cover. Because the Church of God, Cleveland, believes wearing jewelry is prideful, and therefore sinful, they refused to mail the magazine to their people. They wouldn't pay for the magazine with this photo on the cover either.

This was a huge problem—a crisis we brought on ourselves. Knowing their position on jewelry, we had made a colossal blunder, which we were required to resolve. Reprinting the magazine was too expensive; so we decided to place a gold medallion sticker over the grandfather's right hand, covering the ring. The medallion announced the inaugural issue of the magazine. The stickers had to be placed on the magazine by hand, which was a labor-intensive job—an undertaking nobody at Living Water was willing to make. Taking the bull by the horns, I volunteered my mom, Brittany, and Brianna to do the work. Everybody at Living Water loved the idea, which effectively solved the crisis.

Having experienced two significant problems with the first issue of *Family Values*, Donald Duncan called a meeting of the art department and informed them that my approval would be required for every magazine or marketing resource produced for our clients. Initially furious that "a salesman" would need to be consulted about artistic decisions, the staff blustered for a few months; but they had no choice. From then on, I was included in all photographic decisions, which was a substantial imposition on my time, adding significantly to my responsibilities, which were already considerable.

At first, nobody was happy about Donald's decision; but I started to like the creative aspects of my job better than anything else. Additionally, I had a talent for it, which the artists recognized. They abandoned their resentment, choosing instead to enjoy the process, which became pleasant for all of us. Because I understood the differences between the ministries we served better than anyone else, the material we produced fit their theological nuances in doctrine to a tee, making everybody happy.

18

Lifting Up Christ Works—Pushing Jesus Does Not

Obviously, launching *Family Values* was quite an adventure, but this wasn't my only duty—not by a long shot. Solidifying the base for *Truthful Living* was also my responsibility. To ensure its continued viability, I needed a large client, which the Billy Graham Evangelistic Association definitely was. Six months after launching *Family Values*, I contacted one of the people I had met at NRB—Johnny Lenning, the producer of *The Hour of Decision*, Billy Graham's weekly radio program.

Being friendly, forthright, and genuine, I liked Johnny the minute I met him, and we remained friends for the remainder of his life. Working out of Greenville, South Carolina, with Cliff Barrows, Billy's right-hand man and master of ceremonies for his worldwide crusades, I pitched the devotional to both Johnny and Cliff one day when I drove over to have lunch with them. Cliff thought *Truthful Living* would be a perfect magazine to use as a monthly communications tool for the entire Graham donor base, which was enormous.

Spearheading the effort, Cliff discussed the matter at length with Billy

Graham, who agreed it was a great idea—especially since it would help people develop a better grasp of God's Word, which was a high priority for the evangelist. To get the ball rolling, Billy wrote Cliff a letter, stating that he wanted to produce a Billy Graham Evangelistic Association (BGEA) version of *Truthful Living*.

It seemed like we had everything in place to add the premiere ministry in the world to Living Water's client base. Knowing how valuable the signed letter from Billy was, Cliff intended to use it—like the Pope's imprimatur—to ensure the project came to fruition.

Cliff asked Donald Duncan and me to meet Johnny Lenning and him in Minneapolis, where we would begin implementation, after getting a sign off from George Wilson, the business manager for BGEA. Salivating at the prospect, Donald and I immediately agreed, realizing this would be the biggest sale we would ever make.

On the appointed day, we boarded a plane in the middle of winter, heading for the Twin Cities to finalize the agreement. When we arrived—amid snow, ice, and biting wind—I had a great reminder of why I never regretted leaving Boston. When Johnny and Cliff met us, they were sporting grins of impending victory, which were only surpassed by our own. We headed off in a taxi for the BGEA headquarters. As we drove through the city, Johnny informed us that George Wilson was a gruff curmudgeon, and Cliff should be the one to do most of the talking, which was fine with us.

Arriving at BGEA headquarters, we were ushered into George's office, where we all sat at a medium-sized table. Unlike some of the palatial ministry offices I had visited, Dr. Graham's headquarters were meager by comparison—even his office, which he used sparingly.

After exchanging pleasantries, Cliff took charge of the meeting and said, "George, I've met with Billy, and he wants to make *Truthful Living* available to our donor base. The list of our best supporters is about

300,000; isn't that right?"

George nodded that Cliff's estimate was correct. As this was transpiring, I caught Donald's eye. Both of us fought hard to play it cool, knowing what a financial boon this would be for Living Water.

Continuing with his presentation, Cliff said, "These donors are the ones Billy and I think should receive the monthly magazine."

George nodded once more, signifying he understood Cliff's intent.

"With the Crusade in Los Angeles being less than a year away, we thought this would be a good time and place to launch *Truthful Living*." Looking directly at George, Cliff asked, "What do you think?"

Devoid of emotion, George replied matter-of-factly, "That would be a good time to start the magazine, if we were going to use it, but we're not."

"But Billy wants us to use it," Cliff challenged—with just a hint of annoyance. "He wrote this letter for me to give to you. It says he wants to have a BGEA version of *Truthful Living*." With this, Cliff handed George the letter—like it was a bearer bond ready to be redeemed.

Taking a minute to look around for his glasses, which he found under a pile of papers on his desk, George returned to the table and read the letter carefully, handing it back to Cliff, when he finished.

Thinking the letter would override George's obstinacy and seal the deal; Cliff repeated confidently, "I think we should start the devotional at the Los Angeles Crusade. Don't you agree?"

With all eyes looking intently at George, he replied, "No I don't; and we're not going to use *Truthful Living*, Cliff."

"But Billy," Cliff retorted imploringly; but George interrupted, not allowing Cliff to protest any further.

With a wave of his hand, speaking authoritatively, George responded. "I don't care what Billy wants. We're not going to use it—period. That's the end of it." With that, George folded his arms brusquely, hunkering down defiantly like a bulldog, daring Cliff to protest further, which he didn't do.

Stunned and deflated—with nothing more to say—the meeting ended awkwardly soon thereafter. As we walked out of the building, Johnny and Cliff were visibly shaken. Both had tears in their eyes as they apologized for how badly we had been treated in George's office. Donald and I tried unsuccessfully to console both of our benefactors but with little success.

Cliff, who had been the only one treated badly, promised to call Billy and have George straightened out. After that, we would be able to get the project back on track. Thanking Cliff and Johnny for their efforts, I promised to follow up with them a week later. With this, Donald and I left, headed back to warmer weather in Georgia.

I called a week later, and Johnny informed me George had killed the *Truthful Living* project. Taking a deep breath, Johnny added, "I'm sorry you had to fly all the way to Minneapolis and waste your time, Cole. I really am. George wouldn't budge, and Billy won't override him. *Truthful Living* is as dead as a doornail."

"That surprises me, Johnny," I replied. "I didn't realize George had that much power."

With a hint of irritation in his voice, Johnny agreed. "I guess George knows Billy better than we do." As our conversation came to a close, Johnny added, "Please tell Donald how sorry Cliff and I are that we wasted his time, too."

"Of course," I said graciously. "I'll do it just as soon as we get off the phone." Hanging up, I realized we had just missed the largest sale we would ever have.

As I thought about the entire situation, I couldn't believe Billy Graham didn't have the gumption to make a decision for his own ministry and stick to it. It made me think he was a weak leader and not nearly as strong as everyone considered him to be.

I remembered how people used to extol the virtues of the continuity of the BGEA leadership team, marveling at how long they remained intact without any major turnover in personnel. I knew the reason why. It was because they all lived in different parts of the country. If Cliff had worked in the same office building with George every day, their working relationship might have lasted a year—not decades.

I believed Billy's response to George indicated how feeble the evangelist's leadership was for quite a while, but I eventually changed my mind. Over time, I came to view what happened from a different perspective. What I had initially considered to be weakness I eventually viewed as strength.

Neither Billy, Johnny, nor Cliff had much business savvy. George did, and he was good at it. It was his responsibility to run the day-to-day operations of the ministry; and BGEA always paid its bills on time, which was a rarity for Christian ministries, including Living Water. George had his own ideas about how to develop the BGEA donor base and was close to implementing an entirely different strategy—one that couldn't utilize *Truthful Living.*

Because Billy had given George the responsibility of running the ministry's business operations, he simply allowed George to do his job without interference—just like President Reagan routinely allowed the members of his Cabinet to run their departments. Reagan provided overall direction but rarely interfered with day-to-day decisions, which proved to be an effective leadership model. Billy had simply done the same thing, allowing George to do his job without overriding him.

Billy wanted to use *Truthful Living*—no doubt about it, but he allowed his desires and his decision to be reversed. Such behavior was something most Christian leaders would never permit. To do so would be an affront to their stature and their authority, which—in their eyes—would amount to challenging God's will. They would have insisted on using *Truthful*

Living—even if doing so proved to be unwise. I witnessed such willful behavior repeatedly over the years and came to recognize it as part of the narcissistic ministry culture that was so prevalent in America.

George did what he thought was best for the ministry, which was at cross-purposes with the idea we proposed for BGEA to implement. That he was secure enough in his position, and in his ability to check Billy's desires, revealed quite a bit about both of them. It showed strength of character that I didn't recognize at first but came to understand. When I did, I admired George for sticking to his guns. I also had high regard for Billy, who allowed George to make the decision he believed was best for the ministry. Eventually, my respect for Dr. Graham increased because he didn't override George and allowed the project to die, rather than impose his will on the situation, even though it was not in Living Water's best interest.

The strength of leadership displayed by Billy was something few Christian leaders would even consider. Allowing a subordinate to question or countermand a directive is rare within Christian ministries. Most of the superstars lack the strength of character necessary to do so. Only a few have enough humility and maturity to permit themselves to be checked. Most prefer to behave like the Queen of Hearts, saying, "Off with their heads," dismissing those who challenge either their wisdom or their decisions. This happens routinely, regardless of how capricious or ill advised the decision might be.

For example, years after I left Living Water, Donald announced that God wanted the ministry to move their headquarters from Atlanta to Birmingham, which disrupted the lives of everybody working for the ministry. Refusing to listen to any dissenting voices, which were numerous, the move was made. Less than two years later, God purportedly told Donald the ministry needed to move back to Atlanta, which caused further disruption. Living Water actually returned to the same building it had vacated; but Donald never acknowledged how impulsive or erroneous he had been, choosing instead to call both moves an act of loyalty and obedience to God, which also meant that those who balked were being disobedient to God's will.

Donald capriciously disrupted the lives of everybody who worked for him, including their families. Rather than admit he had been wrong, he chose to redefine reality, assigning God's will to his position, which injured numerous people in the process. To this day, there are many who remain bitter because of Donald's capriciousness, which the ministry leader continues to justify as God's will.

* * *

The summer following our meeting in Minneapolis, to show their appreciation for all I had done, when Billy Graham held his Crusade in L.A., Johnny Lenning and Cliff Barrows invited me to attend. I sat on the platform, right next to the huge podium, where the religious leaders, movie stars, pro jocks, and choir sat—just a few feet away from Billy Graham.

Seeing the mass of humanity at the L.A. Coliseum was as exciting as it was surreal. I listened to every word Billy spoke to the spiritually hungry crowd. When he finished and asked people to come forward, I was disappointed and thought that few would respond. To me, his address was weak—rambling aimlessly from one point to another. It seemed like he had just thrown it together, spending very little time in preparation.

Finally, a few people came forward—followed by a few more. Then hundreds came—followed by an avalanche of penitents who made their way up front. In all, at least 7,000 people came forward that night.

Johnny turned to me and said, "I knew this would be a strong showing. Billy was really good tonight."

I was shocked but nodded my head in agreement—as I watched multitudes make their way forward.

As I watched the sea of humanity respond from my elevated position, I actually saw my ex-wife making her way forward with tears streaming down her face. I could not have been more surprised. At first, I couldn't believe it was really Barbara. During our marriage, she had never shown the least bit of interest in spiritual things—not once.

Seeing the sorrow on her face, I was deeply touched and started to cry myself, but I didn't want her to see me. I didn't even know she was in L.A. She didn't know I was there either. We hadn't spoken for several months, although someone told me she had recently experienced a nasty break up with her jealous, possessive boyfriend—one that necessitated a restraining order. Hearing this didn't surprise me, but I was relieved she was rid of him. He was nothing but trouble, and I knew it.

To remain unnoticed, I moved behind the choir, as they accompanied George Beverly Shea, who sang the chorus, "Just as I am," while thousands continued to come forward. Standing behind them made me less visible, while also putting me in the midst of the music, which I had come to love. Barbara came within twenty feet of me, but she never noticed me.

This was her time with God, and I knew it. It had nothing to do with me. I didn't want to interfere in any way, which would have been inappropriate. Nevertheless, I was deeply touched to witness the mother of my children putting her life in the hands of Almighty God—accepting Christ as her personal Savior. Who wouldn't be moved by something as tender as this?

As I drove away several hours later in my rental car, having stayed until nearly everybody left, I internalized a valuable lesson—one I've never forgotten. A Bible verse kept racing through my mind; "When I am lifted up, I will draw all men unto myself." That's what happened at the Coliseum. God did the drawing—not the persuasiveness or eloquence of the messenger. It's never the other way around.

Billy Graham lifted up the Lord, and the people came—thousands of them—including the only woman I had ever truly loved. His eloquence had nothing to do with people's responses. He told the audience God loved them and wanted a relationship with each one of them—nothing more. It was the only thing he did well, but it was the key to everything that followed. Once again, I started to cry, which was hazardous, since I was driving 70 mph. on Highway 101, but I couldn't help myself.

I also realized something else. In my bitterness about Catholicism, I had failed to provide the spiritual leadership my family needed to survive, leaving a terrible void in the process. Barbara used Jeffrey to fill that empty space. Acknowledging that I was more culpable in our divorce than I had ever been willing to admit, I continued to cry, purifying my soul as I drove. I knew that before getting involved with another woman, I needed to work on becoming a stronger spiritual leader. If I didn't, I would end up with another mess on my hands instead of what I truly desired.

As I reminisced about that evening in L.A. hundreds of times throughout the years, I came to realize something else. When ministries present nothing but the Gospel, wonderful things happen. When they "promote" Christ, nothing good comes from it. In fact, all hell breaks loose—literally. Lifting Christ up works—pushing Jesus doesn't. This may seem like it's just a subtle difference, but it isn't. It is an entirely different thing.

19

An Asset I Might Need on a Rainy Day

Being invited to sit on the stage at the Los Angeles Crusade, where Billy Graham's career began in 1949, was an empowering, transformational experience. I had never seen anything like it before in my entire life—not even close. I watched the power of the Holy Spirit extend to people from every walk of life, touching them precisely where they needed, at exactly the right time.

It was wonderful. With the added surprise of watching my ex-wife respond, coming forward with thousands of others, I knew this was an important moment. It was several years before I would learn precisely how important, but to say I was gratified would be an understatement.

The next time I spoke with Barbara, which was more than a month later, she called to ask if it would be okay to stay in Midge's suite above the garage for a long weekend. Brittany and Brianna loved it when their mom and little brother came, so I was happy to oblige. I wanted to tell her I had seen her at the crusade, but I didn't. To have broached the subject seemed out of place, despite my curiosity. More than anything,

I wanted to be careful to not violate my boundaries with her. What happened was for her to tell and not for me to ask. Because she didn't mention it, neither did I.

Coming from Catholicism, I knew she was at least as private about such matters as I had been several years earlier. When it comes to "sharing" a testimony, Catholics are as reticent as Baptists are eager. I knew this, of course, having felt similarly just a few years earlier. Because of my work with Christian ministries, I wasn't nearly as reserved about my spiritual experience as I used to be.

Being a participant in the Los Angeles Crusade is what most people thought my job consisted of routinely. Everybody believed I experienced one amazing Christian incident after the other, but that simply wasn't true. I did have some amazing times—make no mistake about it—but they were few and far between.

Instead, by working closely with dozens of ministries, I came to see their dark side—the ugly underbelly carefully concealed from the public. What I witnessed made my job difficult. Coming to terms with this never ceased to be a challenge. It was far more difficult than having responsibility for expanding Living Water's client base. If I had known what I was getting myself into when I took the job, which I didn't, I probably would still be teaching English literature, rather than writing a book about the clay feet of evangelical Christianity.

* * *

Working for Donald Duncan, who I considered to be one of the best Bible teachers in America, was always an adventure. There was no telling what crazy idea he would come up with next. Most of the people who worked at Living Water dreaded Donald's brainstorms, which they referred to as schemes. They understood that—whatever his idea happened to be—it would undoubtedly mean extra, thankless work for them. When it came to implementing one of his new initiatives, in the unrealistic timeframe Donald insisted upon, his motto was always "crash and burn."

This referred to others crashing and burning, never him. Because of my temperament and sense of adventure, I loved his innovativeness. Perhaps it may have been because I was still relatively new to the job. The wilder his schemes became, the better I liked them. Although I was never certain whether Donald was having a brilliant idea or a crazy one, his visionary leadership appealed to the crusader mentality in me, which was becoming one of the most dominant aspects of my personality.

During my time with Donald, I recognized he was one of the most enthusiastic, creative people I had ever known. Secretly, I loved his manic leadership style. Others chafed under it, resenting his constant disruption in their daily routine, but I enjoyed the challenge and the excitement. Although he may have been one plumb off center, I liked that about him. Most of the people working for Living Water clearly did not, but I certainly wasn't one of them.

One day, while attending a marketing meeting, Donald unexpectedly announced we were going to start selling advertising space in the magazines. He intended to produce an eight-page, full-color centerfold insert for each devotional, which meant eight ads would need to be sold numerous times a year. When he made this announcement, I was intrigued. Others whined, choosing to lament the downside of commercializing the devotionals, rather than look at the upside of how much income it could generate.

Regardless of the strong dissent expressed by my immediate supervisor, this was more than an idea for Donald; it was a directive. Looking straight at my boss, Donald informed him that it would be his responsibility to sell the ad space for all three of the devotionals, beginning immediately. This would equal more than a million insertions per ad for each sales cycle, which was a substantial amount of advertising for a Christian publication.

Casting a contemptuous look at Donald, my boss balked. Condescendingly, he replied, "I'm not going to do it. I'm the V.P. of Publications—not a space rep!"

Taken aback that he had been rebuffed so decisively—not expecting such open defiance—Donald sat brooding in stunned silence. Instantly, the meeting turned tense and ominous.

Without thinking about the potential ramifications, or weighing the pros and cons, being as impulsive as I was the day I threw the tennis ball of out the window in Sister Anna Catherine's Latin class, I blurted, "I'll do it."

Turning to me, without altering his expression, Donald replied, "Fine, Cole, you can do it."

Instantly, my supervisor's eyes darted at me menacingly. Unable to retrieve my words—like I was unable to retrieve the tennis ball—I had to stand behind my assertion. Unfortunately, I made an enemy out of my immediate supervisor, which was never my intention.

Having missed this non-verbal exchange between my boss and me, Donald continued. "You'll need to make a personal visit to each Christian publisher in America, and there are a lot of them. It will keep you busy; that's for sure."

"I understand," I replied confidently, but I really didn't. I just liked the idea of participating in a thrilling new adventure—that's all. In some ways, I was still a little boy playing The Cisco Kid.

"These publishers are all over the country," Donald continued. Looking at me squarely, he added, "You'll need to get on a plane and rack up a bunch of miles. It's essential to keep in contact with each of them regularly."

"Okay," I said, still eager for the challenge that awaited, but already wondering how I could possibly manage this and still be Mr. Mom to Brittany and Brianna.

"It will be a hard job, Cole," Donald added. "But you'll get to know everybody in the Christian publishing industry, which I think you'll enjoy quite a bit."

By the time he finished describing how difficult the challenge would be, which my supervisor obviously understood, I was nervous that I had bitten off more than I could chew.

Although I didn't realize it at the time, by accepting Donald's challenge, I had ensured my boss's future at Living Water would be coming to an abrupt end. By refusing to comply with Donald's directive, which I had jumped at, my supervisor was terminated a short time later.

I had no idea this would happen. Nevertheless, I've always felt responsible for his dismissal. I wondered if I had been a brownnoser that afternoon? I didn't think so, but what brownnoser ever does? That I still feel guilty about what happened probably answers my question.

Once my supervisor was fired, I was promoted, replacing him, which I didn't want or expect. He was an excellent administrator. By taking on his job as well as my own, with the added responsibility of selling ads, I had to work harder than I ever had in my life. It was quite a test. I loved the selling aspects of it, as well as the creative work, but I loathed being an administrator. It was time-intensive and boring. Even worse, it sapped my energy and my motivation.

Despite this, I worked hard, especially at selling, redoubling my efforts to ensure that the advertising initiative became successful. As I started calling on publishers throughout the nation, I repeatedly flew from coast to coast, as well as from North to South. Donald was right. I was on a plane constantly, racking up over 700,000 miles on my Delta Frequent Flyer account in the following three years. I wanted an adventure, which is exactly what I received—no doubt about it.

My largest advertising client was Ludlow Randolph. Calling on Dett, when I flew to Orlando, was one of my favorite trips. He was interested in our new initiative, understanding its potential value at once. He knew the ads would be seen repeatedly by thousands of prospective consumers, making what we had to offer a great advertising vehicle. As a result, he became my best customer. Having to visit Ludlow Randolph allowed me to travel to Orlando regularly. I even had the opportunity to play basketball once in a while with Mark Wade, which was a lot of fun.

On one of my trips to pitch Dett, he introduced me to the President of Ludlow Randolph—Benny Lessner. Benny liked me. In fact, he took an immediate personal interest in me. I liked Benny too. He always seemed to have time for me when I came, which made me feel important. Benny thought I would make a good addition to his company down the road, which was very flattering. I kept this tidbit of information in the back of my mind, knowing it might come in handy some day.

At the time, however, I was far too busy to give serious consideration to making a transition. I had ads to sell. It was a difficult job, but I loved it. Plus, I ended up generating substantial revenue for Living Water. Maintaining such a high profile throughout the Christian marketplace provided me with a measure of status I had never known—a degree of importance that was exhilarating. Finally, I was coming into my own professionally, although my compensation didn't come close to matching my effort.

* * *

There was another problem. Because the art department had the responsibility for producing the graphics, the ads created additional work for them. It was quite a bit of extra work actually, but this wasn't something Donald considered to be a problem. Why should it be? He didn't mind putting another burden on the staff—one without added compensation I might add. As you can imagine, this generated resistance and resentment. It was the type of thing Donald did routinely, creating acrimony and friction throughout the staff.

During one of our production meetings, several people from the art department complained that there wasn't anybody skilled at writing advertising copy. Because there wasn't, this created a production bottleneck. Once again, I said I would do it, which I did. Remembering that one of my college professors had said I possessed "excellent writing skills," I volunteered to do the job—much to the relief of everyone. Truthfully, it took me less time to write the ads than it did to listen to everybody complain about them not being written.

Therefore, beginning with the first ad I ever sold for Living Water, I wrote the ad copy as well, which everyone seemed to like, including the clients who purchased the space. I did so well that writing copy became a part of my job at Living Water and has continued to be a part of the work I have done ever since. One time, I did the math and figured out that I had written copy for over 1 billion pages of advertising in my career, which is something I never considered to be part of my skill set.

Like always, I simply did it because the work needed to be done. My problem was just like Ado Annie's in *Oklahoma!* She complained, "I'm just a girl who cain't say no." In some ways, I felt the same way. Overburdened, I needed to balk, but I never did.

20

With Little Light and Less Saltiness

After maintaining this frantic pace for several years, being quite successful, I finally ran out of steam, crashing and burning in the process—just like everybody else who ever worked for Donald Duncan. Being employed by a ministry, where the wages were substantially lower than in the private sector, I was also sinking financially, going deeper into the hole. The cost of raising two girls was substantial, and I wasn't able to make ends meet, despite making my division at Living Water quite profitable. I still loved travelling, but doing so meant I had to be away from home frequently, which conflicted with my parental responsibilities. Being under substantial stress, I realized something had to give.

At Living Water, my conflicts were more than financial. Functioning within a culture that continued to cater to Duncan's extravagant tendencies began taking a toll on me emotionally. I was burned out.

Our executive VP was another problem. Nothing passed Owen Yeager's discerning eye—nothing. For example, being treated for cervical cancer, a secretary named Prudence Latham missed work quite often.

Becoming suspicious—for whatever reason—Owen pieced together that two other women were also repeatedly absent at the same time—one after the other, but never all three together. This piqued Owens's curiosity, so he began a clandestine investigation to discover what was really happening.

In chapel, I remembered that we prayed for Prudence's full recovery every week for a year, never considering there might be anything fishy about her illness. Who would?

Despite the universal concern for her wellbeing, Owen discovered Prudence never had cancer. It was all a ruse. She concocted the entire story to obtain sympathy and attention from her friends, family, and co-workers. It also allowed her the opportunity to be absent from work without missing any pay.

How Owen figured things out I'll never know, but he did. He also discovered much more. Prudence's two dearest girlfriends—both of whom worked at the ministry—gave her all the sympathy she needed. Apparently, they provided her with more than friendly compassion. Like a queen bee, Prudence buzzed from one woman to the next, bestowing nectar on each, driving each crazy with jealousy toward the other.

Owen, moral purist that he was—with investigatory skills worthy of the FBI—uncovered the whole sordid affair and planned to fire the lot for unexcused absence and immorality on company time. The entire incident was hush-hush, which meant it was all anybody talked about. Such a scandal was far too juicy to be kept quiet. Everybody whispered about it to anyone who would listen, and everyone did.

Finally, someone went to Donald. He intervened, sparing the job of each, which seemed magnanimous and compassionate. By the end of that day, shortly after everything had been simmered down, I walked into Donald's office and shut the door behind me. I sat down with an expectant expression on my face and waited for him to speak.

Knowing why I was there, he informed me that he had talked at length to each woman about her "sinful behavior." After that, he counseled each individually for over an hour. By the end of the counseling session, each promised to stop her immoral behavior and never repeat it. With this, Donald smiled at what he had been able to accomplish in just one afternoon.

In his mind, he was certain the lesbian problem was a thing of the past, and all three women would seek suitable men to marry.

I was dumfounded. To clarify that I had heard him correctly, I asked; "So, you think they'll be straight from now on?"

"Absolutely," he replied with confidence. "Each has repented of her lesbianism. I read them Romans 1:26, which says it's a sin."

"Donald, do you really believe they will change their sexual orientation?" I asked once again.

"Of course. I've counseled with each of them and shown them their error."

I just nodded my head. There was nothing left for me to say.

As I left his office, I thought, *Donald believes these women have changed their sexual orientation because "he" has counseled them.* That was the key—his counseling. His self-importance was so elevated he really believed what he had said.

I was delighted none of the women lost their jobs because each was very competent, but I never believed they changed their orientation—not for one minute. They simply became more circumspect about their behavior, especially at work, which was appropriate.

I had never seen Donald's Aristotelian flaw as clearly as I did that day. Others frequently mentioned his Messiah complex, but I never witnessed it more vividly than with this incident. There was a narcissistic streak in him, but Donald's self-absorption wasn't about trivial things like prestige, notoriety, private jets, clothes, or jewelry. His was more subtle; but it was there, nonetheless, a deep-seated pride about having a "superior" relationship with God. It made him—and what he had to say—more important than others. He was a victim of his own giftedness, which left him isolated, with virtually no peers, at least in his own mind.

People from the outside can't imagine how difficult it was working in an environment like this, but it was. I had to deal with numerous Christian leaders who ruled their ministries like a medieval lord would rule his fiefdom. Most could give a stirring message about being a servant of God, but that's all it was—a message. What they proclaimed wasn't real—not in their personal lives anyway. They could talk the talk quite well, but that's all it was—talk. Generally speaking, walking the walk was a rarity for the aristocracy of evangelicalism.

Instead of being servants, what I witnessed was men and women who arrogated God's authority to themselves, while pursuing a lifestyle generally reserved for titled nobility. Instead of being genuine and humble, they took a detour from the simplicity and purity of God's calling, choosing instead to produce empires and monuments to their own grandeur. At the same time, each would maintain, "All the glory belongs to the Lord," fooling multitudes with their disingenuousness.

It isn't that they were lying—not really—at least not consciously. Drunk with the success of their accomplishments, they actually believed their personal goals equated to Almighty God's purpose, producing a Christianized version of narcissism that was often self-deprecating. They talked about God's will, but they were so consumed with their own grandeur, it was as if they were saying, "Give your money to God, but be certain to use my address."

Aiding them were their knights, the lesser nobility—many of whom routinely took advantage of their enhanced positions of personal power for sordid gain. The lesser nobility behaved arrogantly while always maintaining a façade of Christian piety—just like Dett did at Ludlow Randolph. Although neither the lords nor their knights would ever smoke, drink, or cuss, none had a problem reaming a subordinate a new one. Crushing the spirit of someone who served them was routine behavior for Christian leaders and their lesser nobility. I witnessed it repeatedly, and each time I remained silent about it, it whittled away a piece of my soul.

Preaching powerful sermons on humility and service, in their day-to-day lives, the superstars of Christianity bore little resemblance to the message they proclaimed. In our society, where moral leadership in the political arena and on Wall Street is woefully lacking, Christian leaders often eclipse their secular counterparts, leading the way in hypocrisy. Practicing greed, they manipulate funds from their followers, while castigating political and business leaders for lifestyles and values that differ little from their own.

When the lives of Christian leaders fail to exemplify the values they promote, is it any wonder political and business leaders follow suit? From this perspective, the "trickle down" theory in ethics and morality is fully operational—but in the wrong direction. With little "light" and less "saltiness," the message of the evangelical lords and ladies often rings hollow.

Knowing this, I had finally had enough of the hypocrisy. So, I left Living Water to work for a Christian financial planning outfit—one where I would make substantially more money.

The name of the business was Covenant Financial Planning—a start-up company led by Travis Keisler. The opportunity Travis presented seemed like the adventure of a lifetime and too good to be true, which is exactly what it was.

21

A Bite of the Forbidden Fruit

When I met Travis, who was the son of a Southern Baptist minister, I liked his business model immediately. It was very enterprising. Plus, everything he did seemed to be well funded.

His goal was to generate sufficient secular clients to help impoverished pastors, permitting Covenant to establish an altruistic ministry outreach. His benevolence appealed to me from day one. Explaining that after a lifetime of service in the ministry—only to retire penniless—most pastors, especially of small churches, were destined to live the rest of their lives in virtual poverty. Bothered by this injustice, he intended for Covenant to do something about it.

Because I was weary of the conspicuous consumption of capital displayed by the lords and ladies of electric Christianity, Travis's altruism resonated with me immediately. I liked the idea of helping destitute pastors—noble men who had done praiseworthy work for decades. Embracing Travis's vision as my own, I also liked him personally. He seemed genuine and unassuming.

Travis was particularly interested in my extensive network within the evangelical community, especially since he planned to expand his small company, taking it nationwide quickly. Because of the value of my contacts, he let me know those who joined him at the beginning would be destined to become extremely wealthy. Each time he mentioned this, my heart leapt, as I entertained the possibility of being among the select few.

When he said, "You're a marketing genius, Cole. We need you at Covenant. If you join our team, you'll help your friends become financially secure; and you'll never have to worry about money again."

"Really?" I responded, as my heart leapt. I couldn't remember a day when I didn't worry about how to pay for things, so I was primed to take a bite of the forbidden fruit, which he held out, tantalizingly.

"Absolutely," he reaffirmed with a knowing gaze.

"You're sure about this, Travis?" I asked once again.

With a warm, credible, and heartfelt smile, he said, "I guarantee it."

"Then, I'm your man," I responded with confidence—ready to become the affluent Christian businessman I was certain God intended me to be. If being easily fooled is the trademark of a naïve Christian, then I must have been nearing sainthood.

"You'll never regret it," he promised with a chuckle.

With that, the deal was sealed. I had finally arrived. I believed every word that came out of Travis's silky, serpentine mouth. I bought the lie completely—eagerly, greedily. In my mind, I was already planning ways to spend the money. I wanted it to be true and never considered the alternative. Just past forty, having never made enough money to support my family adequately, this was an answer to my repeated prayer. It had to be.

I became the Vice President of Marketing for Covenant Financial Planning, making $50,000 a year—plus bonuses, which was quite a bit of money at the time. I received a new Cadillac Sedan DeVille as a company car. I was also made a member of the board of directors, which appealed to my ego. Becoming more self-important by the day, I had finally arrived, marketing genius that I was.

As I thought about what the future would hold, I smiled, believing it would be very bright. Embracing my newfound status among the rich and affluent, I was so tickled I walked with a swagger like a gunslinger itching for a fight. The Cisco Kid was back in the saddle again.

* * *

Because Covenant was best known among Southern Baptists, Travis and I flew to Dallas in our corporate plane—piloted by him—to attend the Southern Baptist Convention. Travis, knowing many of the leaders, was a welcomed confidant in the inner circle of the denomination's conservative wing.

It was hot in Texas, and the contentiousness between the conservatives and moderates made it seem even hotter. This was the year that would determine the direction of the denomination for decades, and each side supported its candidate for president vigorously. If the conservatives won, they would have a majority on the board of directors for the first time, enabling them to gain control of everything. A victory would also mean the inerrancy of the Scriptures would be established, leaving the moderates with no safe place of refuge within the fastest-growing denomination in America.

The conservatives nominated Charles Stanley, the popular pastor of First Baptist Church of Atlanta and the superstar of a major television program, *In Touch*. The moderates nominated Bill Self, who was also a popular pastor from Atlanta. Because the stakes were so high, this was the largest convention ever held—with the outcome of the vote uncertain. Because nobody could accurately predict the victor, each side had its messengers prepared for the impending battle—like a crucial vote before Congress.

I was in the thick of things within days of having assumed my new position at Covenant, which was very exciting. The stage was set, and everybody knew it. The future of the Southern Baptist Convention was the prize—along with ownership of numerous seminaries, universities, and billions of dollars in property. The stakes couldn't have been higher—with the networks covering the convention like it was the deciding primary of a presidential election.

Although this convention was purported to be a spiritual conclave, it certainly wasn't. It was as political as it could possibly be. There was significant animosity, but none of it was straightforward or openly confrontational. Pastors don't display their emotions like others. Instead, they choose to cover their anger with smiles as disingenuous as those of Cinderella's stepsisters. At the Southern Baptist Convention, passive aggressiveness was an art form.

Being a part of the inner circle, Travis had been invited to the conservative strategy session, and I accompanied him. As both of us sat in this top-secret meeting—the conservative's inner sanctum—we listened intently. I learned that Billy Graham had just sent Charles Stanley a telegram. It said the evangelist would vote for Dr. Stanley, if he had not been conducting a Crusade in Eastern Europe. The telegram's purpose was meant to be an encouragement to Dr. Stanley—nothing more.

Judge Paul Pressler, the conservative strategist and power broker, had the telegram in his hand, holding it up victoriously. He said, "When we nominate Charles the day after tomorrow, we're going to hold this up and read it out loud."

"That's great," several replied in unison. Others grinned, muttering their approbation.

Continuing, Pressler said, "There are still quite a few messengers who remain uncommitted. This may help swing them to our side and secure their vote for Charles."

Everyone sitting around the table agreed—everybody except for me. Although not a part of the inner circle and the youngest person in the room by a decade, I raised my hand cautiously—like I would have in Sister Anna Catherine's Latin class.

"Yes," responded Pressler, looking at me curiously.

Repressing my nervousness, I said, "Judge Pressler, I like your idea; but I think I can improve on it, if you're interested."

By the look on the faces of the others in the room, I thought I might have overstepped my bounds; but Judge Pressler motioned for me to speak, which I did.

"If I were you, I would leak the telegram to the press in the morning." By making this suggestion, I gained the immediate attention of everyone. "If you do," I continued, "it will undoubtedly become a major news story. Billy Graham has never taken sides between the conservatives and moderates until now."

"But that will give the moderates a chance to counter the effects of the telegram, won't it?" the judge asked, but I could see I had stirred his thinking.

"Yes, Judge, it will," I replied. "But the power of Graham's endorsement will also have time to build over the next two days, rather than just a few minutes between the nomination and the vote. Everybody will be talking about it. By leaking it, you will maximize its impact, and the moderates will be on the defensive until the vote is taken."

When I finished, Judge Pressler didn't respond. Instead, he looked at another person at the head of the table. The man nodded his head just once. This was all that was needed. Pressler immediately changed the topic and never returned to it.

Early the following morning, the telegram was leaked to the media. It became a major news item, receiving more coverage than any of us had anticipated. Recognizing they had just received a mortal wound, several moderates tried desperately to contact Dr. Graham to implore him to recant his endorsement; but he couldn't be reached while preaching behind the Iron Curtain.

By the time the vote was taken, Charles Stanley won handily. With his election, the balance of power shifted irreversibly to the conservatives, who have become firmly entrenched ever since. Dr. Stanley probably would have won anyway; but like a Forrest Gump character, I played a "nameless, faceless role" in the process—a role Charles Stanley never knew about and probably never will.

22

Two FBI Agents Knocked on My Front Door

Upon returning victoriously from the Southern Baptist Convention, which was the high point in my career at Covenant Financial Planning, I began putting together an extensive marketing plan, which I was convinced would develop a substantial client base. My concept and marketing strategy was sound.

The problem was with the leader of our company—Travis Keisler. I believed we were creating a legitimate business; but we were not—a realization I became aware of one evening about two months after my employment. This was when two FBI agents knocked on my front door at 9:30 p.m. for "a little chat." Stunned to see them, I became enlightened as I listened to them explain what was "really happening" at Covenant. Apparently, the agents believed my surprise was genuine, which it was.

As I became aware of Keisler's fraudulent behavior, my surprise turned to indignation. Promising full cooperation, I agreed to be "interviewed" several days later at the FBI's office in the Richard B. Russell Federal Building in downtown Atlanta. Needless to say, I didn't sleep much, knowing my world had just been turned upside down.

When I arrived two days later at the appointed time, I was ready for the interview. I never considered retaining a lawyer. I didn't need one; I was sure of it. I hadn't done anything wrong. Plus, retaining counsel might make it appear as if I did have something to hide. At the time, I believed the bureau was like one of my favorite old-time TV programs, *The F.B.I.*, starring Efrem Zimbalist, Jr.

As I reflected about my decision several decades later, my mindset seemed pretty naïve—even for me. Nevertheless, I planned to be completely transparent and forthright—regardless of the consequences. It just seemed like the right thing to do, so that's what I did.

When I sat down for the interview, which was more like an interrogation, the severity of the situation became crystal clear. Although I was one of the investors defrauded by Travis, this is not what bothered me the most. My financial loss was miniscule when compared to what others lost.

What galled me was Travis had used me to vouch for him with everybody in the Christian community. He used the confidence my friends and colleagues had in me to cheat them, and I gave him the "Good Housekeeping Seal of Approval" wherever we went. This was my value to the company—not being a "marketing genius." When I realized how badly I had been deceived, I felt like a complete fool—an assessment I richly deserved. For months afterward, I castigated myself for being so blind, finally admitting that my avarice—my lust of the eye and the boastful pride of life—had been my undoing.

During my interview, I explained that Travis had lured me away from Living Water by offering me a salary of $50,000 a year, a lucrative performance bonus, and a new Cadillac—with leather seats. At the time, I was making $28,500 and drove a faded blue 1980 Pinto station wagon, which my girls referred to as "The Crapinator."

When the FBI investigation finally concluded—exonerating me

completely—I was relieved this unsettling episode was finally behind me. The entire process lasted three months—each day being a living hell. Although I hadn't participated in anything illegal and had been kept in the dark about what was really happening, it was intimidating to be part of a criminal investigation—no question about it.

Candidly, it was more than nerve-racking; I was scared to death, especially during the interview. This was serious business. I couldn't even muster a smile. It was hard to keep from being incontinent. My legs shook constantly, and I wanted to vomit, even though I had done nothing wrong and had nothing to hide.

Everything Travis said to potential investors was a lie, and he needed me to authenticate his deception as the truth. My presence validated his deceitfulness. I introduced him as a man whose "passion in life" was to provide Christ-centered financial planning for pastors and ministry workers—a man who was gifted at multiplying money invested in his company.

It was all a lie, and I helped him spread it—like a prostitute spreading a sexually transmitted disease. Travis brought the illusion of wealth—just like a whore brings the illusion of love. I was his pimp—an unknowing pimp but a pimp nonetheless. Just thinking about my complicity in his fraudulent scheme made me sick—some "marketing genius" I was.

My good friend, Johnny Lenning, from the Billy Graham Evangelistic Association, invested his life savings with Covenant—only to lose everything. Johnny never would have made this financial commitment without my endorsement, which I gave without hesitation. Johnny, like all of the others, including me, never saw a dime of our investment again. I ran into Johnny often after his loss, which he could ill afford; but he never blamed me for a thing, which made me feel worse than if he had been angry.

Travis used Johnny's life savings to support his lavish lifestyle—a lifestyle that included a corporate plane, which Travis used as his personal toy. Nothing was invested in blue-chip companies as Travis had promised. Like a ravenous glutton, he consumed everything.

One man who had invested nearly $100,000 with Covenant became suspicious and started asking hard questions, which Travis couldn't answer satisfactorily. When Travis hedged about returning the man's money, the investor went to the FBI.

Once the bureau became involved, Travis's scam unraveled quickly. I went from making $50,000 a year to making nothing overnight—literally. Nevertheless, during my interview with the agents, I answered every question they asked—as did the vice president of sales, another dupe like me. When everybody in the small company had been interviewed, the FBI planned to indict several people but not the vice president of sales or me. Fortunately, being fools worked in our favor—not against us.

The Bureau arrested Travis, taking him out of his house in handcuffs in front of his horrified wife and children. That got his attention. To his credit—and unlike most cons—Travis came clean, admitting his wrongdoing. He took complete responsibility for the fraud, telling the FBI none of the rest of us actually knew what was happening.

Within a short period, he accepted a plea bargain and was quickly sent to prison, where he served three years. The whole nauseating episode ended as quickly as it began—much to my relief.

About five years later, I saw Travis at a men's breakfast meeting, where he was busy putting together a "foolproof" investment for young Christian businessmen. His captivated audience included many family men, who were eager to make their mark in the world—in other words, gullible fools like I had been. I could see it in their lustful, materialistic eyes. It was a look that resembled mine just a few years earlier. In their minds, they were already calculating their profit—just like I had done.

Taking the leader of the group aside, I informed him of my experience with Travis's "foolproof" schemes. The leader told me Travis had been "up front" about his past. The man said Travis had repented and was eager to make up for his previous misdeeds.

When I heard this, I thought, *Travis is conning these people by telling them he is a "redeemed" con.* Shaking my head in disbelief, I thought, *Christians will believe anything—just as long as Jesus' name is mentioned as part of the deal.*

Nevertheless, my persistent warning, which was a prediction of financial disaster, must have resonated with the group's leader. Shortly afterwards, he insisted Travis submit to an in-depth personality assessment, which Travis took. It revealed that Travis was a man who was incapable of feeling empathy for those he cheated. With this realization, the men's group dropped Travis like a hot potato, but this didn't bother my former boss. Travis just moved on to the next group of naïve Christians, giving them his same "redeemed con" testimonial.

* * *

Being jobless, as well as having been a fool, I felt deflated. I had to relinquish the new Cadillac Sedan DeVille and return to driving the Crapinator. This didn't bother me. In fact, I was grateful to have everything about this distasteful episode in the rearview mirror.

Sitting in the living room late one evening, feeling a little lost and disconnected, wondering what I would do next, the phone rang. It was Barbara, and she was in tears. Alarmed, I put my troubles aside and asked what was wrong with her?

"It's Jeffrey," she said. "He's dead."

"What?" I replied—completely taken aback—knowing how young, energetic, and fit her ex-husband was.

"He's dead, Cole. He's dead!"

"But he was in such good health. What happened?" I asked.

After a long moment, she answered. "Someone garroted him. He was murdered!" When she divulged this, she fell apart, crying her eyes out.

I sat quietly for quite a while, trying to assimilate this shocking news, while she continued to be emotional. There was part of me that resented how deeply she had loved Jeffrey, even though their marriage had been over for quite a while. I suppose it was residual jealousy that I wouldn't admit was real. Despite this, I was grateful she sought me out for comfort. I could tell how badly she was hurting, so I made a commitment—right then and there—to do whatever was necessary to support her. After all, she was the mother of my children, and I was her oldest and most-trusted friend.

When she finally gathered herself, calming down quite a bit, she acknowledged her marriage to Jeffrey had been problematic from the day they had their son. To avoid parental responsibility, he had begun seeing someone else, which didn't surprise me. Apparently, his new lover was married, and her husband wasn't as civilized about his wife's infidelity as I had been, choosing the Mafia's method of strangulation to end Jeffrey's life. Garroting was a horrible way for Barbara's ex-husband to die.

While going through our divorce, I entertained numerous vengeful thoughts, including murder, but I never would have acted out on any of them. Obviously, this spurned husband did, or he hired someone else murder Jeffrey for him. So far, according to Barbara, nobody had been arrested for the crime.

That evening, I must have talked to Barbara for at least an hour. She told me Jeffrey had been living in Reno, but she hadn't spoken to him for quite some time. He never saw his son, Chance, nor did he ask about the preschooler, which I couldn't imagine. Such self-absorption was beyond my comprehension. It was heartbreaking for the little boy.

It also made me sad for my ex-wife, knowing how alone she must feel, living in Las Vegas. If I considered myself to be a fool for getting involved with Travis Keisler, I wondered how hoodwinked Barbara must have felt for marrying a man with so little character?

While we talked, I wanted to ask her about her relationship with the Lord, but I didn't. Since she still had not brought up the subject—not once in two years—neither had I. Choosing wisdom over curiosity, I continued to remain silent.

For quite a while after our initial conversation, Barbara called frequently, which I encouraged her to do. She needed to vent and to grieve, which I understood. Being reciprocal, I told her everything about my imprudent escapade with Covenant, and she listened, offering me comfort, support, and solace.

It seemed like we were developing a true friendship—not a superficial one, which both of us obviously needed. In her time of despair, I was there for her. I thought this might be difficult, but it wasn't. I was happy to be available. Besides, being out of work, I had plenty of time on my hands.

23

Driving Evangelicals to Their Knees

Knowing I needed to find work quickly, I put in a call to Dett at Ludlow Randolph, hoping to cash in on my "rainy day" chip. Immediately interested, he said he was having a meeting that afternoon with Benny and would inquire about what was available. I was very grateful for Dett's friendship and for his willingness to help. Having a guy like him in my corner was very reassuring.

As our conversation was winding down, Dett said, "Don't take another position, Cole. I feel certain we can find a place for you. Just give me a few days to work things out. Can you do that?"

"Of course," I answered. "I don't want to be pushy, but things are really tight. I don't have any savings. What little I had, I lost with Travis, so I need to find something fast."

"I understand completely. I'll get right on it," Dett assured me, putting my mind at ease.

After disconnecting, being certain things would work out at Ludlow Randolph, I didn't make any additional phone calls. What would be the purpose? Instead, I went to the YMCA and played basketball, which I had not done for quite a while. It felt wonderful to have some time to get away from all of my troubles and just play ball, like I was still a kid.

But the following morning, I could barely walk. My legs felt like rubber bands. When I got out of bed, I actually wobbled, which was a pretty good indication of just how out of shape I was. Despite this, I took 800 mgs of ibuprofen and went back to the Y later that same day. It was great. Basketball cleared my mind like nothing else, but being older, there was a physical price to pay for such strenuous exercise—a painful one.

I didn't hear from Dett for the rest of the week, which both surprised and concerned me, so I called him again the following Monday morning. Once again, he assured me he had nearly everything worked out and asked me to sit tight. I was beginning to get a little nervous, but I took him at his word, spending my time at the Y playing basketball rather than searching for a new job.

The following two weeks, Dett gave me the same story. Each time, he informed me that he was making progress, but he never actually made me a job offer. He just hinted about what was being discussed. Wanting to believe him, I clung onto the hope that he was putting things together.

Since it had been a month since my last paycheck, my mom was forced to help us out, which she really couldn't afford to do. Besides, I was unwilling to accept money from my mother for very long. I didn't like the way it made me feel. Being jobless—just hanging out at the YMCA— was also beginning to affect my self-worth adversely.

Finally, putting a position at Ludlow Randolph on the backburner, I started making calls to everyone I knew, which is what I should have done a month earlier. Once I did, things started rolling quickly. One publisher offered me a sales job immediately, but it necessitated a move to Kansas City, which I really didn't want to make. Neither Brittany nor Brianna would want to move so far away from home either. Knowing this, I didn't even mention it to them, but I did keep it as my back-up plan.

Finally, a friend who owned a creative agency, specializing in serving the Christian marketplace, made an intriguing suggestion. Joel Dawson, of Equipity Creative Concepts, asked, "Cole, you are the person who has developed all of the publishing relationships for Living Water, aren't you?"

"Yes," I said, adding, "I know just about everybody in the industry."

"Do you have a 'non-compete' with Living Water?" he inquired.

"No. We never even discussed the subject," I assured him.

"Then, why not use your contacts to create something for yourself? Have you ever considered doing that?" Joel asked.

"No, I haven't," I admitted, but I was beginning to entertain the idea, which was intriguing.

"If you can get the publishers and some of the ministries to go along with the idea, you could create a Christmas catalog featuring their products. I think it might work. What do you think?"

"I think you're right," I agreed, as the wheels in my mind began to churn.

"You could get ministries to customize their own version—just like you've done with the Living Water devotionals. If you did this, you would be creating your own business. What do you think?"

"I think it's a great idea, but there's one problem. I don't have the funds to stay afloat until something like this starts paying off." Sarcastically, I added, "I would have to sell one of my daughters—just to make ends meet."

Confidently, he replied, "That's where I can help. I'll underwrite the project, and we'll split the profits. What do you think?"

I thought it was a brilliant idea and told him so. Meeting with him later that day, we worked out the details. Starting the following morning, I began making calls to promote my new *Equipity Christmas Catalog*.

Dett never did get back with me, as he promised he would, which I never understood. It still seems bizarre. I suppose I should have learned from this, but obviously I didn't.

* * *

As I was beginning my new venture, in my relentless effort to put numerous deals together quickly, I was on the phone constantly. Expecting several return calls from my West Coast prospects, I wasn't surprised when the phone rang at 10 p.m., but it wasn't a potential customer returning my call. It was Barbara, and she needed to talk to me about Jeffrey.

By now, his murder was more than a month old, but there still hadn't been an arrest in the case. Like Barbara, I assumed the crime was one of passion and the jealous husband would be charged, but that didn't happen.

Barbara was very concerned about the situation and didn't believe there would be an arrest. Apparently, Jeffrey's paramour was married to someone in organized crime, which meant the police were unlikely to pursue the culprit vigorously. Obtaining a conviction would be even less likely, so Jeffrey's murderer would probably remain unsolved.

As you can imagine, this bothered my ex-wife, who wanted to emote about how unjust this was. I listened—like always.

This turn of events was very unsettling for her. It bothered me as well. Like Barbara, I realized Jeffrey had been involved in a clandestine sexual escapade, but he may have participated in things far more sinister too. Voicing my misgivings, I told her she needed to be extra careful. There was more here than met the eye; I was sure of it. Agreeing with me, she promised to be extra cautious.

When she hung up, I said a prayer for her and for Chance, asking

God to protect both of them. Despite doing this, I couldn't shake how apprehensive I was.

* * *

The goal for my new job was to produce an *Equipity Christmas Catalog*, but it was already September, which in the printing world is already Christmas. That's because there is so much lead-time necessary to get everything done. For most people, undertaking a project of this magnitude, with so little lead time, would have been impossible.

Because I didn't have the option of thinking this way, I knew I had to make it happen. So, that's exactly what I did. I made it happen.

I began by calling several of my friends on the West Coast who loved the idea and committed to participate, if I was able to put it all together, which I assured them I would. To make my catalog financially viable, I needed to print at least 500,000 copies. Talking to friends around the country, I received commitments for 125,000 catalogs within two days. It was a good start, but that's all it was—a start.

To help me, Joel gave me the name of one of his friends—a pastor at a large Baptist Church in Charlotte. Suggesting I drive up and call on him, I said that I would. It was a solid lead, and I needed all the potential clients I could get.

Leaving early the following morning, I sold Joel's friend 25,000 catalogs before lunch. Since it was so early in the day, with time to spare before heading back to Atlanta, I drove over to PTL to see if Jim and Tammy Faye Bakker's ministry might be interested. It was a cold call, which no salesperson likes to make, but I needed a big client to make my project financially viable.

I had never been to PTL, which was beautifully laid out with state-of-the-art television equipment and a hotel. The grounds even had a mini-shopping mall. It was truly an impressive facility—full of lively, energetic, and purposeful people.

I really didn't expect to get anywhere with my pitch; but much to my surprise, their marketing people loved the idea and committed to purchase 250,000 catalogs right on the spot. I was flabbergasted but thrilled nonetheless.

This is what I have always liked about charismatic ministries. They can make an immediate, impulsive decision and stick to it. I felt very confident driving home in the Crapinator—my Pinto station wagon—knowing I had come close to making the impossible happen in less than four days.

With commitments for 400,000 catalogs, selling the rest was easy. I ended up printing 625,000 catalogs, which made my new venture profitable from day one.

I still had to finalize my deals with the publishers, but this was even easier. When I called Dett and pitched him, Ludlow Randolph bought half of the available ads. By making such a substantial commitment, other publishers followed suit. In my numerous conversations with Dett about the catalog, he never brought up the subject of me working for Ludlow Randolph, which continued to bewilder me.

Once I had everything sold, I had to write ad copy for each of the products, which required an entire weekend. Once the copy was finalized, Joel's team did the photography, created the layouts, typeset everything, and pasted up the boards. After getting approval from the clients, we ran film, and printed the catalogs, putting them in the mail on October 21st—just six days later than the date we targeted. Within days, the orders started flying in, and we began fulfilling them, making the project an immediate success. We were pleased; so were the ministries and publishers who participated.

This was a great time in America. It was easy to be successful. After nearly two terms of Ronald Reagan, the country was experiencing a surge of prosperity and patriotism that many thought was impossible, but it was happening.

For Christian ministries, it was a great time as well. Prosperity reigned. People donated generously. Plus, they bought Christian products in abundance, ensuring my new endeavor would be a long-term success.

As I thought about what the following year would bring, I smiled in spite of everything—blissfully unaware that I had jumped from "the frying pan into the fire." I was about to become part of a shocking scandal—a scandal that would rock the world of electric Christianity, driving evangelicals nationwide to their knees.

24

Pray for Fluffy

The first week of January, representing Equipity Creative, I drove the Crapinator to PTL and presented the idea for a spring catalog to Jim Bakker's marketing team. I even had a comp created to show what the front cover would look like. Knowing how visual they were, I suspected my proposed cover might intrigue them, which it did. They loved the idea.

Because the Christmas catalog generated nearly $500,000 in revenues and only cost $100,000, including product fulfillment, they were ready to listen to whatever I had to say. Best of all, from their perspective, there was no extra work required by them. It was all done from our end. This meant my stock was sky-high with the PTL marketing team—especially with my main contact, Paul Chambers. They committed to buy another 250,000 catalogs to be mailed to their top donors. I also presented our new devotional magazine, which PTL showed interest in customizing.

Back at Living Water, when a new salesperson paid a visit to PTL, my friends at the ministry told the representative they were busy and I was taking care of them anyway. Showing the woman the catalog I had produced, the Living Water representative brought a copy back to the office. When Owen Yeager, the ministry's Executive V.P., was informed I was in direct competition with them, he had a conniption fit. After calming down, he called me immediately.

"Cole, this is Owen," he said. "How are you?"

"Fine, Owen, and you?" I replied warily.

Casting pleasantries aside, he added, "I've been better." Without pausing, he got right to business. "I've just learned you sold a spring catalog to PTL, which should be *our* client, not yours. It's our intent to sell them a devotional and to do their catalog work as well."

Unwilling to accept the validity of his assertion as accurate, I countered. "Why don't you ask them who their marketing consultant is? They'll tell you it's me—not you or anybody else from Living Water. Feel free to make the call. I'm perfectly happy for you to speak with *my* client."

"That won't be necessary. This is between you and me," he said, trying to intimidate me, which he had done successfully dozens of times in the past. "It's unethical for you to have contacted them, and you know it."

"Why is it unethical, Owen?" I retorted. "I don't have a non-compete with Living Water, do I?"

"No, not in so many words. Not legally, you don't." After a short pause, he added,

"But it's still unethical." "Why? Just because you say it is?"

If he had been honest, this is exactly what he would have admitted—but he wouldn't. With nothing further to discuss, the phone call ended abruptly a few moments later.

He wasn't just a little miffed that I had created a competing catalog, taking away advertising business from Living Water, he was also furious that I had begun to siphon off devotional business as well. Within a few months of my departure, I closed six accounts for our new devotional, which Living Water thought should have been their clients.

When my conversation with Owen concluded, I was shaking. I had held my ground with my former boss, who loved to be a bully; but I never enjoyed confrontations like this one. Realizing the altercation had permanently burned my bridges with Living Water, I redoubled my efforts to make Equipity Creative successful—especially at PTL.

When I left Living Water, Owen thought I would be a good little boy and disappear like all of the others he had been responsible for forcing to resign; but that's not what happened. Instead, I became more successful than ever. Living Water was never able to compete with me, especially with the catalogs. Eventually, they abandoned their efforts, leaving it all for me.

Despite this encounter, I wasn't interested in being combative with my former employer. I was far too busy to be petty. Making certain the *PTL Spring Collection* was a success became an all-consuming task. Making Christmas profitable was one thing, but replicating profitability with a spring catalog was quite another.

I was at PTL so often Jim Bakker actually thought I worked there. At a marketing meeting one day, he asked where I was, which surprised me because he never even bothered to learn my name. He never spoke to me—not once. I don't suppose I was important enough.

His inquiry was also interesting because I never thought I would end up doing business with him. I remembered the first day I saw Bakker at the National Religious Broadcasters Convention years earlier, sauntering through the hall with an entourage of sycophants, trailing in his wake. Now I knew many of his employees quite well. They didn't seem like sycophants at all. Nearly all of them were wonderful, selfless people who wanted to use their talents to serve the Lord. I liked them, and they liked me.

Continuing to reminisce, I also remembered Tammy Faye walking by ten minutes after her husband, wearing her patented, industrial-strength mascara—with a platoon of fawning underlings who laughed on cue at every quip she made.

I remember thinking, *What a pair*. I couldn't imagine how anybody could take them seriously. Now, they were essential to my livelihood—go figure! Like the Virginia Slims commercial, I could have said, "You've come a long way, baby."

Once, when I made a trip to Charlotte for the spring catalog in mid-January, Paul and I walked by the TV set where Jim and Tammy Faye were taking a break from recording. Each star was in their respective dressing rooms, where stylists were busy enhancing their glamour. When I looked at the set, I noticed a dog at the foot of the sofa that looked alive but wasn't. It never moved.

My curiosity getting the better of me, I pointed at the dog and asked, "What's that?"

Turning his head, Paul Chalmers smiled mischievously. "That's Fluffy," he said.

"Fluffy?" I replied, still curious. "Why is Fluffy not moving?"

"Because Fluffy is dead."

Laughing, I said, "That explains part of it, but why is Fluffy on the set?"

"Because our donors don't know that Fluffy is dead."

Far more curious than ever, I retorted. "I'm clueless about all of this. You know that, right?"

Laughing, Paul pulled me aside. In a conspiratorial tone, he confided, "A while back, Fluffy got sick. Tammy Faye was very upset. One day, during the broadcast, she wailed, 'Please pray for Fluffy,' which thousands of people did. Jim laid hands on the dog and prayed for Fluffy to be healed, but Fluffy didn't get better. She died."

"Okay, but I still don't understand why you have a stuffed dog on the set."

"Cole, you don't get it. Jim thought the dog's death might make people lose their faith in the ministry, so they stuffed Fluffy instead of admitting the truth about what happened."

"You're kidding?" I replied incredulously.

With this, Paul nearly fell over laughing. He finally admitted, "No, I'm not kidding. It's the truth—I swear it is. Sometimes, they move Fluffy during breaks, but she's always there. I've told them how bad it will look, when the truth finally comes out, but nobody will listen."

"Unbelievable" was my only comment, ending the conversation by walking into the men's room.

* * *

Returning from Charlotte that evening, my answering machine was full—maxed out at twenty-five calls. Surprised, I started listening to each. As I did, my curiosity turned to apprehension, as I realized that nine of them were from Barbara. She was obviously upset and needed to talk. Putting her needs above all others I returned her call immediately.

Answering on the first ring, Barbara said, "Cole, I'm so sorry to keep calling you like this, but I don't have anywhere else to turn."

"Don't worry about it, Barbara. I'm glad you called. What's wrong?"

When I responded like this, she started to cry, which she hadn't done in our more recent conversations. I was prepared to let her cry for quite a while, but she stopped shortly thereafter. Gathering herself, she sighed deeply and announced, "The woman Jeffrey was having an affair with has gone missing."

"Missing? What do you mean exactly?" I asked.

"She's vanished. Nobody has seen her for over a week, and I just learned about it. Something has happened to her, Cole. I'm sure of it. I can feel it," Barbara added.

When she said this, my insides went cold. She was right. I felt the same way. Warning her to be cautious, I said, "I need to be candid with you. I think there is much more to this than meets the eye. Something is seriously wrong. Don't you agree?"

"Yes, I do."

"Do you have any idea what it might be?" I pressed.

Without hesitation, she opened up. "When Jeffrey and I moved out here, while I was still pregnant, he got involved in things that weren't legal. He didn't think I knew about it, but I did. He loved the intrigue of the seedy side of life, but he never involved me in it. I swear he didn't."

"I believe you," I replied, trying my best to be supportive, as well as protective.

"Thanks, Cole. Anyway, he got in—way over his head—and it got him killed. I think this is why Trixie is missing. I'm sure she's dead too," Barbara added.

"The woman Jeffrey was having an affair with is named Trixie?" I asked incredulously.

"Yes, I thought you knew," she answered.

"No, this is the first time you've mentioned her name," I said, trying not to laugh, which Barbara would have considered inappropriate. Although tickled, I didn't want to offend her. Moving the conversation along, I asked, "Are the police looking for her?"

"Yes, but I doubt they will find her. She's been murdered, Cole. I'm sure of it," Barbara asserted.

"I think you're right," I said. Pausing for a minute, I asked, "Do you think either Chance or you are in danger?"

"No," she replied immediately. After a short pause, she added, "At least, I don't think so."

When she added her caveat, my insides froze. She was concerned. I could tell that she was; so was I. "Barbara," I admonished, "you need to be vigilant. Watch everything you do. Promise me you will!"

"I promise, Cole," she replied, and I could tell she was pleased by the level of my concern. She was definitely scared, as was I.

A few minutes later, after we disconnected, while I was brushing my teeth before going to bed, I thought: *Today I have been introduced to Trixie and to Fluffy*. Despite the seriousness of the situation, the humor of it got to me. I started to laugh and couldn't stop, which can be very messy, when you have Colgate in your mouth.

25

A Funeral Atmosphere Permeated

Logically, I didn't think anything would happen to Barbara or Chance, but the people responsible for Jeffrey's garroting and Trixie's disappearance were neither rational nor reasonable. They were vicious and vengeful, making them unpredictable and dangerous. To make matters worse, they appeared to have police protection. No arrests had been made, and Trixie's vanishing became old news as quickly as Jeffrey's murder. Because Barbara didn't notice anything unusual in her routine, which I quizzed her about repeatedly, my apprehension began to abate.

Despite my disquietude about Barbara's never-ending drama, my focus had to remain on producing a quality spring catalog. So far, I had ten clients under contract, including PTL.

In mid-March 1987—once again affluent enough to afford plane fare—I flew to Charlotte to handle some last-minute details before we printed the spring catalog. When I arrived at Hartsfield Airport for my 7 a.m. flight, nearly every seat was filled with reporters and cameramen. I asked someone from CBS News what the excitement was all about.

Turning his head toward me, he replied, "We're going to Charlotte for the Bakker scandal." Having answered my question, the newsman walked away.

Because of unfolding events, there were no empty seats on the plane. While boarding, the air was electric with anticipation. I can't remember being more apprehensive about the future than I was during my short flight, including being fearful for my ex-wife's safety.

Bakker was going down, and the sharks were circling to make certain they received their fair share of his carcass. Sitting next to me in the middle seat was a NBC cameraman. He was nearly as large as Owen, my former boss. Even worse, the cameraman was unkempt. He placed his huge camera between his legs, taking up all of the room, forcing me to shrink in my seat, which is what I felt like doing anyway. The cameraman looked like he washed his hair once a week, whether he needed to or not. I suspect he bathed even less often. Cringing, I did my best to not touch him, which added to my misery.

After picking up my rental car, I drove straight to PTL where the media frenzy was at a fever pitch. One reporter asked me a question as I started to walk into the communications building. When he did, another twenty raced over to see what was happening. I was so anxious I didn't say a word but scurried hastily into the building, which was off limits to the press.

Walking into Paul's office, without first being announced, I intended to demand an explanation; but I stopped before uttering a word. When I saw the look of despair on his face, I could tell how badly he had been crushed. My self-concern evaporated. Instead of being confrontational, I knew I needed to be supportive of him, as well as of the others. Everyone I saw that day at PTL shared his look—a look of despair, mixed with dread and disbelief. It reminded me of how I must have looked when Barbara informed me about her infidelity.

When I was there one week earlier, everybody was energetic, full of life, and purposeful. Now a funeral atmosphere permeated everything, eclipsing the bright, energetic faces I was used to seeing.

Within ten minutes, the entire marketing team assembled and made a decision to go forward with the catalog, hoping the Bakkers could weather the storm. With their firm commitment to honor the terms of our purchase order, Equipity moved ahead with the project as well, printing the catalog two days later.

During that fateful meeting, none of us accurately comprehended the gravity of the situation. We just hoped things would return to normal, but they never did. Nothing was ever the same at PTL again. The allegations against Bakker, especially the sexual ones, proved to be true, and they were simply too grievous to overcome.

A few days later, we mailed the *PTL Spring Collection*, which was the last direct mail project Jim and Tammy Faye Bakker ever produced. Initially, it was so successful Jim became encouraged that his base of supporters had not abandoned him—in spite of the daily barrage of negative news stories, nearly all of which focused on his rampant financial impropriety and sexual dalliances. Bakker became so optimistic, because of the catalog's strong showing, he summoned Paul into his office one day and said, "Call Cole and tell him how grateful we are he has put together such a successful catalog."

When Paul made the call, which was supposed to encourage me, I thanked him. By this time though, no amount of encouragement could help. Each of us knew the final days of Bakker's reign at PTL were coming to an end.

Paul's call grieved me more than anything else. I was sad for him because it was the end of a dream. I was distressed for myself because I was worried we might not get paid for our work, despite the assurances of the PTL marketing team. When the conversation ended, I reflected on what Paul had said and realized this was the only time Jim Bakker ever referred to me by name.

During my subsequent journeys to PTL, which were frequent, I could see how difficult it was for my friends to cope with the daily stress of their situation. The emotional carnage was written on each of their faces. It was like every revelation of perfidy whittled away another piece of their souls, exposing raw nerves, precipitating emotional hemorrhaging.

Confident, self-assured people became shells of their former selves, as they tried to stabilize their lives and their careers in the aftermath of Bakker's fall. None of them knew what was transpiring behind Bakker's veil of deception—not really. They were dupes—just like I had been at Covenant Financial Planning. They believed in Jim and Tammy Faye personally and in the ministry of PTL. Having been so badly deceived, many took a step back in their walk with the Lord, choosing to become marginal believers from that point forward. It was how they dealt with the pain of having been misled so badly. Their disillusionment reminded me of my own.

It's difficult for people who have experienced religious abuse to ever trust again. It's as if their souls have been molested. Such a violation changes how one views life from then on. It's why so many abused people turn to alcohol, numbing prescriptions, pornography, and promiscuity. Each medicates the pain from being wounded. By turning to vice—to self-defeating behavior—many become addicted to its fruit, eventually twisting the core of their characters. Outwardly, wounded people maintain a thin veneer of propriety, but inwardly, their hearts drift further away from their first love. Many never return.

I wish what happened at PTL had been the only example of spiritual carnage I witnessed during my many years of working for Christian ministries, but it wasn't. I saw similar instances repeatedly.

Unfortunately, abusive situations are the rule at large ministries, rather than the exception—the secret Christian organizations conceal as they cast aside their wounded, replacing them with people who are younger, more naïve, and more trusting. Refusing to change their self-serving ways, such ministries go through people repeatedly. It's a pattern of mistreatment that seems endless.

26

A Ten-Inch Stack of Paper

About a month after we mailed the catalog, Bakker was forced to resign as the president of PTL. He summoned a group of Christian leaders to assume the reins, including his old nemesis, Jerry Falwell. Bakker also asked Rex Humbard, the original TV evangelist from the 1950s, to help out. Many were surprised Falwell would accept Bakker's invitation, but Jerry realized the enormous potential of the PTL Television Network and couldn't resist.

Rex Humbard was another story. Having produced a devotional for his ministry, while at Living Water several years earlier, I knew Rex pretty well. He was a warm, gracious gentleman—unaffected by his celebrity status.

Once, when I visited his ministry in Boynton Beach, Florida, there were some technical problems with the production of his TV program. While they were fixing it, I visited with Rex for several hours. During this time, we had a long, enjoyable conversation.

When the technical issue was resolved—just before Rex returned to finish his show—he said, "Cole, I've got to get back to work; but before I do, I want you to come into the conference room and lead us in prayer. Will you do that?"

"Certainly," I replied without hesitation—surprised but honored he would even consider asking me. I followed him into the conference room, which was filled with his staff—all prepared for prayer.

Joining hands, circling the conference table, Rex said, "Cole, I've promised to pray for these people by name." With that, he pointed to a ten-inch stack of paper—an IBM printout of names. The stack must have contained at least 5,000 entries.

"Please put your hand on the names and pray for them," Rex said solemnly.

At first, I thought he was joking; but he wasn't. He was dead serious. He wanted me to pray for a stack of paper. To me, this was so funny it was all I could do to not break out in laughter; but mirth wasn't an option. It was one of those moments when you have to be serious, despite every fiber in your body wanting to erupt spontaneously—like laughing at a funeral. Being Irish didn't help. I bit my cheek—literally, causing enough pain to squelch the impulse. Then, I prayed fervently for the stack of paper, believing I had no choice—none that was acceptable anyway.

Excusing myself soon thereafter, I thought I would laugh all the way back to my hotel; but I didn't. By then, it no longer seemed humorous. Instead, I felt icky—like I needed a shower. People who believed in Rex by the thousands asked him to pray for them "by name." It was a commitment he promised to fulfill. I wondered how many of them would believe Rex had kept his promise? I also wondered how many would have been offended, believing they had been consciously misled?

* * *

The leaders Jim Bakker assembled to keep things together at PTL quickly fell apart. They bickered about everything—worse than Democrats and Republicans. To his credit, Rex went to one or two meetings and then decided to withdraw, which was the smartest thing he ever did. Falwell, who was in conflict with the charismatic group, led by Richard Dortsch, went to court to gain ownership of PTL's donor list. The federal court was needed to sort things out because the Christian leaders couldn't do it among themselves, which is a sad commentary about men who repeatedly criticized the federal government for infringing upon their religious liberties.

At the same time, in an attempt to generate much needed operating capital, Equipity agreed to create another catalog for PTL—long after the Bakkers were gone. The day the court's decision about the list's rightful owner was to be handed down was a busy one for the media. Hundreds were camped out at PTL, which had become a common occurrence. As they anxiously awaited the court's decision, I loaded the entire list of names—250,000 Cheshire labels—in the back of the Crapinator and drove back to Atlanta to have them placed on the catalogs for mailing.

While driving and listening to the news in the early evening, numerous approaching vehicles interrupted me, flashing their high beams and blowing their horns. Because the labels in the back of the Pinto were so heavy, oncoming vehicles thought I had my bright lights on, which irritated numerous motorists on my long drive home.

Because we still had not been paid by PTL for the spring catalog, Equipity was on shaky ground financially. When I accepted the job, I came to be a blessing but feared I would be a curse instead. Worst of all, I had no idea what the future would hold.

Most people know what happened to Jim Bakker. He went to prison for a couple of years; and Tammy Faye eventually married the man who built most of PTL. The staff—people like Paul and others—fell on hard times. Their commitment to "the cause of Christ" was so intertwined with Bakker's purpose many became disillusioned and apathetic. For quite a few, things would never be the same. With their lives shattered, numerous marriages failed.

To some, the carnage at PTL was shocking but not to me. Having been through it before, I knew what the consequences would be. They were predictable.

As I watched one life be ruined after the other, my heart ached for my friends; but there was little I could do to help. From the depth of my soul, I knew it was Bakker who had let them down and not God; but I didn't know how to convey this simple truth—not in a way that didn't seem to be trite or sanctimonious. Unfortunately, each person from PTL had to weather his or her emotional storm—mostly alone.

Still nervous about the outstanding invoices from PTL, which came close to six figures, I was sitting in my office one afternoon deep in thought, when the phone rang.

"Cole Cassidy," I answered—like always.

"Cole, this is Barry Milton at CBN—Pat Robertson's ministry."

"Hi, Barry," I responded curiously.

"Cole, I don't think we've ever met; but I'm very impressed with the work you've done for PTL. I just got off the phone with Paul Chambers. He has given you a resounding endorsement."

"That was nice of him," I replied. "He's a great guy."

"He says the same about you, which brings me to the purpose for my call." Pausing for a moment, he continued, "I'd love to talk to you about how you can help us at CBN. Do you think you could come up to Virginia Beach for a visit?"

"Absolutely," I said without hesitation—my sales instincts humming. "I'll come up next week. What does Wednesday look like for you?"

"Ah, Wednesday would work just fine."

"Great, I'll buy you lunch," I said. With that, I set the appointment, realizing a new adventure was about to begin.

The Bible says, "love covers over a multitude of sins." In business, sales do exactly the same thing.

27

I Will Be the Next Commander-in-Chief

Flying to Virginia Beach the following week, I met with Barry and his marketing assistant—a really interesting guy, who I would work with closely for several years. His name was Darryl Dijon—pronounced like the mustard.

Barry was a sharp, handsome, buttoned-downed businessman, who looked like he would have made an ideal political candidate. Sophisticated, personable, and self-assured, he had an urbane manner about him that placed him in the upper echelon of management at CBN. As intelligent as he was humorous, Barry left Beacon Hill Press, where he had been the president, to assume the same position at CBN Publishing. As the ministry's newest executive, Barry was a firm believer in the vision espoused by Pat Robertson—CBN's founder and superstar.

Darryl, on the other hand, was in many ways the exact opposite. Constantly fighting a weight problem and nearly oblivious to fashion, he looked like the first cousin of Vito Corleone. The similarity was in looks only—not in character. Darryl was genuine and kind. Plus, he had a world-class sense of humor, which made us good friends from the moment we met—just like Pete Chalmette and I were at Ludlow Randolph.

Because Darryl was open and candid, he frequently spoke his mind, which created trouble for him repeatedly at CBN. Like all Christian ministries, CBN had its own version of political correctness, which Darryl routinely breached. Never intending to do so, he frequently offended his superiors by just being himself.

Being direct with his cutting insight, Darryl recognized subtle flaws in many of the plans of his superiors. Pointing them out, however, was rarely solicited or welcomed. Although this kept him in hot water constantly, he never seemed to learn his lesson. He couldn't; being a brownnoser simply wasn't in his nature.

On his fortieth birthday, he had his ear pierced and started wearing a small diamond stud, which irked the ministry's leadership—all of whom dressed as if they were walking advertisements for Brooks Brothers—just like their leader, Pat Robertson. Pat actually measured the worth of a man by the quality of his watch and the style of his shoes—withholding respect from those who didn't measure up to his standards—people like Darryl and me.

Darryl was a mess, infuriating many, while endearing himself to quite a few others. I liked both Darryl and Barry at first sight and never changed my opinion about either. Both were first-class human beings—as were the people who worked for them.

At our first meeting, I explained to Barry and Darryl how the catalog worked, which interested them because they were looking for new ways to generate sales for their fledgling publications division.

Because PTL was unable to continue with the catalog program, Paul Chambers suggested CBN take their place, which ensured Equipity would have the major client we needed to carry on our operation. Despite having his career derailed at PTL, Paul made sure to look out for me. You can't be a better friend than that.

By the time I left my daylong meeting at CBN, Barry had made a commitment to create a *CBN Christmas Collection*. Because it was already late summer, we needed to get the ball rolling quickly. Darryl made plans to fly to Atlanta for a photo shoot one week later—accompanied by two of his assistants.

Returning to Atlanta the following day, I knew I had substantial work ahead of me to prepare for their arrival. My photographer was a nervous, artistic Jewish guy, originally from New York. I had been using him for quite some time. His artistic eye was fabulous, as was his attention to detail. I enjoyed working with him, but his studio was very artsy. He displayed numerous photos that weren't pornographic—not exactly—but they were definitely risqué. With Darryl Dijon and his two assistants headed to Atlanta, I insisted my photographer take down the photos—fearful of offending my new clients.

Because I had just met Darryl and didn't really know him very well, my intention was for everyone from our Equipity team to go out of his or her way to be warm, friendly, and ingratiating. Working diligently to achieve my goal, I picked up our guests at the airport and drove them to the studio. After enjoying a pleasant lunch at a nearby restaurant, we began our work, which was estimated to require a two-and-one-half day photo shoot. It was the first time a major client had insisted on being present when we did the photography, so I was naturally concerned that all would go well.

Within thirty minutes of everyone arriving at the studio, while we were still adjusting the lighting for our first shot, my photographer turned to Darryl and said, "What do you think about Pat Robertson running for President?"

I could have throttled him—just like I throttled the Jewish kid who spilled the beans about Santa Claus, when I was young and believed

Santa was real. I would have gladly killed my photographer and claimed it to be justifiable homicide. I had expressly forbidden him to ask that question on at least three separate occasions, but he asked it anyway.

While we were creating the catalog, Pat Robertson was busy garnering presidential backing to succeed Ronald Reagan. Robertson had an army of enthusiastic Christians who zealously supported his nomination—some from within his ministry. At one chapel, which was mandatory for his staff, Pat announced he would be the next President of the United States. He said, "God has told me I will be the next Commander-in-Chief." During this chapel, Pat displayed an overhead map with states colored as favorable or unfavorable to his candidacy. It also revealed how he planned to accomplish the task God had set before him.

While some were enthusiastic about Pat's candidacy, most of the country was aghast at the possibility of having a president who would "rebuke a hurricane" rather than prepare for it. Additionally, there were many Christians who were adamantly opposed to his plans to abandon his ministry for politics—many of whom were from his donor base at CBN. When the presidential primary was held in Virginia, Pat didn't even carry his own precinct, where CBN was located and most of his staff lived. Evidently, not everybody believed Pat was God's man for the job, including those who knew him best.

Nevertheless, my photographer had asked the question, which everyone in the studio heard. As soon as it was "out there," all work ceased, and everybody turned to listen to Darryl's response.

Looking first at the photographer and then at me, Darryl said, "I don't want Pat to be President because I don't want his wife to be the First Lady."

When he said this, you could have heard a pin drop. Nobody expected this response, nor did anybody know how to react to it. Finally, one of Darryl's assistants started to giggle—just a little. When she did, everybody laughed so hard tears rolled down their cheeks, including me. From this precise moment, I knew Darryl and I would be great friends for a long time.

Darryl had plenty of reasons for not liking Pat's wife, Dee Dee. As part of his responsibility, Darryl manned the West Coast desk during the CBN fundraising telethons, which were aired several times a year. Because of the backdrop, the viewers thought Darryl was in California, providing news coverage in that part of the country; but he was just a few feet away from the moderating anchor—as well as from the East Coast desk.

Each telethon, which continued for many days, was exhausting. One evening, Darryl went into Pat's green room, where there was plenty of food. While there, the security guard encouraged Darryl to make a sandwich. Bringing the sandwich—with nuts and chips—back into the studio, along with a second sandwich for the woman who sat next to him at the East Coast desk, Darryl and his friend nibbled as time would permit.

Walking through the set, Pat's wife, Dee Dee, spotted the half-eaten sandwiches. Grabbing them, Dee Dee threw both sandwiches into the trash, scolding Darryl and the woman caustically. As she walked off, Dee Dee snapped, "No food is allowed in the studio." Embarrassed, Darryl felt the sting of her reprimand the remainder of the evening.

As fate would have it, the following day, Dee Dee returned to the studio with her daughter and granddaughter. All three were eating ice-cream cones. Miffed by her hypocrisy, while still feeling the sting of her rebuke, Darryl confronted Dee Dee. In front of numerous people, he pointed to the ice-cream cones and said sarcastically, "I thought there wasn't supposed to be any eating in the studio? Or doesn't ice cream count?"

Instantly, Dee Dee gave Darryl a look as frosty as her ice cream cone. Then, with a look of pure malice, she turned and marched out. Darryl had won the battle; but it was a pyrrhic victory. Dee Dee never forgave him—nor did she forget the incident. Among the lords of evangelicalism, which, in this case, included the "Ice Queen"—Darryl's favorite name for Dee Dee, there were two sets of rules—those for peons and those for the entitled nobility.

Darryl had foolishly pointed out the double standard. Dee Dee assumed everyone understood the rules did not apply to her, but Darryl confronted her double standard, criticizing her for her entitled behavior in front of everyone. Like the little boy from Aesop's fable, Darryl said, "Look, the 'Ice Queen' isn't wearing any clothes."

Considering herself to be above criticism, regardless of what she did, Dee Dee never considered explaining her actions to an insignificant commoner like Darryl. Why should she? In his naïveté, Darryl never understood the double standard, and it cost him dearly. He had made a powerful enemy out of the superstar's wife, sealing his fate at the ministry.

Although Darryl didn't know it at the time and wouldn't know it for quite a while, there would be no future for him at CBN. From then on, he was a "dead man walking"—like a prisoner on death row with his eventual termination certain. Blissfully ignorant, Darryl went about his job—oblivious to the political realities at CBN. It's why I liked him so much.

Back in Atlanta, the photo shoot went well, and we produced an excellent catalog for CBN. When we mailed it, the orders were significant. Pleased with the results, Barry made a commitment to produce a spring catalog, building on the success of their Christmas effort. Sighing with relief, I was grateful that the future looked bright again.

* * *

Shortly before the New Year, with Jeffrey's unsolved murder now a cold case, the torso of a woman's body was discovered in a remote area of Golden Eagle Regional Park—just outside of Reno. The head, hands, and feet of the woman's body were missing, making identification of the remains nearly impossible. When Barbara called to inform me about this development, my apprehension for her safety skyrocketed.

Although unconfirmed by the police or coroner—long before DNA would have made identification easy—both Barbara and I knew the torso must have been Trixie's.

At the time, Barbara's son, Chance, was just four year's old. Nevertheless, I was also concerned for his safety—young as he was. Fearful of the following generation exacting revenge, the mafia often murdered the male offspring of their enemies. I certainly didn't want to see this could happen to him. Although it seemed remote, I considered the possibility to be real. Not wanting to be overly dramatic, I kept my concern to myself, but I also increased my intercessory prayers for the boy's safety.

He was just a kid—a good kid. He had nothing to do with his father's immoral and illegal activities. Chance had difficulty even remembering his dad. In fact, as much time as he spent at my house, I was the only father figure he had.

I knew Barbara and Chance were in a bad situation. Something had to give. I was certain of it, but I had no idea what that might be.

28

Do You Know Who I Am?

Because of Pat Robertson's Presidential candidacy, which involved considerable public scrutiny—complete with massive negative media coverage—the donor base at CBN deteriorated dramatically, despite Pat's persistent assurance he would win the election. He was firmly convinced God had promised him victory.

Our first catalog had been a great success, but by the following spring, Pat's popularity took a nosedive, even among his ardent supporters. As a result, the *CBN Spring Collection* was a financial disaster. Believing everything would be recouped the following Christmas, Barry authorized another catalog, which didn't do nearly as well as the one from the previous year. This meant CBN remained at least 120 days behind in paying their bills, which placed quite a burden on Equipity. At the same time, Barry needed the cash flow from the catalog to maintain his operation, which continued to deteriorate. Nevertheless, with limited options, he kept moving forward.

Intent on finding a solution that would work for all of us, I flew to Virginia Beach to discuss CBN's debt, which had come to exceed six figures. Upon arrival, I spent the morning with Barry trying to determine how we were going to get paid, which he fully intended to do. I understood his dilemma. He was in a difficult financial position, largely based on Pat's grandiose political aspirations.

As we finished one item and were about to start another, Barry looked at his watch and said, "It's almost 11:30." Having no idea what this meant, with a puzzled look, I shrugged my shoulders.

Smiling at my confusion, he said, "It's prayer time for everybody in the ministry. We need to wrap things up until after lunch. Will you join Darryl and me for prayer?"

I could tell he hoped I would respond positively, which I did. Without hesitation, I said, "I'd love to."

With this, we closed our notebooks and walked down several long corridors, arriving at the prayer meeting a few minutes later, which had already started. We entered the large meeting hall through a side door. When I walked in, I was stunned by what I saw, or more accurately, by what I heard.

The room was large—filled with nearly four hundred people—all speaking in tongues at once. I have never had an experience like that in my entire life. I was uncomfortable from the moment I entered the room until I left thirty minutes later. It sounded more like a chicken coop than any prayer meeting I had ever attended. Chaos reigned. Nothing was discernable. I felt overwhelmed—smothered by Pentecostal exuberance. I was emotionally unprepared, but I couldn't reveal how horrified I was. To have done so wasn't an option. Because we were there to pray, that was exactly what I did. Bowing my head, I prayed. "Lord, please make this prayer meeting end!"

* * *

By this point in my career, I was no rookie to evangelical Christianity, but being in "the chicken coop" freaked me out. Years earlier, when I was a new believer, I went to a charismatic meeting with a friend. While there, a man approached me and said, "Sir, the spirit of lust is in your left shoulder blade."

Turning to him, I replied, "I might have it, but it's certainly not in my left shoulder blade."

My response offended the guy, who skulked off muttering something unintelligible. Although I thought that experience was weird, it had only been with one person—not four hundred.

After my episode in the chicken coop, I made certain to never visit CBN, when they had corporate prayer. To avoid "Prayer Meeting," I scheduled my meetings for other days of the week and always in the afternoon—just to make certain.

The next time I visited, Barry asked if we could pray at the end of our business meeting. He wanted to ask God to bless us with additional sales to pay off CBN's outstanding debt. This request certainly resonated with me, so I eagerly obliged.

As we began, there were five men in the room, including me. When the first person started praying, it wasn't in English. It was in tongues. When he finished, the person sitting to his right followed. Each person prayed in tongues, going around the room until it was my turn—the last of the five. By the time they reached me, I was as apprehensive as Cary Sullivan had been—the kid who dropped Jesus on the floor at my First Holy Communion.

Although everybody had their heads bowed, I could tell they were looking at me out of the corner of their eyes. Darryl had a slight grin on his face, which let me know he understood my discomfort. With no alternative, I began to pray, using my Irish sense of humor to deflect from how uncomfortable I felt.

I muttered, "Frere Jacques."

Was this it, they must have wondered, as their ears perked up? Encouraged, they suspected I had finally received the gift? As their curiosity mounted, I continued.

"Frere Jacques." Then, I broke into song.

Frere Jacques.
Frere Jacques.
Dormez vous?
Dormez vous?
Sonnez les matines!"

At this point, Darryl started laughing. Then, everybody laughed, including Barry, which showed that—despite the stress from their financial difficulties—they were upbeat, could enjoy life, and didn't take themselves too seriously.

I couldn't speak in tongues, and I wasn't going to fake it. Not knowing what else to do, I decided to make light of the situation rather than intensify things, by making them feel as uncomfortable as I did. That they were willing to accept my response humorously was why I liked them so much and did everything in my power to make them successful. The French song contained all of the non-English words I knew—other than the Latin declensions—thanks to Sister Anna Catherine.

* * *

Fortunately, CBN was not my only catalog customer. At one point, Equipity was serving fifteen different ministries simultaneously, customizing the contents to meet the specific needs of each. In addition to my responsibilities for writing advertising copy and helping with the creative design, I continued to travel nationwide selling space ads to the publishers, as well as visiting each of our clients. Needless to say, I was a busy guy.

In fact, I met with Dett quite often. On several occasions, he renewed his efforts to recruit me, but I definitely wasn't interested.

One of my smaller customers was an Assembly of God ministry in the Seattle-Spokane area. This church broadcasted regionally on Sunday's, and also funded a modest food program in Nicaragua, which fed dispossessed people, during the time of the Sandinista Junta.

The pastor of the church, Jerome Campbell, was the real deal. Warm, unassuming, and humble, he served his people, while never becoming overly self-important. Although a busy man, he always had time for me, which made visiting him enjoyable.

On one of my trips, I walked into his office with a smile. By the look on the pastor's face, I could tell he was clearly distressed. As he rose to greet me, I noticed his hands were shaking. Because he was clearly rattled, I didn't waste time with small talk. Immediately, I asked him what was troubling him.

Pastor Campbell said, "I have just had a twenty minute conversation with Jimmy Swaggart, and it was unnerving."

"Why?" I asked.

Pastor Campbell explained. "We have a small ministry that feeds people in Nicaragua and other parts of Central America. Jimmy has a very large food program that does the same thing. Our program helps some people; his helps many more."

"I'm aware of this," I replied.

"Apparently Swaggart's organization missed a shipment of food," Pastor Campbell continued. "So, he wants me to give him our food, so he can feed his people, instead of us feeding our own."

"You're kidding!" I exclaimed, clearly surprised.

"I wish I was." Taking a moment before continuing, Pastor Campbell added, "And do you know what else? He actually expected me to comply with his request, which was much closer to a demand."

"Unbelievable!" I replied.

Becoming a little agitated, as he thought more about his conversation with Swaggart, Pastor Campbell continued. "There's more, Cole, much more. Do you want to hear it?"

"Of course," I replied. I wanted to know everything.

Calming himself, he continued, "Swaggart said to me, 'Do you know who I am?' Then he repeated himself. 'Do you know who I am?' I answered, 'Yes, I know who you are. You're an Assembly of God pastor just like me. That's who you are. That makes us equals.'"

I was glued to every word Pastor Campbell spoke. Nodding my head just once, I encouraged him to continue.

"Then, Swaggart said, 'No, I'm much more than that. We're not equals. Every week I preach to more people than Jesus ever preached to in His entire ministry—millions more.'"

"What!" I exclaimed, as my jaw dropped—shocked by what I had just heard. "You can't be serious. Did he really say that?"

"Yes, that's exactly what he said. With God as my witness, those were his exact words," Pastor Campbell reiterated.

"That's incredible," I replied. After pausing for a long moment to take it all in, I added, "What he said isn't arrogant; it's blasphemous!"

"I couldn't agree more, Cole," Pastor Campbell concurred. After a moment to reflect, he mused, "With pride like that, Brother Jimmy is certain to take a fall sooner or later."

I nodded my head solemnly, agreeing with his conclusion. Having worked for ministries for years, I didn't think anything could surprise me, but I was wrong. This did; it surprised me a lot.

29

Entry into My Soul

Less than six months later, Jimmy Swaggart's sexual escapades were exposed for the entire world to see. When he fell, Swaggart was at the pinnacle of success, by far the most influential television evangelist, except for Billy Graham. Swaggart's plunge shocked the entire evangelical world.

Bakker's scandal wasn't surprising—not really. Because of persistent negative news stories over a long period of time, many saw it coming. Robertson's foray into politics was just a temporary setback, but Swaggart's crash caught nearly everybody off guard. Worst of all, his promiscuity with prostitutes was a pattern of misconduct—not merely an isolated incident.

As soon as the news became public, Swaggart went into full damage control. Crying in front of his congregation and television audience, pleading for forgiveness, he recovered for a short period, but when he was caught with his pants down again, it was all over for him. Being the brunt of numerous coarse jokes, he became the laughing stock of the entire nation.

As several news stories surfaced about his out-of-control sexual addiction, everybody seemed to recognize who he really was—that is, everybody other than him. He had preached to millions about turning their lustful desires over to God, wagging his finger in the face of his audience, scolding sinners mercilessly. But his admonitions were for other people—not for him. He couldn't control his own problem, but he was too proud to humble himself and seek help.

After being "outed" several times for wagging something other than his finger, he finally told his audience that what he did in private was his affair and nobody else's. When he responded this way, being self-righteous about his indefensible conduct, rather than being self-effacing, his following evaporated. His supporters abandoned him in droves, leaving him with a large ministry and very few contributions to support it.

Just like PTL, Swaggart's ministry withered quickly, becoming a shadow of its former self. His tumble hurt everybody, especially his vendors, but it also impacted other faith-based ministries. As the level of trust for TV evangelists plummeted, it created economic difficulties for all of the lords and ladies of evangelicalism, including CBN.

Because the finances were grim in the publication division, Barry was forced to let Darryl Dijon go. There just wasn't enough income being generated to support his executive position. Undeterred by his dismissal, Darryl applied for numerous positions at CBN. Skilled, bright and talented, he was certain he would be offered another job within the ministry. Applying for several openings in the months that followed, Darryl was repeatedly turned down. Ever the optimist—like the Energizer Bunny—he kept applying for one job after the other.

On one of my final trips to CBN, after Darryl had been terminated for quite some time, Barry pulled me aside and said, "Cole, you're still friends with Darryl, aren't you?"

"Yes," I answered, uncertain about why he had asked.

"I think you ought to talk to him," Barry advised. "He keeps applying for jobs at CBN, but nobody is going to hire him. The word is out on Darryl."

I just looked at Barry, uncertain about how to respond.

Sensing my confusion, Barry added, "It's come down from the top that nobody is to hire Darryl. So, he's just wasting his time applying. He needs to move on. He'll never work at CBN again—not in any part of the ministry. You would be doing him a big favor to let him know this."

I was stunned. Nevertheless, I was grateful for Barry's candor. "I'll let him know," I promised, and I did.

Barry's advice was unequivocal, so I passed it on to Darryl later that evening, when I had dinner with him at his home.

Flying back to Atlanta the following day, I thought about Darryl's situation. He paid a heavy price for being forthright. By confronting Dee Dee, challenging the "Ice Queen's" double standard, he sealed his fate. It was the kiss of death for a peon like Darryl. By correcting her, Darryl ensured his employment at CBN would end just as soon as a convenient opportunity presented itself.

Knowing Darryl as well as I did, I don't believe he could have behaved any differently. I liked that about him. Nevertheless, the way he was treated, which was financially difficult on his family, certainly didn't display Christ-like business principles. People working in secular positions are treated more fairly and respectfully than Darryl was.

Seeing the handwriting on the wall—thanks to Barry's candor—Darryl found a job with another ministry soon thereafter and moved west, where he and his family have thrived ever since.

* * *

Barry's publication division continued to be delinquent with its payments to Equipity, which now had its own cash flow problems. After I produced a spring catalog, which proved to be my last, Equipity refused to pay the printer, saying they delivered an inferior product. Since the bill was for nearly $100,000, the printer was left holding the bag for a substantial amount of money.

Appealing to me to settle the situation, I confronted my business associate about it. He was adamant that Equipity was not going to pay the bill. This put me right in the middle, with no way to resolve the situation amiably. There was nothing wrong with the print job. It wasn't unacceptable. In fact, it was excellent. Equipity didn't have a leg to stand on, but they obstinately refused to write a check, choosing to stiff the printer instead.

With no alternative, the printer filed suit and asked me to testify on their behalf, which I agreed to do. It was the right thing to do, although it certainly wasn't in my best interest. When I told my friend I was going to testify against him, my decision ended our relationship, leaving me with no future catalog business or a paycheck. Despite this personal setback, I had to tell the truth in court. I had no alternative.

In life, there are very few occasions when you are required to make a black and white decision, knowing the outcome will be self-injuring, but it does happen. For me, this was one of those times. I was in a situation where I had to do the right thing for the right reason—with no wiggle room. I was forced to stand for the principles I espoused, and that was precisely what I intended to do.

Despite the negative ramifications, I was certain the Lord would take care of me. All I needed to do was be straightforward and honest. This was a test of my character, and I knew it. There was no way out for me, other than to stand for the truth. My choice was clear—right versus wrong.

Packing up the things in my office, under the watchful eye of those who had come to despise me for my intention to be forthright, I loaded everything into the Pinto and headed home—jobless again, feeling depressed and a little flaky.

My last day was on a Friday. That same night I had a date with a lovely woman I had been seeing for quite some time. She wanted our relationship to deepen. By telling her about what had happened and how I felt about it, this would be a perfect opportunity to take our relationship to the next level.

Perhaps I should have been stronger, but I wasn't. I felt needy and weak. I wanted to talk. I needed to have someone make sense out of what was happening. I needed to be held and to be told everything would be okay. I needed someone to validate me—to assure me I wasn't to blame for things falling apart. I felt like crying and needed to be with someone who was safe. I needed to release all of my debilitating emotions. What I needed was a woman.

When I arrived at her house, I fully intended to allow her to be there for me, which she desired. But I couldn't do it. Feeling a check in my spirit, I deferred. The truth is, although I liked her a great deal, I didn't love her. So, I couldn't grant her entry into the privacy of my soul. To have done so, despite being as needy as I was, would have been unfair for both of us.

Unaware of what was transpiring inside of me, she smiled and asked what we were going to do for the evening? I suggested a movie, allowing her to make the selection. When we sat down in the theatre, I had the opportunity to think about things. Once again, I reproached myself for being out of work, wondering what I would do next.

I don't even remember what the movie was about. It seemed like there was more chaos in my life than order. Fearful of financial uncertainty, I felt peaceful one minute and fearful the next. I wanted to be confident, but I was acutely aware of the enormous financial requirements necessary to take care of Brittany and Brianna.

I also wondered what God's purpose was in all of this. I speculated about what it might be, but I didn't have a clue. Regardless, I knew I had to remain upbeat. I couldn't succumb to self-pity, which I knew would lead to depression.

Dropping off my date at the end of the evening, kissing her softly—but devoid of misleading passion—I headed home. I was thankful the girls were spending the weekend at the lake with their friends, which afforded me the solitude I needed to reflect. When I went to bed, I wondered what was going to happen next.

As so often happens in life, I didn't have to wait very long.

30

I Started Planning Our Escape

When I finally put my head on the pillow, my mind was racing. I thought slumber would elude me, but I was wrong. Mentally and emotionally exhausted, I crashed and slept hard.

Dead to the world, I was startled awake by a persistent knocking noise at 4:47 a.m. At first, I didn't know what was happening. I thought I was dreaming, but the knocking continued. Finally, realizing the noise was coming from the front door, I immediately became alarmed. Since my daughters were not at home, I was fearful something had happened to one of them, experiencing the panic that every parent knows so well.

Hastily putting on my robe and slippers, I practically bolted to the front door to see what was wrong. By the time I arrived, I had convinced myself one of my girls was injured or dead, and the police were there to inform me about the tragedy. Turning on the porch light, I saw Barbara standing there, holding her son, who was now much too big for her to carry. Opening the door for her, she smiled at me imploringly. Unable to speak, with quivering lips, she started crying.

Taking Chance from her, I motioned for her to come in, which she did. I was grateful the taxi driver stayed to make certain Barbara was safe. I nodded my head to him in appreciation, as he drove off.

Being silent—intent on not awakening her son—I walked to Brittany's room and laid Chance on her bed. Taking off his shoes and socks, I covered him, ran my hand through his hair, kissed him on the forehead, and backed out of the room silently, closing the door behind me, knowing he would sleep for hours.

When I walked into the living room, Barbara was sitting on the couch, crying her eyes out. Taking her right hand, I held it firmly for a long time, allowing her to release all of her pent up emotions. She finally regained enough composure to take off her coat. Not having seen her in a while—nor hearing from her—I wondered what was going on.

I assumed she had begun a new romance, which bothered me a little, but this wasn't what it was. Looking at her, I could see she had gained a little weight, which surprised me nearly as much as her unexpected arrival. She had always been perfectly trim, but not now. I wondered if she was pregnant and that was what was upsetting her?

Turning to me, she said, "I didn't have any place else to go. I hope it's all right that I came here."

"Of course, it is," I assured her. "You're always welcome, Barbara."

When I said this, she started crying again, and it was quite a while before she could stop. When she did, she announced, "Jeffrey's murderer intends to kill Chance and me. I'm sure of it."

"What!" I exclaimed—my protective instincts becoming acute.

Explaining, she added, "About two months ago, there were some things out of place in my apartment. At first, I didn't think much about it, but then I realized someone had been there. Nothing was missing, but my bills weren't in the order I left them. When I saw that, I knew for sure something was wrong."

"Did you call the police?" I asked.

"No, not after the way they've handled Jeffrey's murder—Trixie's too. I didn't think it was wise to let them know I was suspicious." Reflecting, she added, "Maybe I was wrong not to, especially since I live in Vegas and not in Reno, where the murders were committed, but I couldn't take the chance. After the break-in, I also suspected my phone might be bugged. That's why I haven't called. I wanted to keep you out of this sordid mess," she added with a weak smile, followed by more tears.

I couldn't believe what I was hearing. I sat perfectly still—totally focused on the story she was divulging.

Regaining a modicum of self-control, with a deep sigh, she continued. "When I realized what was happening, I kept my eyes open from then on. About a month later, the same thing happened again. That's when I knew for certain someone was stalking me. The following week, when my agent booked me for a weeklong gig at the same hotel where Jeffrey worked in Reno—at double my normal rate—my antennae went up. To get me to commit to an out-of-town engagement, they offered free childcare for Chance, which is something none of the other casinos have ever done."

"You're kidding?" I replied.

"I wish I were, Cole, but I'm not. I made the commitment, pretending that I was very excited about the opportunity, but that's when I realized neither Chance nor I would survive the experience. From that moment, I started planning our escape." Looking at me, she added, "I had my agent tell them I preferred to drive, rather than fly, and that I would keep a log of my miles and expenses along the way. I did this to keep them from realizing I had become suspicious."

"That was very resourceful, Barbara."

Smiling at me, she continued. "Yesterday morning, Chance and

I headed to Reno on Highway 95. I watched to see if we were being followed. Just as soon as I was certain we weren't, I turned around and headed back to Vegas. Because we were expected in Reno by 1 p.m., I didn't have much time. The day before, after paying all the bills I had, bringing everything current, I destroyed every record of my existence, especially my phone bills. I shredded everything, dumping the contents in four different receptacles."

Listening to her, I was mesmerized. Her account sounded like something out of a James Bond thriller, but it wasn't. This was real, and so was my concern.

Barbara continued. "When we got back to town, I went to the bank and withdrew everything I had in savings, cashing in my entire life. It's quite a bit," she added. Standing, she opened the front of her blouse and unfastened a thick money belt, handing it to me.

I couldn't have been more surprised. Smiling, I said, "So, you haven't gained a few extra pounds?" Wisely, I refrained from mentioning I suspected she might have been pregnant.

Surprised by my response, she smiled and said, "Cole, you can be such an ass!"

Equally surprised, I laughed heartily. "What's your point?" I replied.

We both laughed at our old joke, despite the seriousness of our conversation. Holding up the money belt, I said, "Why don't I lock this up where I keep my shotgun?"

Nodding, she replied, "If you don't mind, that would be wonderful."

Immediately, I went to my bedroom closet and put the money belt beside my weapon. Returning, I sat down beside her, motioning for her to continue, which she did.

"Once I had the money, I went to the airport, abandoned the car, and bought tickets for Chance and me to fly to Chicago. When we arrived, I destroyed all of the identification I had for Barbara Varner and bought tickets to Orlando, using my old Barbara Cassidy identification. Although my driver's license was expired, I hoped they wouldn't look too closely. They didn't. So, Chance and I flew to Orlando. Then, we flew here on another carrier—just to be safe—finally arriving at your front door. I used cash for everything. As an added precaution, I didn't call to tell you I was coming. My goal was to vanish into thin air, and I hope this is precisely what Chance and I have done."

Having finished her story, she gazed at me, knowing I would have questions.

Curious, I asked, "But can't they trace you as Barbara Cassidy?"

With a sheepish look, she replied, "No, they can't. Jeffrey insisted I never mention my previous marriage. It's why I still had my old driver's license. I took it out of my wallet and put it in a drawer. I planned to destroy it but forgot about it. It wasn't until I started planning my escape that I remembered I still had it."

"I'm glad you did."

"Me too," she replied, letting her guard down enough to yawn.

Looking at her, I could tell she was wiped out. So, I said, "Brianna's room is a mess—like always—but it will have to do. Why don't you get some sleep? We can talk again after you've rested."

Standing, she said, "Thank you, Cole. I didn't know where else to go."

"You did the right thing coming here. I'm glad you did. Nothing is going to happen to you—or to Chance—not when you're with me. I guarantee it. When I put your money away, I unpacked my shotgun and loaded it."

When she heard this, feeling safe and protected, she started to cry again. A long moment later, she hugged me hard, kissed me on the cheek, and headed to our youngest daughter's room to get some sleep.

* * *

I slept fitfully for the rest of the night, finally abandoning the effort. Both Barbara and Chance slept until noon, which didn't surprise me; especially since their body time was three hours behind Eastern Time.

Barbara was the first to get up. When she walked into the kitchen, I handed her a cup of freshly brewed coffee, with half & half and no sugar—just the way she liked it.

Taking it, she took a sip, said nothing, but smiled warmly with her eyes. By the time she finished her second cup, she was ready to start talking again, but she didn't get very far before Chance walked in, hungry and wondering where his sisters were.

I made both of them sausage, eggs, and cheese grits, which each ate heartily. I'm a good cook, by the way. I don't believe I've mentioned that.

Once they were finished, Chance sat down to watch cartoons, and Barbara and I resumed our conversation. This time, it was my turn. I told her about my catalog business—how it had disintegrated and how I was unemployed. Even worse, I told her I had to testify against Equipity, which was very troubling. We talked for several hours, or more accurately, I talked. While doing so, she helped me fix numerous things around the house, which actually made doing my Saturday chores enjoyable.

Later that afternoon, I called Brittany and Brianna to tell them their mom was at the house, which meant both wanted to come home immediately. That evening, we all ate at Pasta Vino, sharing a huge pizza, fried calamari, and a salad. On Sunday, Barbara took all three of the children to see *Aladdin*, which had just been released. With the pressing needs of the kids, we didn't have the opportunity to talk further for quite some time.

With our daughters home, Barbara and Chance moved into Midge's place, where they intended to stay for a while. The girls were glad to have their mom around; so was I.

* * *

Bright and early Monday morning, I received a call from Dett at Ludlow Randolph. He told me he had heard I was no longer with Equipity and asked if I could get on a plane and come meet with Benny Lessner and him about my future. Shocked to hear from him, coupled with no other prospects for the future, I said I would be delighted. So, I booked a flight for early the following morning, leaving the girls with their mom.

When I arrived, Dett brought me straight to Benny's office. Upon entering, Benny stood, shook my hand, and said: "Cole, it's good to see you. When I heard you were no longer with Equipity, I told Dett to get hold of you right away. You slipped through our fingers before, and I don't want that to happen again."

Flattered, I replied, "Thanks, Benny, I really appreciate it."

"You're welcome. I've got to run, but Dett is going to make you an offer. I want you to take it. I have plans for you at Ludlow Randolph. I've always had plans for you. This is where you belong."

When he added this was "where I belonged," I felt like tearing up, but I didn't, obviously. Having felt unwanted in so many areas of my life for so long, Benny's affirmation touched my deepest desire—to belong.

After our meeting ended, Dett took me to lunch. While there, he made me an offer. He told me my job would be calling on ministries on the East Coast, producing marketing materials for them, using Ludlow Randolph's product line exclusively. He added that since I would be on the road a lot, it made more sense for me to work out of my house in Atlanta, which had direct flights to every place I needed to travel, rather than move back to Orlando. I liked this part of my job description a lot.

Striking a deal, I flew home on Wednesday morning—once again employed—this time by a major publisher. Cisco was feeling pretty good again. I thought things had stabilized, but this was nothing but an illusion. My life was about to change again . . . dramatically!

31

Of Course, I Did—Duh!

On Thursday morning, after Brittany and Brianna went to school, Barbara took Chance to the babysitter, returning to the house shortly thereafter. With all three occupied for hours, she looked at me nervously and made an announcement. "There are some more things I need to discuss with you." Becoming quite serious, she added, "This can't wait, Cole. I need to tell you everything. I can't hold it in any longer."

When she said this, we were in the kitchen. Taking the phone off the hook to make sure we would not be interrupted, I waited for the annoying hi-pitched beeping to stop. Then, I sat at the kitchen counter, across from her, giving her my complete and undivided attention, honoring her request without saying a word.

Taking a deep breath, she began. "Cole, there are so many things you don't know, but I feel compelled to tell you everything."

After she said this, I just nodded for her to continue. "I've never told you this, but I invited Christ to come into my life nearly three years ago.

I didn't say anything because I wanted to make sure it was real and not just an emotional response to my neediness after Jeffrey's murder—also the mess from that other guy, you know, the possessive one."

I just nodded my head that I remembered her jealous boyfriend. How could I forget?

"You didn't have any idea I became a Christian, did you?"

"Actually, I did," I replied. "The night it happened, I was a guest on the podium at the Graham Crusade in L.A. I saw you from behind the choir, but I didn't let you know I was there."

Dumfounded, with her mouth wide open, Barbara replied, "You were there?"

I nodded my head, affirming that I was.

"Why didn't you say something?" she asked, a little vexed.

"Because it was your time to be present with the Lord. It had nothing to do with me. To have interfered in any way wouldn't have been in your best interest. I knew that, so I just kept my mouth shut."

"But you've never said anything since then either!" she snapped, in a cross tone.

"Neither have you," I replied, holding my ground. "I wanted to many times, but I never did. I couldn't initiate that conversation. It wasn't my place to do so. You can see why, can't you?" I asked.

She didn't respond. Instead, she raised her right eyebrow—something she always did, when deciding whether or not to be angry. She could go one way or the other, and I knew it. All I could do was hold my breath and wait. Finally making her decision, she nodded her head that she did understand. She let it go, as the brief moment of tension between us passed. Once it did, I started breathing again normally.

Going to the coffee pot a minute later, she poured herself another cup and asked if I wanted one.

"No, my eyes are floating," I replied.

Smiling at our longstanding joke, she resumed our conversation. "Working in Vegas is like being in a pit of snakes. You have to watch every move you make. When Jeffrey and I first arrived, all I could see was the glamour and none of the decadence behind it. After his murder and the Graham Crusade, all of that changed. I can't explain it, but I wasn't the same person anymore. I needed to be certain the changes were permanent though. At first, I wasn't sure they would be, but now I am."

"I can see the difference," I replied. I intended to say more—to provide her with substantial validation—but she cut me off.

"Don't interrupt me, Cole," she scolded. "This is hard enough without getting sidetracked." Holding up her hand imploringly—like a cop directing traffic—she added, "Will you just listen, please?"

Nodding that I would, I motioned for her to continue.

Becoming very serious, she said, "Cole, I have been badly deceived—about everything. I knew I needed to start over, so that's exactly what I've done. I focused on raising my son, saving money, and ridding myself of the tinsel mentality that made my life a wasteland. I didn't get involved with anyone, which was surprisingly easy. You may not believe me, but it's true."

When she said this, she stopped and scrutinized my face, trying to discern if I was skeptical about what she had said. If I had been, she was ready to do battle. I could see it in her eyes.

I wasn't surprised though—not really. I understood completely, having made the same decision several years earlier.

Changing direction—much to my relief—she continued. "Because of what I've done, I need to make amends to you." Taking a deep breath, she said, " Cole, I'm sorry for having betrayed you so badly. I didn't know how excruciating the pain was for you until I experienced it myself. I'm sorry; I really am."

I had waited so long to hear her say this. I had dreamed and fantasized about it. Now it was here, but it was not enunciated on a mountaintop at sunset, as I had dreamed, but across from me at the kitchen counter. It felt deeply gratifying nonetheless.

Continuing, she added, "I've never told you this before. I should have, but I haven't. So, I'm telling you now. I was wrong—dead wrong. It wasn't you; it was me."

"It was both of us," I interjected, despite my commitment to remain silent. Having spent substantial time in counseling, I needed to "own my part" in the marital break-up, and I did.

"Thank you for admitting that, Cole. I know there is some truth to that, but we were not equally responsible. Can we at least agree about that and move on? I have a lot more to say."

I nodded that we could.

As I thought about this conversation many times afterwards, replaying it repeatedly in my mind, I realized this was all that was required. With mutual forgiveness, this massive wound to each of our souls had been lanced, allowing the malice to drain away peacefully. Now, healing could begin in earnest. At the time, I was too dumfounded to respond, but I came to realize that both of us had matured appreciably by this simple—yet difficult—act of letting go of the past.

When she asked for my forgiveness, I assumed this would be the end of our conversation, but it wasn't. She had quite a bit more to say.

"Thank you, Cole. I knew this was how you would respond. I was sure of it," Clutching her heart with both hands, she added, "I'm so grateful." Both of us remained silent for quite a while after that, as she drank her cup of coffee, but I could tell she wasn't finished. Sitting still, I just waited, but it was a peaceful wait—not one filled with foreboding or trepidation.

Her eyes became misty, but she was determined to proceed. I could tell she was a woman on a mission. "Cole, I knew you wouldn't shame me. I was certain of it. I've seen how much you've matured and how well you have raised our daughters. I'm so proud of you."

When I heard this, I started to cry. I couldn't help it. When Barbara saw how emotional I had become, she walked over to my side of the counter and held me, allowing me to cry for quite a while. At first, what she said felt surreal, but it also felt good and normal. I loved being validated by her. It was the best feeling in the world—a feeling I had actually forgotten.

Finally pulling away, she returned to the other side of the counter. Standing tall, she announced: "There's more."

"Okay," I said, "Bring it on." I felt a little punch drunk from all that had transpired, but I smiled, finally being able to tap into my Irish sense of humor. I expected her to laugh, but she didn't. Instead, there was apprehension in eyes, perhaps even fear. Obviously, she was nervous about what was coming next.

Taking a deep breath, coupled by a leap of faith, she announced, "I want you back, Cole. I want all three of you back—you, Brittany, and Brianna. I know I've made a mess of things, but it will never happen again. I promise. That's all in the past. Since the Crusade, I've focused on being the person who I am looking for is looking for, and that person is you."

"What?" I asked, making her repeat her last sentence several times, until I finally got it straight in my mind. It meant she wanted someone who shared her values and commitment, and I was the only one who came close. Although this was deeply gratifying, as you can imagine, she still wouldn't allow me to respond. There was more, and she needed to get it out.

"Cole," she said, "After inviting Christ into my life, the only man I thought about being with was you. I couldn't get the need to reconcile out of my mind, so this conversation is more than about making amends.

I've grown to love you again, and I hope you can learn to love me too. In time, I think you can. So, let me just ask, plain and simple: Will you think about taking me back?" After a brief moment, she added, "Not just me, Chance and me. We are a package deal."

When she said this, she stopped and looked at me imploringly. I was about to speak, but she held up her hand, telling me to hold my thought. To deflect from the tenseness of the moment, she added playfully, "You might as well. We already live here. Besides, we're on the run and don't have any place else to go."

Following suit, I laughed out loud, which turned into tears. Unable to speak, filled with emotion, I didn't say a word, but I did the next best thing. I simply nodded yes. This was what I wanted too. I think it's always what I wanted, although I had given up hope that it would ever come to pass.

Retrieving a napkin from the counter, she wiped my eyes and my nose. Putting it down, she reached up and kissed me. It was the first time in six years, but it was electrifying—just like our original kiss at the University of Massachusetts many years earlier.

* * *

Afterward, I wanted more affection—a lot more. What can I say? I'm a man whose engine had finally been turned on, after sitting in the garage for a long time. But that's not what happened. We had too much to discuss to get sidetracked. Knowing what I had in mind, Barbara suggested we both take a shower and get cleaned up—mine, a cold one. Then, we could go out for lunch.

Her idea seemed like a good one. Standing up, I put the phone back on the receiver. It rang less than a second later. Shrugging, because I didn't want to talk to anybody but Barbara, I answered. It was Dett.

"Cole," he said. "We're ready for you to start next Monday, but there is one little glitch."

"What is it?" I asked—immediately focused on my livelihood.

Trying not to rock the boat, Dett said gingerly, "Instead of making you a full-time employee, we need to start you out as a full-time consultant. The pay will be exactly the same; so will everything else, but you won't be an employee."

Bewildered, I asked, "Do you mind telling me why?"

"It's because of the lawsuit the printer has against Equipity. Benny wants to be careful to not get Ludlow Randolph involved in any way, and you're definitely involved. When this is settled, we'll change your status from consultant to employee. I promise we will. I want to be perfectly clear about that."

"Okay, I think that can work," I said, not sure how else to respond.

Ending the conversation soon thereafter, I told him I was looking forward to being in Orlando with him the following week. As I went to take my shower—my hormonal engine once again back in neutral—I couldn't imagine there would be a problem with Benny and Dett's temporary solution. As I would soon discover, however, it ended up making me an indentured servant without rights or recourse for two years.

* * *

After showering and getting dressed, while Barbara did the same in Midge's bathroom, we went to lunch at Goldberg's—one of my favorite spots. Hungry, I ate a bacon cheeseburger with extra crisp fries. Predictably, Barbara had a salad with dressing on the side. Where calories are concerned, men and women are not equals—not even close—but I'm grateful.

When we were full, Barbara pulled out a manila folder from her enormous handbag and laid it on the table. Becoming serious, she said, "I love your house, but it's your house—not our house. I don't have any ownership, which won't work. Besides, it's too small for all five of us."

"I was just thinking about that," I replied. "But with you out of work and me beginning a new job, I don't think we can afford a bigger one. We'll just have to make do for a while. I don't think we have an alternative."

"I have a better idea," she said. Inside the manila folder she pulled out a drawing for an extension to my house. It showed a large master bedroom, complete with a huge bathroom—one with his and her sinks and water closets.

Looking at it, I couldn't have been more surprised. It was perfect and would add significant value to the property.

Barbara said, "If we could build the addition, it would make it our home—not just your home." Looking deeply into my eyes, she added, "This is important to me."

"I understand, Barbara. I love your idea. I really do. When we get our finances in order, we'll do it. I promise we will." I meant what I said, which she could tell.

"But, I want to do it right away, Cole."

"I know, but we can't afford it," I reiterated.

"Yes, we can. I'll pay for it," she added.

On a day filled with surprises, this was the biggest. I didn't ask her how—not verbally. I didn't need to—the incredulous expression on my face conveyed my message perfectly.

Crinkling her lips mischievously—one of her most endearing looks—she said, "You haven't opened up the money belt to see how much is in it, have you?"

"No," I said emphatically. "That's your money—not mine. I would never do that."

Shaking her head playfully, She retorted. "I knew you wouldn't. You're so predictable." Raising her eyebrow again—this time playfully—she added, "When I cashed in everything at the bank, I received $100,000 in thousand dollar bills and $40,000 in hundreds. This renovation will cost between $45,000 and $50,000. We can pay cash for it, and I can be a stay-at-home mom and finish raising the kids. This is what I want. What do you think about my plan?"

Floored by her proposition, I tried to regain my equilibrium but couldn't. Instead, I just nodded my head that this was what I wanted as well. I also realized I would finally be free from the fear of economic uncertainty for the first time in my adult life, which was a great feeling.

After paying the check, I opened the folder again to have a second look at her architectural enhancement. In the lower right hand corner, I noticed a Las Vegas firm had produced it. Pointing this out, I asked her when she had the drawing made.

She replied, "After the first break in, but I've kept it in my purse at all times. I didn't want anybody to find out about it."

"So, you've known for quite a while I would take you back?" I asked, somewhat seriously but far more playfully.

Standing to leave, putting the drawing back in her purse, she said, with her crinkled smile, "Of course, I did—duh!"

32

What Happened in Vegas Stay in Vegas

As we walked out of the restaurant, Barbara stopped, looked at me and then at her watch. Scrutinizing me closely, she asked, "You're not going to change your mind about this, are you?"

"No," I replied emphatically.

"You're positive?"

"Absolutely," I said, and I meant it. "Will you change yours?"

She just shook her head, while she studied to study my face. "What about Chance? You won't," she started to ask, but I cut her off.

"Barbara," I said emphatically. "I'm already the only dad Chance has ever known." Again, I meant every word I said, being completely forthright.

When she heard my clear response, touching the deepest desire of her heart, it evaporated any hint of apprehension she may have been harboring. Looking up at me tenderly, I could see love in her eyes for the first time in years. Although Barbara was never one for public displays of affection, she clutched my hand, interlocking her fingers with mine, squeezing firmly. It was at that precise moment we became a married couple again. It was our bonding experience. Although brief in duration, it was a powerful moment—acting like solder to bond two pieces of metal.

Looking at her watch a second time, she said, "We still have an hour-and-a-half before I have to get Chance and the girls get home from school. If we hurry, we can get the marriage license and have our blood work done."

"Kind of like the way they do it in Las Vegas, huh?" I teased.

Mischievously, she responded to my light-hearted banter. "That's right—just like Vegas. Or would you rather wait until after you get back from Orlando a week from now? I can hold out; can you?" She knew the answer to this question, which made it rhetorical.

Instead of continuing the repartee, wasting precious moments, I replied, "I'll drive. I can get there faster than you." With this, I turned and headed for the car, while she looked in her purse for her lipstick. Sporting a knowing smile, she followed, but it was difficult for her to keep up with me. I'm sure you can figure out the reason why. A moment later, I turned on the car, put it in gear, and raced downtown.

* * *

That evening, after dinner, we sat down with all three children and told them what was about to happen. Needless to say, they were surprised, but they were also thrilled. Secretly, kids from divorced families want their parents to get back together. Some openly say so. The only difference is ours were having their desires realized, which was evident by the smiles I saw around the table.

When Chance was told he would have his own room, he beamed. Barbara intended to enroll him in E. Rivers Elementary School as

Chance Cassidy, discarding their last link to Jeffrey. Chance wasn't sure he liked the idea of changing his name—not until Brianna told him it would make him her real brother. When she told him this, idolizing his older sisters, he became much more enthusiastic.

Later in the evening, I called my mom to tell her the news, which I thought would surprise her, but it didn't. I had prepared myself for a stinging rebuke, but it never came. She responded by saying she had expected it and wondered why it had taken so long, making me the one who was surprised. Nevertheless, I was grateful. Without having to be asked, she said she would book an open-ended flight and come down to help, staying as long as she was needed.

After we disconnected, thinking about our conversation, I marveled at the wisdom of my mom. Now in her late seventies, I intended to offer her the mother-in-law suite as her permanent home. Barbara thought this was a good idea too, but she wasn't ready for Midge to move in until after the renovation was complete. According to Barbara, until the construction was finished, we would need all of the dust-free space we could get.

The following morning, I found one of my basketball buddies, who was also a minister, and asked him to perform the ceremony early Friday evening. Without hesitation, he agreed. With this, everything necessary had been placed in motion for our wedding.

With the kids in attendance, along with my mom, we were married in the living room of our house. Despite being put together in haste, everything was lovely, largely because of my mom.

The moment Midge walked in the front door, she made herself useful. Actually, she did more than that. She took charge. In the living room, she placed flowers everywhere, lighting the room with ivory candles that cast a warm glow on everything. Midge even prevailed upon one of my old girlfriends to sing.

How she accomplished that I'll never know, and I doubt I'll ever ask. Not having been informed beforehand—just like everything else concerning the ceremony—I was surprised when I heard Bridget's voice. Apparently, Barbara knew because she welcomed Bridget with a smile, hugging and thanking her for helping out on such short notice. Wisely, I kept my mouth shut and just went with the flow.

When Barbara walked in, I couldn't believe how beautiful she looked, nor how blessed I felt that each of us had been given a second chance. If anything, she was prettier than when I first married her, or at least she looked better to me. I suppose that's all that really matters, isn't it?

This time, when I promised to cherish her, I understood what was necessary to do so, and I owned enough of myself to fulfill my pledge. After the ceremony, which was charming, Midge stayed with the children, while Barbara and I flew to Ponte Vedra for a short honeymoon.

One week earlier, I was unemployed and didn't have a clue about what the future would hold. Then, just seven days later, I had a job, although it was as a consultant and not a full time employee, and I was married. I had a new son, our house was scheduled for renovation, and my mom was making the decision to move into her suite full time. Life often comes at you fast but rarely at a frenetic pace like this.

* * *

In a relay race, the handoff of the baton is the most critical part of the competition. If it's accomplished correctly, everything works smoothly. To those watching, it seems effortless. When the handoff isn't done right, it looks awkward and disjointed. Often the baton falls. If this happens, the team is disqualified.

The goal of our remarriage was to make the transition smooth and effortless for everyone involved, and that's precisely what we accomplished. Learning to pass a baton requires practice. For a marriage to be successful, both parties must have character, which requires a great deal of practice to establish.

For Barbara and me, we learned our lessons by trial and error—both dropping the baton before we learned how to pass it correctly, but we did learn. This is what growing from our mistakes produced—a richness that neither of us had ever experienced.

From the moment Barbara said, "I do," she poured herself into our family and into our relationship, choosing to serve, while never keeping score. I've learned that those who have been forgiven much have a greater capacity for love. Barbara's love manifested itself in hundreds of little ways—few of which escaped my notice.

Remarrying Barbara wasn't rolling the dice, hoping things would work out the second time around. Having lived through the degrading consequences of her poor choices, she used her second chance wisely, and the rest of us became the beneficiaries of her positive character changes.

* * *

When our brief time together in Ponte Vedra was over, I drove Barbara to the airport in our rental car. She had to catch a flight back to Atlanta. When I left her, I headed south on I-95 to I-4, then west to Orlando, where I was prepared to begin my new challenge at Ludlow Randolph. Freshly married and newly employed, I wondered what adventures awaited me.

I arrived at Ludlow Randolph just in time to have lunch with Dett and Pete—both of whom had been waiting expectantly. I didn't even get a chance to go to the restroom before we headed out.

Once we were seated at the restaurant, after having excused myself,

I didn't say anything about getting married. I wanted to see how long it would take before one of them noticed I was wearing a shiny new wedding band.

It didn't take long. Just as soon as I held up my menu to make a selection, Dett noticed it.

"Cole, you're wearing a wedding band?" he stated—like it was a question.

"That's right," I smiled, or more accurately, beamed.

"You're married? When did that happen?" he asked, with keen interest. This was followed by numerous questions, all fired at me in rapid succession. "Why didn't you mention this before? Do I know her? How long have you been planning this?"

Dett would have made a great game show host for *Twenty Questions*. He was relentless. I couldn't answer his inquiries as quickly as he asked them. I finally gave up and started laughing. So did Pete.

Then, I told them about how Barbara and I had gotten back together—a story that fascinated both. I didn't tell them about Jeffrey's murder though, nor did I mention anything about Barbara abandoning her former life, essentially skipping town. Barbara and I decided to let what happened in Vegas stay in Vegas.

We did this—not out of shame—but out of caution. We were concerned that Jeffrey's murderer was still looking for Chance and her.

While in Ponte Vedra, suspecting that being a stay-at-home mom might lose its luster, Barbara and I also discussed alternative career pursuits for her. Although music was her passion, she would never be able to sing again professionally. Those days were over. She was too well known in the world of performing arts. Tracing her whereabouts would be much too easy for those looking.

After Dett, Pete, and I had lunch, we went back to the office to develop our strategic plan to sell Ludlow Randolph books to its evangelical client base. Originally, I had expected to spend the afternoon doing paperwork with human services, but this wasn't necessary—not on this trip anyway. Being a consultant, there was no paperwork for me to submit other than to give my address and Social Security number.

Returning to Atlanta late Wednesday evening, I discovered Barbara had already chosen a contactor to begin the remodeling. The renovation was scheduled to start the following Monday. When she announced this, after giving me a quick kiss at the front door, I must have looked like a deer, frozen by the glare of a car's headlights. Smiling and squeezing my hand, like I was a grade-schooler, she laughed.

"If you want to make an omelet, you have to break some eggs," she announced. Then, she patted my cheek, turned, and walked back into the kitchen.

I wasn't the only one caught in the whirlwind of Barbara's activity. She used my mom to be the chauffer before heading back to Boston a few days later. Being Mr. Mom for years, I thought I was busy with my role, but I was lethargic compared to the energy my wife produced, making our new lives more comfortable. To get everything done smoothly and quickly, she was the Energizer Bunny on steroids.

The following ten weeks were a blur. The renovation was supposed to require no more than six weeks, but contractors never tell you the truth. Once they begin, they think they have the advantage, but ours was no match for Barbara's tenacity and grit. She handled the subcontractors like she was a professional hardhat, withholding pay until things were done to her satisfaction. Fair but firm, she had to listen to whining and moaning routinely from those who always had their hand out, begging for more.

During the renovation, the girls moved into Midge's place, while Barbara and I took the second bedroom and Chance the third. The girls loved their newfound independence, but they were grateful when the omelet was complete and things got back to normal. The renovation wasn't the only project Barbara tackled. She made arrangements for Midge to sell her home in Wellesley, which my mom could never have done on her own.

As part of her divorce settlement with Jeffrey, Barbara received substantial child support. Not wanting this monthly payment, which was funded by Jeffrey's life insurance trust fund, to come to our house, she redirected it to a bank in the Cayman Islands. This anonymity provided a further level of protection—just in case. This would never have occurred to me, but people from Las Vegas learn how to do things like this all the time. The additional funds helped out considerably.

With what I made, coupled with Chance's child support and a small amount of rent from my mom, which she insisted on paying, we had enough for Barbara to be the stay-at-home mother she always wanted to be. With all that was happening, I don't know how she could have worked outside the home anyway. Her plate was full—far more so than mine.

Planning long term, she invested the remaining $87,000 from her money-belt in the stock market, being aided by a Christian financial planner—a real one. Taking care of everything required quite an effort on her part, but she made it happen. She created an environment that allowed our family to thrive, and she did it in a record amount of time. Honestly, I didn't believe she could achieve what she did so quickly, but she did. Thinking about it, I believe it would have taken me a year for me to accomplish what she did in three months.

Now, we just had one more hurdle to jump before I could become a full-time employee at Ludlow Randolph and our lives would run smoothly—the litigation between the printer and Equipity.

33

An Unspoken Irrelevancy

I worked for Ludlow Randolph for nearly a year before the case involving Equipity was finally placed on the court docket. By that time, I had discovered working for Dett was not nearly as pleasant as being his casual friend, nor was it as rewarding as being courted by him for employment.

I also realized a full-time consultant's position was not nearly as prestigious as a consultant who comes to town every month to inform senior management about things rank-and-file employees already know. Aware of how I was beginning to feel, Benny told me several times he had plans for me "once the messiness" of my court appearance was finally put in the "rearview mirror."

From my perspective, the trial wasn't nearly as significant as it seemed to be for everybody else. I felt like I was the one on trial—accused of some heinous felony—rather than simply being a witness for the plaintiff in a case involving civil litigation. To me, it was just one afternoon away from work, but it meant much more than this to my superiors. Although it surprised me, my impending testimony definitely impacted my standing at Ludlow Randolph.

It affected me in other ways as well. My old friends at Equipity let it be known how treacherous and traitorous I had become, trying to make the trial about me and not about them. Bemoaning how much money they lost by backing my last catalog, they griped to anyone who would listen. Their purpose was to shift the responsibility for their actions away from them and place it on my shoulders. Like sleazy politicians, they refused to be accountable for their wrongdoing, choosing to point their collective fingers at me instead.

I had seen similar behavior before. Once, at Living Water, we had a particularly dismal quarter. It was so poor a payroll was delayed a week on two separate occasions, which is the kiss of death for any ministry. Rather than accept responsibility for the mismanagement that created the situation, Donald Duncan said revenues were off because "there was sin in the camp." At chapel, he berated the entire staff, telling us our personal behavior was displeasing to God, who was withholding His financial blessing because of our sinful behavior. When Donald finished his chastisement, he asked the wrongdoer to identify himself or herself, fully expecting someone to do so. When no one did, he said the guilty party could come by his office and confess his or her indiscretion—just like I had to do as a teenager. No penitent came forward though, infuriating Donald.

For several days, the staff gossiped among themselves about who the culprit might be, which did nothing other than justify their penchant for misanthropy. Eventually, many came to resent Donald's attempt to shift the responsibility away from himself—where it rightfully belonged. The staff in accounting—who understood the real reason for the downturn—became particularly resentful.

The people from Equipity were behaving very similarly. In

conversations with several of my ministry clients, they challenged my actions. "How can Cole testify against his brothers in Christ? It's not biblical?"

This argument resonated with several, causing me problems. That the reasoning behind the charge was ludicrous didn't matter. In the minds of several, it was wrong for me to testify against a believer no matter what. Essentially, it made Christianity seem like a clique, where we were supposed to cover for each other, rather than insist upon doing things honestly and transparently.

Equipity was wrong about this—no doubt about it. My responsibility was to be truthful, candid, and forthright about what happened—nothing more, nothing less. Although I viewed this as a black and white issue, others didn't. What resonated with them was my betrayal of "Christian brothers."

When one ministry in Chattanooga challenged me about my intentions, I had finally had enough. Although they approached the subject gingerly, my impending actions were definitely being called into question.

Not interested in speaking in veiled terms, I became direct. "The guys from Equipity complained they lost money on my last catalog, didn't they?" I asked.

"Yes," Mack answered. "Actually, they said they lost quite a bit."

"That's what they have been telling anybody who will listen," I replied. "But let me ask you this: If they didn't pay for the printing, but kept all of the money from the orders, how could they have lost money?"

The answer is they couldn't have, but nobody from Equipity ever mentioned this. When I did, Mack's face changed expression, as he realized he had been duped. He hadn't thought about it that way.

Continuing, I said, "If they were willing to take the risk, which they did, shouldn't they also be willing to accept the responsibility for the results?"

Looking at it differently, clenching his jaw in agreement, Mack nodded his head that they should.

Once he agreed, I changed the subject to the role I was about to play. "My responsibility is to do the right thing, causing no harm to the innocent, isn't that correct?"

Mack nodded his head again.

Continuing, I asked, "Just because the printers are non-believers doesn't mean it's okay to cheat them, does it?"

My question was rhetorical, but Mack answered it anyway, saying it was not.

Then I asked, "Which is worse, lying under oath to 'spare my brothers in Christ' or telling the truth? By being forthright, I will let the non-believers see that not all Christians are willing to cheat them. Which is a better testimony?"

Although my questions were rhetorical, Mack continued nodding his head, indicating he finally understood why I was behaving the way I was. In the end, he encouraged me to move forward, saying he would pray for me to stay strong.

For me, this was a "right vs. wrong" issue. That it was even a topic of discussion was troublesome. It actually revealed one of the deep-seated problems in evangelical circles, where normal rules of ethical behavior don't apply. Among the evangelical superstars, there is an unspoken assumption that they are above the mundane requirements of fiduciary responsibility, and they bristle whenever they are challenged about being financially negligent.

Is it any wonder that my childhood profanity began to rear its ugly head? I think not!

* * *

When the day of the trial arrived, I appeared as the prime witness for the printer. The people from Equipity—whom I hadn't seen for more than a year—were also there. As the defendants, they heard every word I spoke, looking daggers at me from across the courtroom. My former friend, who was the most venomous, sneered at me contemptuously from the start of the proceedings to finish, hoping to intimidate me, but he didn't. It made me more resolute.

Telling the truth under oath was my goal, and that's precisely what I did. I told the judge the catalog printing was excellent, meeting the same high standard of quality the other catalogs produced by the printer had met. I was straightforward about everything. When I finished telling my story, I expected a vigorous cross-examination, but opposing counsel didn't ask me anything—not even one question.

At the end of the trial, the court ruled in favor of the printer and ordered Equipity to pay the print bill, but they never did. This didn't surprise me. Equipity remained adamantly self-righteous, despite the court's verdict. They never even tried to understand the printer's perspective. To do so would have required admitting culpability, which my former employers would never do.

The printer had done everything correctly but was cheated out of being fairly compensated. I continued to do business with them for years afterward, but they remained distrustful of Christian businessmen from that time forward. I couldn't fault them for feeling the way they did. Such behavior is common in the world of Christian ministries. Not paying for completed work occurs routinely. Vendors get stiffed repeatedly and are expected to take the loss gracefully. It's a sad commentary but a true one. Nearly everyone who has ever worked for a Christian ministry knows this is true.

In the evangelical world, confessing personal sin to God is highly valued, but making amends for wrongdoing is rarely mentioned. Somehow, people have come to believe God's forgiveness is all that is required. If they have it, they don't care about the people they've wronged along the way. They're forgiven; that's all that counts. Making restitution becomes an unspoken irrelevancy.

I wish this assessment was inaccurate, but my years of experience have shown me it's true. It's also one of the reasons why Christianity is unappealing to so many, especially to vendors who have experienced what Christian ministries—and the superstars who lead them—are really like.

In numerous similar situations, the lords and ladies of Christendom gerrymander the truth in their favor, justifying behavior that cannot be excused, victimizing their vendors in the process. But the vendors are not the only parties who end up being abused. Ordinary people—those who selflessly work for these ministries—become casualties as well.

Witnessing injustice firsthand grinds a person down. It constantly whittles away at a person's soul—one painful slice at a time—until little remains. Those who witness rationalized sin are left wounded, jaded, bitter and scornful. They become a shadow of their former selves, ceasing to serve the Lord from a joyful heart.

This is what happened to me. Each of these distasteful episodes debilitated me a little at a time. One by one, they chewed me up and spit me out, wounding me deeply in the process. To counter the negative effect, I had the consistent witness of what God had done in the life of my wife. My family became my joy. Working for Ludlow Randolph ceased to be a calling. It became my job—a necessary one, but a job nonetheless.

* * *

Once the trial was over, I expected my status to change from consultant to employee, but the topic wasn't even addressed. Although the trial had been a regular topic of conversation before it happened, when it was an event in the "rearview mirror," it was like it never occurred. It left me in limbo—where Cary Sullivan would spend eternity, according to my childhood priest.

After waiting for a month, I finally asked Dett about changing my status. He said I would have to wait a while longer because there was a company-wide hiring freeze.

"But Dett," I replied, "I've already been hired, haven't I? My salary would be the same as my monthly consulting retainer, so I don't see what the difference would be. Do you?"

"Not really," he said reassuringly. "But this is what I've been told. You'll just have to sit tight a little longer. That's all I can tell you."

"I didn't know there was a hiring freeze?" I asked.

"It's because business has been sluggish. We're not advertising the freeze, but it's real." To end my inquiry, he added. "These are Benny's orders. They've come straight from the top."

With no choice, I was forced to accept the status quo, but it gave me an uneasy, queasy feeling to do so.

* * *

By the end of the fiscal year, Ludlow Randolph had turned the corner, producing one of its most profitable years ever. Our division had done particularly well, so Dett was feeling his oats, strutting his stuff, and grinning like a Cheshire cat. Our success was attained because of an enormous sale Pete made to Grayson—one of Billy Graham's organizations. Acy also made a nice sale to the Crystal Cathedral, and I made one to Concerned Women for America. Dett took credit for each of our accomplishments, of course.

Seeing numerous new faces in the building the next time I was in Orlando, it was obvious the hiring freeze had been lifted. Walking into Dett's office and closing the door, I inquired about my employment status again.

This time, he didn't skirt the subject. Responding immediately, he announced, "Cole, we're going to keep things the way they are. You'll remain a full time consultant from now on. That's the way it's going to be."

His words stung, as he knew they would. By this time, however, I had learned to see through him. I knew exactly who he was, and he knew that I knew. By going against his word, he was essentially sticking it in my face, daring me to challenge him, which he knew I couldn't. I needed the job, and I wanted Barbara to continue being a stay-at-home mom. Because our nest egg couldn't be touched—not without incurring massive financial penalties—we lived from paycheck to paycheck, just like most American families. Missing a payday wasn't an option.

In my meeting with Dett, I knew any protestation would be counterproductive, so I simply nodded my head, stood, and walked out of his office. As I was leaving, with my back turned to him, I noticed his reflection in the mirror. Still seated behind his desk, he was sneering triumphantly. It was a look of pure malice—aimed directly at me—and it made me wince.

34

A Myriad of Wounded Believers

From that moment forward, nothing was the same for me at Ludlow Randolph. How could it be? When I saw Dett's malevolence reflected in the mirror, I knew there would be no future—not working for him.

Although I continued to do my job and actually enjoyed some aspects of it, I realized my situation was tenuous at best, despite Benny's assurances to the contrary. Dett would make certain Benny's desires would never came to fruition. What I witnessed—Dett's unmasked hatred—was real. It was a look of pure Evil, and it was chilling.

When I returned to Atlanta, I sat down with Barbara and told her the entire story. She had become my most trusted confidant, along with Pete. Having been in the entertainment industry for years, especially in the Mecca for cutthroats, Barbara had seen it all. Nothing surprised her—not even the duplicity of evangelicalism's hierarchy.

After listening to me patiently, she took a deep breath, looked deeply into my eyes and said; "Cole, you are good at what you do, maybe even great. You're very talented. Everybody knows it. It's why your clients trust you."

A little surprised, my astonishment must have shown.

Crinkling her nose, she said, "You don't realize that, do you?"

She was right; I didn't, but I began to ponder the validity of her affirmation.

"It's true, Cole. It's also why you get so many non-business calls from all over the country. Your friends know you'll be honest with them. Do you know how rare that is?"

Obviously, I didn't.

"Cole, this is why Dett keeps you around. He needs you to make him successful. His intentions aren't much different than Travis Keisler's. Travis needed you to vouch for Covenant Financial Planning, didn't he?"

"Yes, he did," I replied.

"So does Dett, but your straightforwardness is your greatest asset. It's also why I love you so much. You are trustworthy."

Barbara's validation touched me deeply, and we experienced a tender moment of connectedness across the kitchen counter.

"Remember to sell yourself first, Cole, not your product or your company," she admonished. "If you do, we will be fine, regardless of what Dett's intentions are. I promise we will."

Our conversation lasted a while longer, but I don't remember anything else she said. All I could think about was—"sell yourself first." The truth of this simple aphorism was riveting. It became etched on my brain, practically becoming my mantra, providing me with my marching orders to move forward. Never forgetting her pronouncement, this is exactly what I have done from that moment forward.

By the time Dett made his decision to get rid of me, I was well prepared, so was my family. Having been self-employed before made taking this risk a little easier. The potential rewards were substantially greater, which I was well aware of, but having five mouths to feed, increased my anxiety—that's for sure.

Although I put my faith in the Lord, it was still scary. With no alternative though, I sucked it up and went forward—just like I had been taught to do when I was a little boy growing up in Wellesley Massachusetts.

* * *

While being a consultant at Ludlow Randolph, I put together marketing packages for Bible products, which I loved. It was very rewarding work, and I had a knack for it. While working there, I also learned a great deal, which I was about to put to good use.

Because they employed me as a consultant and not as an employee, I didn't have a non-compete agreement with Ludlow Randolph like everybody else. This worked to my advantage after Dett released me. It meant I could compete against them. I could go head-to-head, using other publisher's products instead of Ludlow Randolph's, and there was no way for them to stop or impede me.

The downside to not being an employee was I had no rights while I was there. Dett could treat me any way he desired with impunity, and he did. The upside was Ludlow Randolph couldn't make any demands upon me once I was no longer consulting for them. I was free to do whatever I pleased, and that's exactly what I did, taking business from Dett's division. He thought my dismissal would hurt me financially, but I turned the table on him and prospered.

In my first year, working as an independent consultant, I developed and produced a project for Billy Graham, marketing the *Scofield Reference Bible* to his constituency, which was the only Bible project Dr. Graham ever promoted. I also developed the marketing program for the *Spirit-Filled Study Bible*, for Jack Hayford, which was the first charismatic study Bible ever produced. Doing work for Thomas Nelson, Dett's chief competitor; galled him—making my successful transition sweeter.

During my second year, I developed a marketing plan for *The Orthodox Study Bible*, helping sell 100,000 copies to Greek Orthodox and Antiochian Orthodox churches. Because my first projects for Cassidy Consulting were all Bible projects, I loved what I was doing. It was great work, and it kept me busy for a couple of years. Working for myself was hard, but by being my own boss, at least I didn't have to attend useless, boring meetings. The best part about being self-employed was no longer being under Dett's thumb. I didn't realize how toxic his malignant personality had become until he was removed from my life, freeing my soul.

In addition to my Bible projects, I secured numerous other jobs, including one that really helped establish my business long term. One of my former co-workers at Equipity, Jeremy Benson, accepted a job at the Southern Baptist Sunday-School Board in Nashville. Soon after being hired, the name of the organization was changed to LifeWay.

In his new position, Jeremy needed some marketing assistance, so he contacted me. Having had our differences in the past, I was surprised he even considered contacting me. When I went to see him, which I did out of curiosity, it seemed like his attitude had changed completely.

When he asked for my help, I considered not accepting the work, but when you start your own business you take what's offered. It's necessary to survive. At first, it was difficult to accept Jeremy's benevolence as genuine, but I soon realized that it was.

Despite my initial apprehension, working for him turned out to be a huge blessing. Suffice it to say his project generated enough income to establish my fledgling business and make Cassidy Consulting financially sound. From the seed capital I generated by working for him, I have sustained myself ever since, replenishing my operating funds year after year.

Jeremy's attitude toward me changed after he suffered the same kind of humiliation I had. He was driven out of Equipity. Experiencing degradation transformed him. Once he reestablished himself, he decided to reach out to me and be a blessing. In the process, he also became a good friend. I never suspected this would happen, but it did.

Reflecting, I asked myself: *Isn't this the way things are supposed to be? Isn't this the way Christians should behave? Shouldn't reconciliation be normal and not unusual? Shouldn't resolving a relationship always be something a believer strives to achieve?*

If Christianity is about anything, it's about forgiveness and reconciliation, which is exactly what happened between Jeremy and me. Nothing was resolved openly. He never verbalized anything, as I had hoped he would. Because it would have been out of place for me to initiate such a conversation—just like it would have been for me to say anything about Barbara's conversion—I remained silent. Nevertheless, Jeremy chose to make amends the best way he knew how—by helping me with my business.

For me, it was an answer to prayer I had not anticipated—from a source I never considered a possibility. As I continued to think about this, I could see God's hand at work, which was particularly gratifying. Having been blessed by Jeremy made me think of ways I could pass my good fortune on to others.

I also thought about how grateful I was that Barbara and I had reconciled. Having been married twice—both times to the same woman—I knew the difference between a good relationship and a bad one. My first marriage had been as miserable as my second one was fulfilling. The difference between the two was our ability to forgive and move forward, trusting each other completely.

Interestingly, we shared the same values both times, but they were better values the second time around. Faith played a key role in transforming our lives and making our second marriage a success.

As I began thinking about my career with a renewed mind, I had an epiphany. I was an expert at discerning duplicity and connivance in the underbelly of evangelicalism. Because of what I had seen, I could curse the darkness like a pro, and routinely did. But, other than counsel a few wounded friends, I hadn't done anything to help those who were victimized by religious abuse.

I realized I needed to do more. I needed to help wounded believers reconnect with God. I needed to light a candle and provide illumination for those who had been hurt. I needed to tell them God was not the author of their abuse—narcissistic, self-serving religious leaders were. When I realized this, I knew exactly what God wanted from me. I had more purpose than just to provide for my family. I had a ministry to perform.

Father Dunnigan was right. I did have an outstanding brain, and I needed to use it wisely—to serve God's purposes—not just my own. What this meant in practical terms I had no idea, but I stopped resenting my career, knowing it afforded me numerous opportunities to help wounded people in crisis.

I certainly hadn't been looking for a purpose, but I found one. Maybe it's the reason why my life has unfolded the way it has. When I told Barbara about the changes that had come over me, she cried, telling me things that provided me with further validation—tender things better left unsaid.

When I informed Pete, he was equally supportive; so was Acy. In fact, both told several of their friends about me—those who had been abused while working for a ministry. As a result, people began to call, and I was always available to help.

* * *

I maintained this good, purposeful attitude until the fateful night when I learned about Crystal Moss's false accusation, instigated by Dett. Because I had been doing the right thing, it was particularly difficult to accept being slandered.

Having to let it go wasn't easy. I was forced to seek counseling to deal with my anger. Barbara was so mad she even joined me a time or two. Being hurt—wounded by a false accusation—I saw a therapist for quite a while before I made any progress. I began to think Pete might have been right. Maybe it would have been better to leave the whole thing alone, but I just couldn't do that. Being wronged, it wasn't part my Irish nature to just let it go—not without a fight.

During a breakthrough session, about nine months after my fateful trip to New York, my counselor said, "Who understands your feelings the best?"

"My wife, I suppose."

Shaking his head, Dr. Petersen said, "What about the Lord?"

"Yes, of course," I replied—a little condescendingly.

"I'm serious," he asserted. "Think about it. Christ was falsely accused; arrested on false charges; and convicted, despite being innocent. Then, He was scoffed at, laughed at, spit upon, stripped naked, tortured, and hung on a cross to die—all by deeply deceived, self-serving religious leaders, whose standing in society was threatened by Him. How could He not understand how you feel?"

I was stunned. I had never thought about my situation in terms like this, but when I was challenged to do so, the sting from Crystal and Dett's defamation began to diminish. Within a short period, my anger disappeared. Everything made sense, and I became capable of forgiving them—Dett, Crystal, and Benny. Once I did, I was able to move forward with my life, which flourished.

If anything, Crystal-gate proved to be a blessing because it helped me identify more completely with those who have been falsely accused—just like I had been. It certainly didn't restore my faith in Mankind, but it definitely deepened my relationship with the Lord.

I was free, doing exactly what I had been created to do. Those who hurt me thought they had won, but this was an illusion. Trusting in their duplicity, each was destined to pay a heavy price for their actions—not just for what happened to me but also for a lifetime of abusing others.

35

To Live in That Much Fear

Despite not having worked for Ludlow Randolph for nearly five years, some of my business still originated from leads provided by its sales team, especially from Pete. Having worked together on marketing projects many times, Pete and Acy understood my value. I helped them maximize their sales by providing marketing tools to reach the end user. Often needing my help, even Dett provided me with leads.

Once, Ludlow Randolph published a book by Bill Gaither—the renowned Christian musician. The book bombed, and Gaither wanted to return nearly 10 thousand copies to Ludlow Randolph, which nearly gave Benny a heart attack. Requiring my help to salvage a disastrous situation, Dett asked me to visit the Gaithers. Having successfully put Crystal-gate behind me, I accepted the challenge, traveling to Alexandria Indiana, at Dett's request.

Meeting with Gaither and his assistant, Thomas Lorz, I suggested we tie the book to a CD, featuring songs from the same era as the book, and sell them as a package, making it a unique product. Listening carefully, Bill said, "That's a great idea, Cole. We're not going to do it, but I like the way you think." He added, "We'll be doing some marketing in about a year. When we do, can we call on you to help us?"

"Sure," I said, disappointed, thinking nothing would come from our meeting. Shortly thereafter, I left—convinced I would never hear from them again.

Because I generated so much of my business from Pete's leads, I accompanied him on numerous trips to ministries in his territory, which was the Eastern half of the nation. Once, we visited Ernest Angsley. When we arrived at Angsley's headquarters, in Akron, Ohio, the first thing I noticed was a large sculpture of a lovely young woman. It was located outside the main entrance. Looking heavenward, she had an angelic expression. Christ was the second statue in the setting. He was kneeling beside her, looking up to her in a beseeching, imploring way, which seemed a little odd to me. It appeared as if Jesus was praying to the woman, which made me feel uneasy.

When the implication of the scene dawned on me, I stopped dead in my tracks, turned to Pete and pointed. "Who is this woman supposed to be, Mary?"

Pausing for a moment, Pete replied, "No, It's Angsley's wife who died a long time ago."

"What?" I said, obviously surprised. "You're kidding?"

"Nope," he replied, as a slight smile crossed his face.

Perplexed, I asked, "Shouldn't the woman be praying to Christ, rather than the other way around?"

"That's what I thought the first time I saw it, too," he said.

As my face grimaced, I was about to ask another question, but Pete cut me off, saying, "There is a lot stranger stuff than that going on around here. Come on. I don't want to be late for our meeting."

With this, he picked up his pace, and we walked straight to the pastor's office, where we were ushered in promptly. Once we sat down,

Pete tried to focus the conversation on business, but Angsley repeatedly changed the subject. He was infuriated by a rival preacher's insinuation that Angsley might be gay. Evidently, the man intended to "out" the TV evangelist.

Sounding very much like he did on TV—Angsley pointed his finger, wagging it threateningly. "If he says I'm a homosexual," he said, "I'm going to sue him. I promise I will."

"I don't blame you," Pete responded, hoping to get the conversation back on track.

"I mean it Pete," Angsley fumed, in his pastoral singsong manner. Repeating himself numerous times, he continued, "I'll sue him, so help me God, I will."

Not having a clue about what was behind Angsley's complaint—nor any idea about its merit—I didn't pay as much attention as I normally would have. I kept thinking; *If he's such a great faith healer, why can't he put some hair back on his head?* The rug he was wearing was one of the worst I had ever seen. I kept wondering if Angsley realized how ridiculous he looked.

I don't remember the product Pete was promoting, but I do remember we had to watch snippets of Angsley' program as part of our presentation. When the healing segment began, Angsley would tap the afflicted person on the head. Immediately, he or she would fall back—slain in the Spirit. During his program, everybody he touched was slain in the Spirit and required being caught by two strong men to ensure nobody was injured falling backward. Where this came from in the Scriptures, I'll never know, but I haven't been interested enough to inquire about it either. Feeling uncomfortable the entire time we were there, I was thankful when we left.

Pete was unsuccessful in trying to obtain business from Angsley, and I was grateful he didn't. While we were there, Angsley spoke exclusively to Pete, never even bothering to make occasional eye contact with me. It was as if I wasn't there, which was fine with me. Although I would have done the work, if I had been asked, I was relieved that it never became an option. Angsley never allowed Pete to complete his presentation, interrupting him repeatedly. Instead, Angsley kept talking about the man who had been slandering him. I was grateful to get on the highway, headed for New York. The entire episode was one of the weirdest I have ever experienced.

* * *

Two days later, we met with leaders from the Salvation Army in Manhattan. Diligently working to help real people with real problems, these selfless Christians made the work of many others seem trivial by comparison. There wasn't an ounce of pretentiousness in anybody I met, which I would have recognized because I ended up working for them for many years.

The following day, we ate lunch with the leadership of the Peale Center for Christian Living—Dr. Norman Vincent Peale's ministry, located in Pawling, New York. Dr. Peale, who was already ninety-three at the time, greeted us, when we arrived. Warm, friendly, and gracious, he smiled, spontaneously displaying the unbridled exuberance that had been his trademark for more than half a century. With his wife by his side, he escorted Pete and me on a tour of the facility before leaving us to attend to other business. As he walked away, I understood why leaders worldwide sought him out for advice so often. His joy for life, as well as his modest, humble demeanor, was more than appealing; it was contagious. I liked the man immediately and never changed my opinion of him.

After Dr. Peale left, Pete and I sat down to meet with his marketing team. The leader, Kirby Johnson—a tall, trim, older man—took charge of the meeting immediately. Being very candid—a rare characteristic for people in his position—he said the ministry needed to use some "outside product" to augment Dr. Peale's books, which were still popular but quite dated. This was music to our ears. Pete had numerous suggestions for ways to help. With me there to explain how to produce an offering in a way that would generate an excellent response, we showed them how working with us would increase their cash flow.

Thrilled with our proposal, we made plans to start working together immediately. Within three months, we rolled out a substantial offering of Ludlow Randolph products, which supplemented the works of Dr. Peale. Our plan worked, generating additional income to further the Peale Center's work.

During a follow up meeting some months later, Kirby became even more candid about the state of the ministry. He said, "Peale Center has no transition plan, if the inconceivable happens—if Dr. Peale dies."

"You're kidding?" I asked, genuinely surprised by his candor.

"No, I'm not. There's no transitional strategy. So far, nobody has even brought it up. The possibility of his passing is unimaginable, unthinkable."

"Well, somebody had better start thinking about it, Kirby," I admonished. "He just celebrated his ninety-fourth birthday a few weeks ago."

"I know, Cole," Kirby replied, but he was unwilling to pursue the subject any further. Not one person at the ministry was willing to discuss what they planned to do when Norman Vincent Peale died, which he did a year later.

In the interim, I continued to develop projects, which were quite profitable, generating substantial revenue by selling new releases from Ludlow Randolph to augment Dr. Peale's books. Our working arrangement was a win-win for everybody, which insured its continuation. At least, I thought this would be the case.

Because sales had been sagging in Dett's division, he was quite willing for Pete and Acy to use me to generate new business. I even met with Dett in Orlando at his office several times. Because he always made his numbers, his standing remained high in Benny's eyes, but that particular year Dett was going to miss his goal badly, which he realized several months in advance. Making matters worse, Dett became sick. He was diagnosed with cancer and began chemotherapy, immediately losing all of the hair on his body.

Because he had thick hair, I was startled the next time I saw him. Not addressing his sickness, other than to tell him I was praying for his complete recovery, we met for several hours about various projects. Sitting across from him—just as I had done when I was a full time consultant years earlier—I noticed that neither his eyebrows nor his eyelashes had fallen out, which seemed a little odd. He hadn't lost any weight either, and his color was good, which probably meant he was winning his war against the dreaded disease.

* * *

About a month after my meeting with Dett, Pete called. He was laughing so hard it was difficult for me to figure out what was so funny, especially since I had begun laughing too. His mirth was that contagious. When he finally calmed down, Pete told me Dett didn't have cancer after all. He never did. It was all a ruse—just like Prudence Latham's cancer had been a hoax a decade earlier at Living Water, although for an entirely different reason.

Knowing he was going to miss the bottom line in sales, Dett feigned his illness to keep his job, which probably was unnecessary, given how tight he was with Benny. The HR department at Ludlow Randolph discovered Dett's perfidy, when they became curious about why they never received any medical bills to pay for his chemotherapy. Once they discovered the truth, they went to Benny, demanding that Dett be terminated.

Knowing his future hung in the balance Dett made a bold move. Dropping everything, he flew to Lynchburg Virginia, for an emergency meeting with Jerry Falwell—Benny's favorite evangelist. While there, Dett told Dr. Falwell that he had never actually accepted Christ as his Savior. Praying with Falwell, Dett invited Christ into his life, returning to Orlando the following morning as a new believer.

Walking into Benny's office, Dett confessed his cancer farce, blaming it on his unredeemed heart, which was desperately wicked. Asking his benefactor for one more chance, now that he was a Christian, Dett promised to never do anything that devious again, which ended the crisis. Dodging a bullet, Dett kept his position.

When Pete heard about the story, he couldn't wait to tell me. Neither of us believed Dett's conversion was real for a second, which is why we found it so humorous. Later, when I told Barbara the story, I thought she would laugh too—just like I had—but she didn't. It didn't tickle her in the least. It made her sad.

Looking at me, she said, "It must be awful to live with that much fear."

Her response couldn't have surprised me more, but it also made me think differently about Dett, who had been wasting his life for years pursuing worthless goals.

36

He's Not Going Anywhere

Making plans with Kirby and his associates at the Peale Center for Christian Living for the following year, I signed a contract and received a purchase order for more than $100,000 worth of business. A short time after Dr. Peale's death, however, there was a changing of the guard at the Peale Center. Kirby was discharged unceremoniously, which happens quite often at Christian ministries. It also meant I had to make an unplanned trip to New York to become acquainted with his replacement.

Meeting with the new marketing director soon thereafter—a man who was introduced to me as a "young lion from Madison Avenue"—I explained in detail the projects his predecessor and I had put in place. Having worked on the creative aspects of one project for a while, it was close to being launched. The new man, whose name was Reggie Buffington, paid close attention to my presentation and thanked me for making the trip to meet with him in person.

A few days after our meeting, I received a registered letter from

Reggie stating that the ministry was taking another direction. They were no longer interested in continuing with the projects produced by Cassidy Consulting.

In a return letter, I thanked Reggie for his time and agreed to stop the projects. In this letter, I also asked for the "kill fee," which was part of my signed contract. It was for $35,000. I signed the letter and sent it to him FedEx.

The following morning, the phone rang, as I suspected it would. It was Reggie, and his voice was an octave higher than when I met with him.

He said, "Cole, I just received your letter, and it's very shocking."

"Why are you shocked, Reggie?" I asked with feigned surprise.

"Because we can't afford to pay you $35,000; that's why," he responded contemptuously.

"But the kill fee is part of our signed agreement," I replied, amiably.

"Well, I don't care if it is or not. We're not going to do your project, and we're not going to pay you the money, either," he stated, drawing a hard line in the sand. "I'll send you a check for $5,000 today, and we'll call it even."

"No way," I replied, as the conversation became contentious. Now that the gloves were off, I added, "I have a contract and have honored its terms. I insist that you honor the terms as well."

Knowing he was in a tight spot, he implored, "Be reasonable, Cole. I'll send you $5,000, and everybody will win."

"Everybody will win?" I queried. "How will I win? I've already spent more than that for a graphic artist and photographer. I've also committed my time to these projects, which I can't replace." Taking a breath, I added, "This isn't going to get ugly, is it?"

"That depends on you, Cole," he replied. "Not me."

"That's not true," I corrected. "I'm committed to honoring the contract. You're the one who intends to breach it." A moment later, I added, "I won't have to take you to court to get my money, will I?"

When I said this, there was a lengthy pause on the other end. Finally, Reggie said, "The Bible says it's a sin to sue your Christian brother. It's better to just take the loss and accept it graciously. You know the Bible says that, right?"

This was the ace of trumps for a ministry, which Reggie placed on the table triumphantly. Whenever a ministry refused to pay for work—or intended to disregard a contract—this response was automatic. Ministries pulled out this biblical passage, which was calculated to end a potential conflict before it developed. By saying it was a sin to sue a fellow Christian, the lords and ladies, or their surrogates like Reggie, used guilt to achieve their ends, while carefully avoiding their role, which was to meet their contractual obligations.

To the luminaries of evangelicalism, it was a sin for a vendor to sue them, but it was never a sin for them to breach a contract. Having gone through this before, I had always taken the loss, but I decided not to be a victim this time. I knew Reggie's purpose was to manipulate me into accepting a substantial financial loss, but I was not about to allow the "young lion from Madison Avenue" to get the best of me.

Responding to his question, I said, "Yes, Reggie, I'm well aware of this passage, but you have a contractual obligation, which I insist you honor."

Sneering, Reggie said contemptuously, "This conversation is going nowhere. Go ahead and sue. If you do, you won't get a dime." With this, he slammed down the phone.

When he disconnected, my hands were shaking. I hated confrontations like this; they were always upsetting. Normally, I tried to avoid them at all costs, but I wasn't willing to be cheated again. Those days were over. The whole episode made me sick, but with my back against the wall, I felt like I had no choice other than to press forward. When I told Barbara about my intentions, she supported me all the way. So did Pete.

* * *

In an effort to increase his profit margin, Benny stopped printing Bibles in the United States, choosing to produce them in China, at a substantially lower cost. Negotiating to maximize his earnings—always desirous of enhancing his bottom line—Benny traveled to the Orient several times. Being able to see the world was a bonus, including eating delicacies he had never experienced.

Unfortunately, his penchant for adventure proved to be his Waterloo. While in China, eating at an out-of-the-way restaurant, Benny was served meat from an infected bovine and developed Creutzfeldt-Jakob disease—an extremely rare degenerative brain disorder—commonly called Mad Cow Disease.

Symptoms from the disease didn't appear until after Benny returned to Orlando. At first, his condition was a carefully held secret, but this didn't last long. His physical deterioration—both physical and mental—wouldn't permit it.

As Benny's disease progressed, he experienced memory lapses, and his ability to think became impaired. Frequently confused and disoriented, his escalating dementia became obvious, producing agitation and personality disintegration. Coupled with involuntary muscle spasms and continuous writhing in his arms and legs, Benny quickly lost his ability to function normally, both physically and mentally.

His demise was swift. The Benny I had known for so many years ceased to exist. Delusional, he was forced to abandon the pursuit of his Christian empire, spending his final weeks in a hospital bed. It was a tragic end—one that gave pause to many—putting justified fear of God in their hearts.

With Benny's unplanned and abrupt departure from Ludlow Randolph, Dett lost his protector. Without his "Godfather" boss to shield him, Dett's enemies circled, waiting for an opportunity to strike, and there was nothing Dett could do to prevent them from doing so.

* * *

A few weeks after my confrontation with Reggie Buffington, I retained a lawyer from Poughkeepsie NY—a man recommended by one of Kirby's assistants who had not yet been terminated. Knowing the fate that awaited my friend, he loathed the "young lion from Madison Avenue" as much as I did.

The lawyer I hired was a really nice guy. Being a friend of the Peale Center's legal representative, my lawyer assured me the case would never go to trial. Feeling relieved, I left matters entirely in his hands, knowing I needed to find a new source of business quickly.

Several weeks later, my "mole" inside the ministry called, barely able to contain his laughter. He said that a big fat cop—with a pinch between his cheeks and gums—had just showed up at the Peale Center with a summons, which had been issued for Norman Vincent Peale, involving the case—Cassidy Consulting v. Peale Center for Christian Living.

He said that when the receptionist greeted the officer, she said, "Dr. Peale isn't here."

"Where is he?" the cop demanded.

"He's over yonder, in the cemetery," she said. "If you want to see him, you could deliver the summons there, I suppose. He's not going anywhere," she added mischievously.

When my friend informed me of this, he laughed so hard he began to cough and had a difficult time stopping. As I listened to the story, my mouth was wide open. Aghast, I was as mortified as I can ever remember being. I couldn't believe my lawyer made such an egregious *faux pas.*

At the ministry, Reggie Buffington was particularly amused. It raised his level of confidence about winning the case. He assumed a buffoon was handling my lawsuit—an assumption I began to share.

In spite of looking foolish by summoning a dead man, my lawyer ended up being quite skilled when he met with counsel from the Peale Center soon thereafter. When the meeting was complete, Peale Center's lawyer called Reggie and informed him that if the case went to trial, Peale Center would lose.

With no choice in the matter, Reggie made a settlement offer of $25,000, which I accepted, ending the matter. Although I definitely stood up for myself, I also burned a bridge at the Peale Center—a bridge I didn't want to burn. Reggie didn't last long after that. "Young lions" rarely do.

If he had allowed me to continue—like he should have—we both would have been successful, but this wasn't his style. Because the marketing ideas were mine and not his, he sabotaged the project, costing both of us dearly. When the dust settled, he was out of a job, and I had lost a major client.

* * *

Once Benny was out of the picture, wasting away from an incurable disease, Dett's enemies at Ludlow Randolph wasted no time in dealing with their long-time nemesis.

One Monday morning, the same day Benny breathed his last, Dett showed up for work and was greeted by two security guards who wouldn't permit him to enter his office. Instead, they escorted him to the boardroom where a dozen senior members of the staff were waiting.

Once Dett was seated, without even being offered a cup of coffee, the acting-president of Ludlow Randolph read a carefully prepared list of Dett's corporate malfeasance, which included nearly everything except for Crystal-gate. Dett's castigation was worthy of a censure by the United States Senate. He wanted to get up and leave but that wasn't an option. To have done so might have put his severance package at risk. He was not willing to do that. Although Crystal Moss' dismissal didn't warrant severance, Dett's did. Being an executive, it was part of his contract. Therefore, he listened, as one member of the staff after the other excoriated him for his reprehensible conduct.

When they were finished thirty minutes later, they didn't even allow Dett to defend himself. The acting-president ended the meeting by calling security, informing them that Dett was to be escorted out of the building immediately. They told Dett that his belongings would be couriered to his house; he wouldn't even be allowed to set foot in his office.

As Dett was escorted out of Ludlow Randolph—never to return—several people clapped, followed by quite a few more. Disgraced, Dett wasn't the least bit defiant as he walked the green mile Crystal had been forced to march several years earlier.

Ludlow Randolph's Uriah Heep had finally been undone. Dett suspected his time at Ludlow Randolph was ending, but he never thought his termination to be as humiliating as it was. Ludlow Randolph had been his entire life. Yet, not one good thing he had done was mentioned. This was a crushing defeat, taking his breath away, wilting his legs.

When he reached his car, he vomited before he could drive off. Since numerous people were watching his departure from their windows, he had hoped to leave before becoming sick, but this wasn't to be. It added appreciably to his humiliation. Shaking badly, he had difficulty placing his key in the ignition before driving out of the Ludlow Randolph parking lot for the last time—a defeated man.

37

We All Have to Start Someplace

Being in business for yourself is wonderful—except for the times that it isn't. Unfortunately, those times can be numerous. The good news is nobody can fire you; the bad news is it is difficult to allocate quality time away from the office to enjoy life—free from business concerns. Your office is always with you. It's the voice in your head—the voice in the back of your mind that is fearful of economic insecurity. When you don't have enough work, or your work will soon end, it whispers; *the phone will never ring again. You're going to be out of work, out of luck, and out of money.* Sometimes, the voice shouts, producing bone-chilling fear—like how I felt the day I learned about the Jim Bakker scandal at PTL.

The more responsibility you have the louder the voice becomes. There are periods when it never stops, while at other times, it almost disappears. But it doesn't, not really; it's always there. For some, it can be debilitating, but it never was for me. Having a strong survival instinct, it drove me forward, never allowing me to take business for granted. Perhaps this is why I survived for so long, while so many of my friends have been unable to survive, working for themselves.

There are also times when tranquility reigns—long periods when everything seems to run smoothly, almost monotonously. You stay busy, but it's with projects you can count on. Occasionally, the action is nonstop, but nothing happens out of the ordinary. When you're self-employed, these are your best times.

Then, when you least expect it, your situation changes, making you long for the tranquility of a monotonous routine. This is exactly what happened the summer after I lost the account at Peale Center for Christian Living. I was clueless about where to get my next major client—a fact the voice in my head reminded me of repeatedly. The Scriptures tell us not to worry, but it's difficult when you work for yourself, especially when you have a large family to feed.

Because I had been self-employed for so long, I was well known throughout the Christian community as a "go-to" person. When there were jobs that needed to be done—jobs that were outside the parameters of what most were willing or capable of doing, I was called in to help. Making a living by doing odds and ends, my business was surprisingly profitable, providing my family with more than adequate income, nearly all of the time.

My settlement from the Peale Center sustained us for a while, but a family of five has substantial monthly expenses. I had several small ongoing projects, but I needed a major client to remain solvent. When things got tight, the Lord always provided. Despite knowing this, I understood why the Israelites murmured in the wilderness. As often than not, I did the same thing.

When I did, revealing my insecurities and apprehensiveness, Barbara would tell me how confident she was in my ability to provide, which was exactly what I needed to hear. Now reconciled for several years, I don't know how I was able to survive, when she was with Jeffrey. I couldn't imagine what my life would be like without her, which I let her know routinely. I didn't know how to cherish her the first time around, but I definitely learned my lesson and was able to do so the second time.

* * *

After he was fired, Dett didn't fare well. The sickness he experienced the day of his termination didn't get better. It got worse. The stress from the pressure he felt turned into diverticulitis, producing stomach cramps and diarrhea. Although excruciatingly painful, he refused to seek medical help, which was a mistake, nearly as disastrous as the one Benny made by dining on contaminated beef sweetbreads.

Dett developed an abscess on his colon and had blood in his stool—a situation that couldn't be ignored. Developing a high fever, he was rushed to the hospital, where he had emergency surgery to drain a huge abscess from his abdomen that had burst, producing sepsis. For more than a week, his life hung in the balance. Unlike his contrived case of cancer, this was real.

Despite talking the talk, while never walking the walk, Dett couldn't con his way out of this. God finally had his attention.

His situation eventually stabilized, but the complications from the diverticulitis required months of healing before he regained his strength. During this time of recuperation, Dett had plenty of time to reflect about his life, which must have been as emotionally painful as his disease was physically debilitating.

* * *

Despite all of my fretful worrying, I still didn't have a major client. Then, one day out of the blue, I received a call from Bill Gaither, requesting me to fly to Indiana and talk with him about marketing a new video concept he had developed—*The Homecoming Series.* When I met with him nearly a year earlier, he had promised to call; but I never believed he would—not really. I had actually forgotten about it. Fortunately, he hadn't.

Seizing the opportunity, I flew to Indiana the following day and met with him—as well as with his assistant, Thomas Lorz. After discussing marketing strategies for his products the entire morning, we ate at a local diner for lunch. It was a Redneck hangout, which was Bill's favorite place—complete with patrons who smoked and parked their 18-wheelers outside. There were also farmers wearing bib overalls. It was great. The ambiance was unpretentious and friendly—just like Bill and his assistant. I loved everything about my day with them, including the food, which was hearty and delicious, especially the banana pudding.

Because their music was Southern Gospel, it was a little too folksy for my tastes—just like it would have been for any Irish Catholic from Wellesley, Massachusetts. Because it helped pay the bills though, I listened. Eventually, I came to love it. Not nearly as snooty as me, Barbara loved it from day one.

Bill wanted me to create a direct-mail kit for their second video from the *Homecoming Series*, which I did; but I also encouraged Bill and Thomas to create a product catalog as well. At first reluctant, they finally agreed a few months later. Starting with a digest-size, 16-page catalog, we mailed it twice a year to their entire list, which at the time contained nearly 75,000 names.

From the first time we met, people working for the Gaithers and I hit it off; and I became an integral part of their operation. Unlike most Christian superstars, Bill was as down to earth as he could possibly be. By far the most creative Christian musician in the industry, which even my wife acknowledged, he possessed none of the pompous, narcissistic or self-serving character qualities I had come to expect from such leaders.

Genuine, pleasant, and humorous, Bill was the same in private as he was on stage, which made him fun to be around.

We had success from the first catalog we mailed and built the Gaither list substantially over the years. I not only had a major client again, I was prosperous and extremely busy for many years, which helped me make a career out of Cassidy Consulting. It also helped quiet that fearful voice in my head. By the fifth year of doing their catalog and other creative work, the Gaither list had grown to over 650,000 buyers; and we mailed a full-size, 64-page catalog—filled with hundreds of products from the *Homecoming Collection*.

Now mailing quarterly, I was so busy with Gaither business I had precious, little time for other clients. Like Ronald Reagan, Bill Gaither believed in the trickle-down theory. Being part of everything he printed, I benefited from this association substantially. Even better, I loved every minute of the work I did.

* * *

Things were going pretty well for Cisco. I was a blessed man, and I knew it. With my marriage restored and my business thriving, as I reflected on the past, I could see that those who tried to hurt me had not fared nearly as well. Shortly after Crystal-gate, it looked like I would be destroyed, but I wasn't. Although this was my perception at the time, it was just an illusion—a snapshot in time that was only accurate for a moment.

The blessings that followed were real and substantial. God had been faithful, restoring me completely—both personally and professionally. Even better, I learned to pass my blessing on to others. Having begun my career in the classroom, being a teacher was part of my nature. I loved helping others; especially those who needed to learn how to recover from being abused by Christian ministries.

Helping them became my passion. I loved helping wounded Christians regain their spiritual footing. Sadly, there always seemed to be a steady stream of those who were used, abused, and discarded by the lords and ladies of evangelicalism. Their stories were heartbreaking, although each seemed eerily similar.

As far as I knew, Dett remained unemployed. He required lengthy rehabilitation to get back on his feet. Benny, who was one of the luminaries of evangelicalism, had been acclaimed far and wide as a hero of the faith, but Dett never reached that plateau.

I often thought of Benny. For a man who was as talented and capable as he was, his grim demise was an apt reminder of just how frail human beings are.

As for Crystal, none of us ever heard from her again. She was gone—never to reenter our lives. I didn't care. After so many years, she became little more than a distant memory—except for the scent of her perfume, that is. Its pungent offensiveness still lingers in my mind as an unpleasant reminder of her toxic nature.

When I reflected about Crystal-gate, which wasn't often, I realized there is never a right way to do a wrong thing. The failure of Dett and Crystal's charade became a poignant reminder of just how foolish folly can be. What looked like victory to these malefactors became the exact opposite, which hindsight clearly revealed. I experienced the triumph of Good over Evil, along with the fruitful qualities it produced, which others could see by the way I lived my life, including my wife, my children, and my friends, especially Pete, and Acy.

Although Pete stayed with Ludlow Randolph, Acy eventually moved on, becoming a voiceover artist. He moved to Manhattan and became very successful, working as the off-camera voice for many TV commercials.

* * *

One afternoon, as I was working in my office, winding up things for the day, the phone rang.

"Cole Cassidy," I answered—just like always.

"Hi, Cole," the voice on the other end responded. It was Dett. Having heard his voice thousands of times before, I would have recognized it anywhere.

"Dett," I exclaimed. "Are you okay?"

"I'm getting better, but it's been a rough road," he admitted. Then he said, "I'm in Atlanta. I had a job interview today, and I wondered if we could get together for coffee in the morning?"

"Sure, I can do that. I'd love to," I replied without hesitation.

Setting up a time and a place, we made a commitment to meet. When I told Barbara, she was as surprised by his call as I was, but she also thought something good might come from it.

The next morning, when I walked into the Starbucks on West Paces Ferry at 9 a.m., Dett was already seated, waiting for me. When I saw him, I was stunned. He was gaunt and pale—a shadow of his former self. More than anything, this confirmed how serious his sickness had been. Although taken aback, I never altered my facial expression, so he had no idea how startled I actually was.

Walking to the table, I smiled as Dett stood, and we greeted each other. After ordering a grande vanilla cappuccino, I joined him at the table, where he had been sipping his black coffee, waiting patiently for me to return.

After discussing his recovery and plans for the future, Dett's face turned somber. It was obvious he had something on his mind, so I stopped talking and waited for him to tell me what it was.

Gathering himself, he finally looked at me and said, "Cole, while I was at Ludlow Randolph, I did a lot of things I'm not proud of. If I hurt you in any way, I'm sorry."

There it was—right in front of me. Dett was apologizing for trying to destroy my life. But it was a generic apology—not a frank admission that he had slandered me with Crystal's false accusation. As I looked at him, I could see how nervous he was. He knew exactly what he had done, but he couldn't be completely forthright. He didn't own enough of his soul to do so. This was as far as he could go and no further. I understood his limitation.

As I sat across from him, I had to decide if his apology would be enough or if I would require more, but thinking about how I would respond lasted no more than a second. It all happened in the twinkling of an eye.

Having made my decision, I replied. "You did hurt me, Dett. You hurt me very badly . . . and for a long time."

Dett just nodded his head, acknowledging he knew what I said was true.

Then, with tears welling in my eyes, I added, "I forgive you."

Surprised that I had responded so quickly and easily, he looked at me appraisingly. Then, he asked, "Do you mean it, Cole?"

"I do. From this moment forward, everything between us is square. I promise it is."

He just nodded his head. With a smile on his face, he said, "Thank you." Then, filled with emotion, his lip quivered and he began to tear up as well.

Because there were so many people looking at us, we felt uncomfortable. So, we wiped our eyes with our napkins and did our best to clean up our act. In spite of its brevity, this was one of the most powerful, healing moments in my life. Although he didn't say so, I suspect it was for him as well.

Later, after leaving Dett at Starbucks, I called Pete to relate the story about what had happened. His reaction was the exact opposite of mine. Pete said, "That apology doesn't mean a thing. If it was legit, he would have been specific. He didn't even mention Crystal Moss, did he?"

"No."

"Then, it wasn't real."

"I understand what you're saying, Pete. I really do, but this is as far as Dett could go—at least for now." Measuring my words, I added, "The Lord accepted you and me exactly where we were. It's no different for Dett. I know this isn't as much as he should have done, but it's a start. I never expected him to apologize at all, did you?"

"No, I didn't," Pete conceded.

After remaining quiet for a long time, I added, "We all have to begin somewhere. This is Dett's beginning—not his end."

Although I didn't convince Pete, as I knew I wouldn't, the seed for their reconciliation had been planted. After we disconnected, something else crossed my mind. Pete and I had just completed a lengthy conversation about Dett, but neither of us had cussed—not once. Perhaps we were beginning to make some progress as well.

Conclusion

The Lords and Ladies of Evangelicalism

Brittany has just begun her junior year at the University of Georgia. An excellent student, she has maintained her Hope Scholarship, which saved Barbara and me a small fortune. She's also in line to become the next president of her sorority, Alpha Chi Omega.

Brianna chose to go to Auburn, despite my pleading for her to go to college in Athens with her sister. Fortunately, her ill-formed decision only lasted one semester. Finishing her freshman year at Perimeter College, while living at home, she transferred to UGA and now lives in an apartment with Brittany. A decent student, Brianna doesn't have a scholarship, which means our expenses for her are substantial, but that's okay. Both girls have turned out to be beautiful young ladies, inside and out. Since they look more like their mom than their dad, this has helped. I see more of Barbara in them as each day passes, which delights me.

We did have some trouble with Chance about a year ago—quite a bit actually. Going to high school at Marist, once his sisters were gone, he started acting out—drinking a lot—becoming defiant, surly, and angry.

Instead of becoming scolding or punitive, Barbara wisely brought him to counseling, which eventually involved all three of us.

Chance had never been outwardly resentful toward me, especially since his sisters always supported me. Whenever a family conflict arose, the girls regularly had my back, and he was never willing to cross them. Smart boy. Once they were out of the house, however, it was a different story.

In counseling, we discovered Chance had been harboring substantial resentment that he blamed on me. He wanted to know who he really was. He wanted to know about his father, Jeffrey, but he thought his mother and I would be opposed. Although nearly a dozen years had passed since they had been forced to flee Las Vegas to assume new identities, we continued to keep this part of his life a secret.

With our son in crisis though, all of that changed. We needed to be forthcoming about his past. In counseling, with his mother and me present, Barbara told him everything, which he deserved to know. It was a long and painful session, especially for my wife. She told me I didn't need to come, but I insisted upon being there. This was my family, including Chance. It was my responsibility to be present and to support both of them, especially her.

Barbara confessed everything. Although it was a grueling session, it was also deeply cathartic. After listening to her story, asking numerous questions to fill in the gaps from what he remembered as a child, Chance felt better about things.

Having sat quietly through the meeting, I finally made a suggestion. "Chance," I said, "why don't the three of us fly out to Vegas and let your mom show you everything she has just explained. If you're up for it, maybe we'll even take a drive to Reno and try and discover everything we can about your father's murder." Looking at Barbara, I asked, "What do you think?"

She looked at me like I was crazy—not at all certain this was a good idea. Because the counselor thought it would provide Chance with the closure he needed to get back on track, we decided to make the trip. Chance loved the idea.

As I told my wife repeatedly after that, we had been living in the shadow of fear for too long. It was time to come out and walk in the light.

Making the trip soon thereafter, we discovered Trixie's husband was dead. Like Jeffrey, this gangster had been murdered in exactly the same way. Jeffrey's probable murderer had been dead nearly five years, but we had no idea this had happened.

Realizing our reason to keep the past hidden was no longer relevant, and hadn't been for years, we felt liberated, which Chance could see. At first, it was more difficult for Barbara and me to accept this change in our situation than it was for Chance. Having to always watch our backs had become a way of life for us. It felt funny to be free, but it also felt good. It was like a physical impediment had ceased to exist, allowing full movement. No longer hobbled because of the past, we felt like dancing for joy.

Best of all, the trip did wonders for Chance. In his eyes, despite everything, Jeffrey had become heroic. Now at peace, our son's acting out behavior abated, which was the outcome his mother and I desired. Within a few months, Chance started dating a really cute girl who kept him in line throughout the remainder of his high school years, much to our relief.

Having business in California, after the three of us drove back to Vegas, I flew west, while Barbara and Chance got on a plane and returned to Atlanta. After concluding my meetings in Menlo Park, I took a direct flight from San Francisco back to Atlanta. On the return trip, I was seated next to a frail, older man who was a Catholic priest.

Because it was a five-hour flight, we began to talk. When he asked about my faith, I decided to be frank. Beginning with the story of my

First Holy Communion, I told him of the fear I experienced as a child about Catholicism. By the time I got to the day of my Confirmation, he stopped me.

Putting his hand on my forearm, with his slightly Irish accent, he said, "There's something I want to say."

"What," I replied, surprised by his interruption.

"I want to apologize to you for the Catholic Church. We were wrong to have treated you this way—all of us. Will you forgive us?"

I couldn't have been more surprised, but I was also touched—deeply touched. Welling up, I nodded that I would. Moving my head to affirm this was all I could do, as my eyes welled up. I was too emotional to speak, and I didn't want to start bawling. Once I forgave Catholicism, and told the priest that I had, the rest of my story seemed irrelevant, so I didn't proceed. Instead, we talked about other things. He was a wonderful man—wise, kind, and funny. It was a delightful trip.

While flying, people often share intimate details about their lives to complete strangers, never introducing themselves to one another. Being anonymous encourages candor. This is what happened on my long return flight to Atlanta. As we approached Hartsfield, I finally said, "My name is Cole Cassidy, by the way, and you are?"

"Father Dunnigan—Father Brian Dunnigan," he said, holding out his hand.

I couldn't believe it. I had just told my story to the priest who belted me in the face, when I was in high school. I wanted to laugh out loud and tell him about the irony of it all, but I didn't. Even better, he didn't recognize my name. To him, I was a complete stranger. I guess too many years had passed, but I definitely remembered him. How could I ever forget?

Because I had just forgiven Catholicism, I didn't want to rekindle any contention either. So, I kept my mouth shut, shook his hand, and hugged him goodbye, when we landed—delighted to have had the opportunity to do so.

The next day, I took a walk from our house up Peachtree Road until I reached Christ, the King Catholic Church. Entering, I blessed myself with Holy Water—just like I had done thousands of times as a child. Then, I walked forward and lit a candle for Midge—my dad too. It was my tribute to them for the value of my upbringing. In many ways, I was still a Catholic. My early years, although difficult, provided me with a moral compass that has served me well throughout life. Now, with my deep-seated bitterness resolved, I was willing to admit this simple, but unmistakable truth: Catholicism had been a blessing to me.

* * *

Now that Barbara no longer feared for her life, or that of her son—with her daughters away at college—she decided to pursue her career again. Instead of working at nightclubs, however, she took a job as the worship leader and director of music at a large church in the area. Not having heard her sing professionally for years, I had almost forgotten how talented she was. When I heard her for the first time, if anything, her voice had become richer with age. When she sang, "Just as I Am," it always brought tears to my eyes.

When Brittany and Brianna came home from college, we didn't have to beg them to go to church like most parents, only to be rebuffed. They couldn't wait to listen to their mom sing. When they did, many of their sorority sisters came, which meant a slew of boys followed. You know how that works.

As I listened to my wife perform, there were things I realized that others didn't. I knew her gift, which had been hidden under a bushel for years, had been restored. No longer fearful, she sang about hope and gratitude to Almighty God for making the wasteland of her life fruitful once again. Understanding this was deeply gratifying. In my heart, I sang along with her, as did the rest of our family.

My mom, who had died about five years earlier, left everything she owned to us. I still miss her. Not a day goes by that I don't think about Midge. She was quite a gal. With what she provided, we were able to pay off the mortgage, which made my role as provider much easier. There are things I miss about being young, including not being able to play full court basketball, but I do not miss the fear of economic security. That's for sure.

I also miss my friends. I lost track of Mark Wade—my basketball buddy who led me to Christ. I have no idea what happened to him, but I do know about Acy, Pete, and Dett.

Acy's career continued to thrive. I don't hear from him anymore, but I do know he landed a role as the voice for the main character in a Saturday morning cartoon show that preschoolers love. It necessitated moving from Manhattan to Los Angeles—a great place for a guy like him to live. Now rich, he has flourished, but neither of his sisters has, which must be a difficult pain for him to bear.

Pete eventually became the CEO of Ludlow Randolph, where he continues to produce quality Christian material, sending business my way consistently. He even reconciled with Dett. Having a conversation similar to the one I had, Dett asked for Pete's forgiveness, but it was a generic repentance again—not a specific one. By this time, Pete had mellowed. Realizing this was the best he would ever receive from our former boss, he accepted it graciously.

Dett eventually took a development position at a Christian college in the Midwest, establishing the Lessner Chair for Christian Business Ethics, providing full scholarships for worthy students from one of Benny's numerous foundations. I don't see him much, but when I do,

I'm glad. I always enjoy seeing old friends.

As for me, Barbara and I continue to thrive. Don't get me wrong. We have our moments, but there aren't many of them. Both of us know how blessed we have been. When Chance goes to college, Barbara and I intend to take a two-week European river cruise, followed by two weeks in the Holy Land.

I continue to work for myself, serving Christian ministries. Having done so for so long, I'm no longer employable. There's no way I could work for anybody. I wouldn't even consider doing it.

Nevertheless, as I witness a new generation of evangelical leaders emerge, I see the same behavior coming from them that I witnessed the first day I walked into NRB and saw *The Jim and Tammy Faye Bakker Show* broadcasted live. Nothing has changed. This generation of superstars continues to seek the lost, while using, abusing, and discarding those who get in their way. Only the lost count—not the Christians they wound in the process. I continue to aid those injured by the lords and ladies of evangelicalism, but there are too many of them for me to help. Nevertheless, I try; I always try.